Paper Valentine

Also by Brenna Yovanoff

THE REPLACEMENT

SMOULDER

Paper Valentine

Brenna Yovanoff

SIMON AND SCHUSTER

First published in the USA in 2013 by Razorbill,
an imprint of the Penguin Group (USA) Inc.

First published in Great Britain in 2013 by Simon and Schuster UK Ltd
A CBS COMPANY

Simon & Schuster UK Ltd
1st Floor, 222 Gray's Inn Road, London WC1X 8HB

A CIP catalogue record for this book is available from the British Library.

PB ISBN: 978-0-85707-814-8
E-BOOK ISBN: 978-0-85707-816-2

1 3 5 7 9 10 8 6 4 2

Printed and bound in Great Britain

www.simonandschuster.com.au
www.simonandschuster.co.uk

ANY MAN'S DEATH DIMINISHES ME, BECAUSE I
AM INVOLVED IN MANKIND.

—JOHN DONNE

1: The Dead Girl

My sister, Ariel, is sprawled upside down on the couch, pointing with the TV remote.

"News 4 anchorman Ron Coleman is totally doing it with special correspondent Cora Butcher," she says. "I bet they make out like hyenas as soon as Jim Dean starts giving the weather report."

Her legs are brown and bony. She's got her sundress hiked up and is in danger of flashing her underwear. Ariel loves the local news in the same practically manic way she loves most things. Like even though it's just half an hour of all the same clichés and ridiculous haircuts, she has to give it her complete, frantic attention, or else it will disappear.

I can hear my mom flirting with my stepdad in the kitchen, arguing over when to stir the rice. The sound of their voices comes in from far away, hissing and buzzing like the signal is fuzzy and I just need to adjust the antenna.

On TV, the anchors are looking serious, shuffling their papers, and I get up to go get a glass of lemonade. I already know how the news lineup is going to go. The feature will be the mosquito virus that's going around infecting people and birds, followed by the latest color piece about how our baseball team keeps losing—but first we have to compare the high temperature for today to the high for yesterday. They've been covering the heat wave every night for the past two weeks.

Instead of the usual graphic of the angry cartoon thermometer, though, the one for the breaking story is a stock photo of yellow crime tape. I stand with my elbows propped on the back of the easy chair to watch. Crime tape means homicide.

The anchor Ron Coleman is doing the breaking story in that broad, unnatural voice that newscasters have, like they come from no place and every place all at once. "And in local coverage, the body of a teenage girl was discovered at the west end of Muncy Nature Park yesterday, leaving many asking the question, 'Is our community safe?'"

Muncy Nature Park is right by our house, but that's not really meaningful or anything. There are ninety acres of it, and it runs straight through the middle of town. It's right by a lot of people's houses.

The news story still makes something tighten in my throat. I try to will the feeling away, going through a little inventory of reassurances, telling myself how it isn't even that shocking, really, and the whole thing would be much more mysterious if it had happened someplace else. The west end of Muncy isn't that far from the train tracks, which makes it not that far from a whole bunch of homeless guys.

The dead girl's name is Cecily Miles. In her school

picture she looks mouse-haired and kind of dorky, but in this fun, goofy way. She would have given you gum or shared her lunch if you forgot yours. She would have been pretty eventually, if she'd had a chance to get her braces off. She was younger than me but older than Ariel—thirteen or fourteen.

"Do you think it was just some random crazy person?" Ariel asks with her head hanging off the edge of the couch. "Like a wandering psychopath or something?"

The way she says it is casual, though, completely unfazed. Nothing really scares Ariel.

She looks strange with her face flipped upside down and her hair brushing the carpet. Gravity distorts her features, and for a second I almost don't recognize her.

I shake my head, leaning on the chair. "No way. When they catch him, it'll turn out to be someone she knew—her creepy estranged uncle, or like a deviant gym teacher or something."

I say it casually, as if it's just that obvious—*whatever*—*I am glitter, I am sunlight*. I've been so good at seeming untouchable these past few months, but now I can't help digging my fingers into the upholstery of the chair. There's a dark flutter in my chest, like a bird smashing itself against a window, and I know what's coming next.

The sleeves of my T-shirt are handmade. They're these scalloped half-moons of white netting that I sewed one day when my friend Carmen was over and we were messing around with some of the damaged merchandise from my mom's consignment store. They used to be a tutu that someone tore a hole in.

The room seems like it's pressing in now. My little white sleeves start to dance and rustle. The air around me is suddenly electric.

First comes the slippery, unsteady feeling, like everything is tilting and the floor is going to slide right out from under me. I stand perfectly still, trying to breathe like everything is normal.

The dry, unnatural cold is next, making the tiny see-through hairs on my arms stand up.

Then comes the whisper very close to my ear. "It's a good theory, Hannah-Bell, but you are one hundred million percent wrong. I bet you anything."

I turn my head like a windup girl, so slowly I can almost hear the bones in my neck, and Lillian Wald is right there next to me with eyes wide as planets.

Ghosts are the kind of thing you go your whole life with everyone telling you they aren't real. I believe in them anyway, because the world is full of things that no one really understands. Mostly though, I believe in them because my best friend died six months ago and now she's with me all the time, materializing silently out of the shadows, creeping closer, reaching out.

She smiles, and her face reminds me of a skull. "You don't seriously think this is the work of a rogue gym teacher, do you?"

I don't answer. The way she's staring at me seems to go on and on, like she's accusing me of something. Some days, it's like she takes every silence personally, while others, she'll forgive me for not talking if someone else is around and might think I'm weird.

"This is no run-of-the-mill pervert murder," she says into my ear. Her face is as sharp and hollowed-out as a moon crater. "It's a thrill kill, baby. All the way."

The sound of her voice sends a chill racing over my neck. I shrug away from her and shiver without meaning to.

On TV, the anchorman is talking about candlelight vigils, looking appropriately sad. "Our hearts are with the Miles family tonight," he says, and then gives the address of a local church where people can send flowers, reminding us that we can reach out to Cecily's family during their time of need. That we all feel this tragedy as one big loving community.

Lillian leans closer, making the sleeves of my T-shirt twitch and flutter like I'm about to take off. "What a load of bull," she says, fiddling with my hair. "We all feel this tragedy like gigantic slobbering gore-hounds."

Her hand tickles a little, but I hold still this time. When Ariel glances over, I smile automatically.

Lillian scowls, waggling her fingers in a devil-horns sign, but Ariel only stares right through her. It's like no matter how many times the universe proves otherwise, I still always expect someone besides me to see her standing there.

✳   ✳   ✳

Lillian weighed seventy-eight pounds when she died.

The outline of her hipbones looked like a basket with nothing in it.

She was cold all the time and always wanted to hug me.

7

It used to be that we were always together, never picking anyone else first, but by then I'd stopped wanting to touch her.

I told myself it was because I might hurt her, which was true—she bruised easily, in dark purple smudges like ink blooming on tissue paper—but that wasn't the real reason. When she pressed against me, her bones felt sharp and spidery, like they might crawl inside me.

When we were little, she was like a completely different girl. We lay in the rope hammock in my backyard and braided our hair together. Hers was black and hadn't begun to fall out. Mine was yellow like butterscotch.

Best friends since forever, Wagner and Wald. She'd flop down in her desk and grab me from behind, squealing my name with her arms around my neck.

I can hear her voice like the cry of a bird, *Hannity, Hannity, Hannity!* I can feel her hands against my throat.

She died in January.

Now it's July.

❊　　❊　　❊

On TV, they've already moved on to the next story, but this one is old news.

"The latest in a continuing epidemic of avian mortality," says special correspondent Cora Butcher, looking heartfelt and serious, but the effect is sort of ruined by her lipstick, which is so red it's almost orange.

She's standing on the front steps of the courthouse and then the camera pans away from her and across the lawn, coming to rest on a scatter of dead crows. They're all over the grass like they just tumbled straight down out of the sky. The cameraman scans the ground, zooming in on a heap of black feathers lying next to the statue of Justice in a blindfold.

The way the crow's eyes are scary and sunken and the way its bones poke up through its skin remind me of Lillian, even though some days she's close to transparent and her own eyes are so wild and bright they almost look like stars.

When our mom calls for us to turn off the TV and come to dinner, Ariel and I leave the living room with Lillian drifting along after us like a helium balloon.

Even with the air conditioning on full blast, the air in the kitchen is warm from the stove, and everything smells like fresh garlic and sweet yellow onion.

My stepdad, Decker, sets a heavy casserole dish in the middle of the table and we all sit down, except Lillian, who crosses to the granite island and hops up on the edge of it. Seeing her in the kitchen is always disorienting. It reminds me too much of how things used to be, nights she'd stayed over and laughed around the table with my family and did all her tricks to fake that she'd eaten something. Later, we would whisper back and forth in my room, then sneak downstairs at two in the morning to lie out in the backyard and look at the sky.

I concentrate on the dish of carrots in front of me and try not to glance in her direction.

"Did you hear what was just on TV?" Ariel says, even though there's no way my mom is going to let her talk about the dead girl, especially during dinner.

9

Things like this aren't normal for a city like Ludlow, but they happen. My cousin Kelly runs a one-hour photo shop over on Coronado Avenue. She's in charge of printing the crime-scene pictures for the district police, and if there's one thing I've learned from hanging out there, it's that a lot more people die in a given week than you'd think. There are a hundred fifty thousand people crowded into a seven-mile stretch along the Coureur de Bois River. For the past month and a half, it's been insanely hot every single day. Someone's bound to feel a little homicidal now and then.

Lillian is wriggling on the edge of the counter, watching Ariel with her eyes wide and her hands clasped against her chest. "I love that your sister is like the darkest munchkin ever."

Ariel soldiers on, even though there's no way Lillian's comment was actually meant for her. No one ever hears Lillian except me. "There was this girl, and they found her by that little cement dam in the nature park and it was all taped off—"

Decker is leaning forward with his hands in fists on the tablecloth, like he wants to fight someone. Like the killer is going to burst into our kitchen right now, this minute, and he will have to scrape back his chair and protect us. My mom is looking way too cheerful, though, blinking fast, and I know she's about to shut down this particular topic. She is the absolute master of avoiding the unpleasant.

"Ariel," she says, sounding dangerously patient. "That isn't a dinner conversation."

"But it's on the news," Ariel tells her, helping herself to salad. "It's a current event, which is like the most basic dinner conversation there is."

My mom sighs, and I know from the way her mouth is set and her hands are folding and refolding her napkin that she's dying to do something totally neurotic, like stay up all night talking about it with Decker, or go around checking all the windows and the doors, or take away Ariel's television privileges. She's going to worry because it's what she does.

"I've already said I don't want you spending so much time watching stuff like that. It's always just the most violent and sensationalist stuff they can find. Why don't you tell us about your music camp?"

I ladle creamed chicken over my rice and give Ariel a look that says, *Please just do it*. She kicks me cheerfully, then launches into a story about how one of the girls in the brass section got in trouble for leaving her phone on in class and it went off during the *Star Wars* medley. But my mom has already stopped paying attention.

She's watching me from across the table, picking at the edge of her napkin. "Did you go to the pool today? You look burned."

I shake my head and tell her how Angelie Baker had two-for-one passes for the activities at City Park, so we walked over and went on the paddleboats.

I expect her to say how stupid it is to waste a whole afternoon paddling around the duck pond and "You should be spending more time helping your cousin at the shop," or

"You need to wear your sunscreen," or "Hannah, you need to stop spending every single goddamned day hanging out with Angelie, because she is as mean as a mean, vindictive cat."

Or maybe that's what I'm thinking.

My mom just nods and scrapes up the last bite of chicken. "You should put something on it so it doesn't peel." She gets up to clear the table, then stops, staring at my plate. "Don't you like your dinner?"

"It's good," I say, studying the line of negative space between a pair of carrot circles and a small triangle of chicken. The line is uneven. Not entirely comfortable. So I move some peas into the gap and balance out the distance.

There are all these things that you do.

Sometime around eighth grade, I got in the habit of always leaving a little bit of everything on my plate. Even if I was starving or at least could have eaten the rest, I'd leave it. Just two or three bites, nothing very intimidating. Manageable. If there was a piece of ginger beef or a few fries on my plate, sometimes Lillian would finish what was left. If the food came from my plate, it wasn't the same as her just sitting down and eating it. It wasn't going to make her fat.

She had this whole list of rules and rituals that, when you got down to it, were nothing but magical thinking. My rituals, on the other hand, were real. They mattered because if I did them right, then sometimes I could actually help her, and now I can't stop, even though there's no good reason anymore.

12

"Are you kidding me?" my mom says. "Hannah, please just eat it."

She's standing over me, hugging her arms across her chest and rubbing at the points of her elbows. Decker and Ariel don't say anything, which for Ariel is basically unheard of.

I look down at the scrap of chicken, and because there's no one else around to eat it, I do.

❊   ❊   ❊

After dinner, I go upstairs to deal with my sunburn, to prove to my mother that I'm still the girl she wants me to be. The girl she can count on. My skin feels prickly and tight, and I shut myself in the bathroom.

As soon as I take out the hydrocortisone cream and close the cabinet, Lillian's there, standing right behind me. It's one of her favorite tricks to pop out from behind doors or come looming up beside me in the mirror. Next to hers, my reflection is sweaty and red. She looks like a cadaver.

"Hannity," she says, wrapping her arms around my neck. "Do you think maybe that girl wound up like me? Do you think she's out there right now, haunting the park or whatever?"

I stare back at her reflection, trying to look unconcerned, but I'm squeezing the tube of skin cream way too hard. Lillian almost never mentions her current situation.

When I finally answer, I know on some uncomfortable level that I'm just echoing what my mom said earlier at the table, but I can't help it. The way Lillian fixates on ugly things makes me feel shuddery, like there's something creeping on the back of my neck. "That's so morbid. Don't even talk about it."

"You would have talked about it last year," she says, holding my gaze in the mirror. "Back when you used to be fun." She presses close against me. Her cheek is freezing. "You used to call me Lyle."

I shimmy away out of her grip and shake my head. "You used to be alive."

It used to shock me, seeing her appear out of thin air, but now it's just normal. When she maneuvers in front of me, her expression is expectant and I wait for her to remind me of how we were best friends, that I have to talk about Cecily or toxic waste or animal testing or genocide or whatever she wants, because I owe it to her. I wait for her to trot out the list of things she's given me, all the ways she plucked me from invisibility and made me matter.

Lillian dragged me along through the land of ironic, up-cycled fashion and three-car garages and bouncy wicked se-quined popularity, and when she died, I was the only one who even seemed to miss her.

All the rest of them, Angelie and Jessica and Carmen, cried and made fancy cards and swore up and down to never ever forget her, but two months later, their lives went right back to normal and I was the only one stuck with what's left: Lillian from the months before she died—all her worst parts.

Now she slouches against the counter, tipping her head back to stare at the ceiling. "Maybe it was a ritualistic sacrifice."

I take the cap off the Cortaid and smear a glob on the bridge of my nose. "Or maybe it was a creepy neighbor. Now could you please just drop it?"

It's a stupid question, though. Lillian can never drop any-thing—not when she was alive, and especially not now that she's dead. Sometimes I think that's the whole reason she's still here—she's weighted down, anchored by all the things she couldn't let go.

I have to believe that, because the alternative is that she's here because of me, which is just blatantly not true.

I am not the kind of person who gets haunted by anything.

2: Monday

Mondays get such a bad reputation, but I kind of like them.

Mondays are when my mom leaves early to do the books at the store, and Decker leaves late for his construction job so he can fix us breakfast.

When I get downstairs, he and Ariel are already in the kitchen making pancakes, and Pinky Ortero is sitting at the table drinking something orange out of a plastic Big Gulp cup from the gas station. It's all over her top lip, making her look deranged.

"Buongiorno," she says, waving the cup at me.

Pinky has red cowboy boots and a silver BMX bike and four brothers. She and Ariel are best friends because they both have what my mother calls "big personalities."

I sit down next to her and watch as Decker lumbers around the kitchen, getting out flour and buttermilk, with Ariel swinging from his neck.

Pinky sets down her cup, reaching to touch one of the sugar-pink roses that are sewn in a tumbling cascade down the front of my halter dress. I spent hours cutting out stacks of tiny silk petals and then stitching them carefully to the bodice and the skirt so they fell in a graceful avalanche, pooling around the hem, just like one they sell at Heléne in the mall for three hundred dollars.

When I wore it to school for the first time, back in April, Angelie said it looked like a flower shop threw up on me, but I just shrugged. The way she said it was like she wanted me to admit she was right or feel stupid wearing it, but I didn't. The dress had turned out exactly the way I'd pictured it. I'd layered the petals so artfully and so delicately they almost looked real, and whenever Angelie came over to do DIY stuff after school, she usually spent most of the afternoon just trying to figure out how to blind stitch an appliqué to her shoulder bag without the fabric bunching.

I've always been better at those kinds of things, though— the sewing and the making. Angelie starts a pattern or a project and then gets bored with it. Sometimes she tries to do something easy, like a tube skirt or a T-shirt dress, but in the end she pretty much always winds up buying most of her stuff at Buffalo Exchange or Urban Outfitters, which Lillian used to say was only, like, three or four steps off from J.C. Penney, and that the only reason she put up with such a blatant lack of originality was that we'd known Angelie forever, and that at least it wasn't Sears.

The kitchen is warm and full of sunlight, making my dress look even brighter than real life.

"You're like a cupcake," Pinky says, and Decker laughs.

He switches on the stove and turns to face me, Ariel still

dangling from his neck. "So, Miss Confectionary, got anything special on the agenda today?"

I smile a sweet-cupcake smile and nod, which is kind of a lie and kind of not. I know what I'm doing (being responsible) and where I'm going (Ariel's music camp, my cousin Kelly's photo shop), but I don't really know how to answer the question. Having someplace to go is not the same as an agenda.

Before Lillian died, I was never out of ideas, and not just because we hung out all the time, but because I was always making things—designing bracelets or hair ornaments out of leftover beads and upholstery fabric from my mom's work.

Now, I mostly fill the time with being helpful and the rest of it hanging out with Angelie and Carmen and Jessica, and the hours spool out like a ribbon I can't find the end of. Even when I have a project or a plan, even when I dress up like Tinker Bell and smile so bright that the light hurts my eyes, everything around me feels sort of like it's winding back on itself.

Across the table from me, Ariel is doing elaborate surgery on her pancake, cutting out a wide psycho smile, biting out eyeholes.

"Where's Katie?" I say, not really dying to know.

Katie Randall used to be at our house all the time, and I know she's in the summer band program with them, but I haven't seen her around much since school got out.

Pinky just shrugs, but Ariel shakes the pancake at me and rolls her eyes. "She doesn't hang out with us anymore. She started to, like, develop. Now she thinks she's better than everyone."

Pinky pinches her T-shirt with both hands, holding it out from her chest and wiggling violently in her chair.

"Don't be mean," I say. "That's mean."

Ariel just shrugs. "Yeah? Well, so's Katie. She said I was a boobless stick, and that Pinky was going to turn into a real porker just like her mom."

That piece of wisdom is pretty much hilarious. Mrs. Ortero is a roundish woman, but it's not like she's huge or anything, and until about a year ago Pinky was so head-to-toe bony she was practically nonexistent. A porker, she is not.

"Twiggy and Piggy," Pinky says, then throws her head back, shrieking like a howler monkey.

Ariel is holding the pancake to her face, looking at me through the eyeholes. And even though she's getting syrup all over her placemat, it makes me laugh. The pancake mask is insanely creepy.

Decker tips another pancake out of the skillet and slides it onto my plate. He's younger than my mom and has a full sleeve tattoo and a shaved head. I know I'm supposed to be weird about him because he's my stepdad, but my parents got divorced when Ariel was three, and Decker is actually kind of awesome.

He gives Pinky the last pancake, then turns off the stove, standing with his back to the cabinets and the spatula still in his hand.

Then he leans his elbows on the counter and looks down

at me. "Your mom and I had a talk last night about what was on the news, and we decided it would be a good idea if you'd take the girls to and from school for a while. Just to make sure they stay safe—just until this guy's picked up. She doesn't want them walking alone."

Pinky and Ariel both make a big thing of sighing, like this is the biggest inconvenience they've ever heard. Since their music camp started, they usually just meet at our house and walk over together. It's been years since Ariel needed a chaperone to go six blocks. But this is exactly like my mom to get worked up about something and then make Decker say the ugly, scary parts, so she doesn't have to.

I nod, waiting for him to say more, but the silence gets longer and he just looks someplace else.

Finally, he runs a hand over his scalp and pushes himself away from the counter. "Okay, I'm taking off. Watch your sister," he says, like Ariel is a television.

❄ ❄ ❄

Just before ten o'clock, I herd Ariel and Pinky out the door so I can walk them over to Harris Johnson High School. As we leave the front porch, it's just the three of us. Lillian might follow me around the house most days or hang out with me at work, but she prefers to avoid the sunlight, which can be kind of a challenge in Ludlow.

I've seen her outside a couple times—at her funeral, and then once on the porch swing when I was over at Angelie's—but it's a lot of work for her, like she has to concentrate really hard just to stay visible. I don't know if that's something that's true for all ghosts, though, or just for her. Even in the last few months before she died, Lillian didn't really like to go outside anymore.

I glance back at the house, and almost think I see her, watching from the upstairs window of Ariel's room, but I can't be sure. It might just be a smudge on the glass.

At the end of our driveway, there's a dead crow lying on the sidewalk. Ariel finds a stick and pokes it.

"Don't," I say. "It's not safe."

Since the virus got bad, the birds are everywhere. They decompose in little black heaps, bones poking through the feathers as their skin dissolves off them. In the papers, the Centers for Disease Control tallies up blood tests and trips to the emergency room. Sometimes people die, but only old people. Or sometimes little kids, which is sad in the same blue, far-off way that Cecily in the nature park was sad. Ariel's not all that little anymore, but still there's no point in taking chances.

"Gross," says Pinky, hitching her backpack higher on her shoulder.

Ariel jabs the bird again, making the sunken body rock stiffly. "It was alive yesterday. I saw it, like, floundering when I took out the recycling."

Its feathers look crumpled, shining with a dirty rainbow, like an oil slick. It smells like chicken dust and dead things.

"Seriously!" I make a halfhearted grab for her arm, but she wriggles away from me. "Stop messing with it."

Ariel rolls her eyes and gives the crow one last defiant

21

poke before shoving it off the sidewalk into the gutter and dropping the stick. It's probably fine, but I kick the stick down into the storm grate anyway, so none of the little kids in our neighborhood will pick it up and play with it. By the time I look up, the girls are already halfway down to the corner of Sherwood and Muncy, and I have to walk fast to catch up.

Ariel is charging along like someone on a mission, but Pinky dawdles, hopping her way through a half-finished hopscotch grid. The squares are lopsided, drawn in three different colors of chalk, and it makes me think of a long rainbow crocodile. The 2 is printed big and floppy and backward.

At Harris Johnson, I stand on the sidewalk and watch Pinky and Ariel until they're safely in through the double doors. Then I cut across the baseball diamonds and out along Coronado to the grimy strip mall three blocks over.

Quality Photo is in a narrow slot between a coin appraiser and a locksmith. I step inside to the sound of the bell jangling above me.

"Oh, thank God," Kelly says from behind the counter, turning with the phone caught between her shoulder and her ear.

Kelly is twenty-seven. My mom says she's crazy to run a business by herself. My mom also says it's crazy to be processing color film when everyone in the whole technologically relevant world uses digital, but to be completely honest, Kelly has never been interested in what's logical or easy.

The strip mall is about forty years old, and you can still

kind of tell that the shop used to be a payday loan place, but it's clean and bright. The walls are painted baby yellow and most of the floor space is taken up by displays of camera accessories and picture frames. The rest of it is filled with big, noisy machines and a smell like vinegar and sulfur and warm moving parts.

Right now, though, the biggest printer is sitting motionless and Kelly is sighing into the phone, writing down part numbers on the back of a receipt. When she nods, the end of her ponytail slaps between her shoulders.

She holds her hand over the mouthpiece and gestures at Matilda Braun, who is made of painted steel and is the oldest, noisiest optical photo printer in the world. "I changed the paper, and now the advance is stuck and Brad can't even tell me why—he just keeps saying that she's old. I know she's old!"

Kelly is always on the phone with Brad from Services. The machines break down every other day, and it's true that some of it's because everything in the shop is really, really old, but sometimes it's because Kelly just isn't that careful. She moves too fast and never remembers that even though there's room for only two prints to move side by side on the belt, Matilda Braun doesn't cut the paper in pairs. Whenever there's a paper jam, there's always another piece.

As soon as I kneel down to pry open the maintenance door, Lillian materializes like black magic, peeking around the corner of the machine.

"I don't even know why you like these things," she says, pointing into the nest of rollers and belts and gears, past the warning pictures taped to the inside of the door. "They're practically cannibalistic."

The illustrations are full of blunt metal slabs and sharp edges. Pinch points like torture devices—hands caught in heavy machinery, crushing all the bones.

"Careful," Lillian says beside my ear. "Don't want to lose a digit."

I look away and snake my hand between the rollers, feeling around for the jam.

The paper is crumpled, lavender from light exposure, and I roll it out carefully so I don't mess up the belt tension. Kelly is good with cameras and with money, but she always handles Matilda Braun too hard.

"Did you get it?" she says, hanging up the phone.

I nod and hold out the crumpled sheet.

"That's it—I'm canceling the maintenance plan. Brad has no idea what he's talking about. Here, come over real quick and let me check the settings on the passport camera."

I stand against the marbled backdrop with my hands flat against the wall. Kelly threatens to cancel the maintenance plan at least once a week.

Over by the register, Lillian is sitting on top of the price list with her legs folded under her, making faces and trying to get me to laugh.

"Chin up," Kelly says from behind the round staring eye of the lens. Her voice is soft. In the real world, she's always going too fast, but with the camera held to her eye, she settles down.

"Good," she says from behind the sound of the clicking shutter. "Good."

When she's done, she prints the test shots on the little tabletop passport printer. The pictures come out in twin squares. Me, looking sweaty and sunburned. The contrast on the passport camera is always way too high, and in the picture my eyes are paler and brighter, silvery like antique coins, fixed somewhere beyond the frame.

Fixed on Lillian.

✳   ✳   ✳

I spend the morning dusting shelves and sticking price tags on packets of lens-cleaning tissue. I'm only allowed to run the printer when the shop is closed, since Kelly has a hard enough time getting customers to take her seriously as it is.

She makes sure all the rush orders are caught up before she takes her lunch break, so the only thing for me to do is help customers and run the register, while Kelly sits on the counter in the back, eating a sandwich and reading *Vogue*.

She finishes just in time to come back out and write up the police order for officers McGarahan and Boles. They're beat cops, in charge of things like doing the community outreach program at school and bringing in the crime-scene film.

Kelly told me once that metro police departments all have their own processing labs in-house, but that means they have to have the paper and the machines and someone to run them, plus the chemicals are expensive and mostly toxic. Ludlow barely has the money for cruisers and body armor. So the police department uses Quality Photo because Kelly's fast and does good work, but mostly they use Quality Photo because the lab technician at Royal Crest said she couldn't do the crime-scene photos anymore.

After the bad ones, Kelly sometimes gets quiet, but she never cries in the bathroom, which is what the girl at Royal Crest used to do before she said she had to stop taking the account.

Boles hangs back, looking at the lens-care display, but McGarahan comes up to the counter, carrying the paper shopping bag that holds their film for the day.

I take the bag from him and sort the film cassettes, arranging them in neat rows, but I let Kelly figure out the print orders.

Everything has to be treated just so, so nothing gets mixed up. Kelly is grievously disorganized when it comes to things like using the right spray to clean Matilda Braun's monitor, or remembering to order more paper towels for the dispenser in the bathroom, but she's very good with numbers.

Officer McGarahan leans on the counter, watching her write down the cases. He's young for a cop, and kind of goofy.

"And what's Hannah been up to?" he says. "Staying out of trouble?"

"Mostly," I tell him, twirling my pen like a parade baton or a magic wand. Like the ghost of my dead best friend is not lounging next to me, pinching the back of my neck with icy fingers.

"Hey," she hisses. "Hey, ask him if he saw Cecily's body. Ask him if it was all horrible."

I shrug her off and shake my head, just a little, barely noticeable.

Boles stands with his back to us, spinning the wire rack where Kelly stocks the photo journals. He has a bony face and a dry, broken voice that reminds me of crows. He's always got that same blank look, like nothing ever shocks him. Lillian says he's a freak, so socially inept that he should have been a mortician. I'm pretty sure I could ask him about the murder, though, and he'd answer. Or at least not tell me I'm being morbid.

McGarahan grins, raising his eyebrows at my cascade of silk roses. "You're a good kid."

I duck my head and smile down at the counter. "You never know. Maybe I'm just waiting for my wild streak to show up."

"You're an old soul," he says, handing me the claim stub for Friday's order, and I can't tell if he's teasing me.

Suddenly I feel the sadness all over me, like being tangled up in a wet sheet, and I have to duck down behind the counter and pretend to look for the finished order, even though it's sitting right there on the bottom shelf. I hate the way it can hit out of nowhere, just because of a word or a phrase, because he said one stupid thing that was probably even supposed to be a joke.

Lillian used to call herself an old soul. She was always talking about all the times that people had told her she was wise beyond her years. As far as I could tell, it was just something people said about girls who were serious and smart.

"Old souls," Kelly told me one time, shaking her head. "Anybody who calls themselves that is just too young to know how young they really are."

Back when she said it, I thought she was being harsh, even though I got what she meant. Kelly doesn't have a lot of patience for loftiness or melodrama.

I think now that she's right. I think people who really are old souls, really wise beyond their years, would never need to praise themselves through other people's words. They wouldn't care about being old souls, because they'd be wise enough to know it didn't matter. Lillian was really smart, but she was never wise.

I stay crouched on the floor behind the counter, first because it gives me time to scrub my eyes with my hands and then because as soon as I'm out of sight, McGarahan says something to Kelly in a weird, fake-casual voice that's so tight I stop breathing.

"Hey, I figure I should give you a heads-up. We'll be bringing in some bad ones—tomorrow or Wednesday, probably."

Kelly laughs. "You know me," she says, sounding brave like a Hollywood cowboy. Like a gunslinger. "You bring it, I print it."

Next to me, Lillian crouches with her knees pulled up, and I look the other way so she can't see my eyes.

"What are you doing?" she whispers. "What's wrong?"

I shake my head and don't look at her, letting my hair fall in front of my face.

"I mean it, Kel." McGarahan's voice has dropped, but

I can still hear him just fine. "It's that kid they found at the end of Muncy Park."

Lillian leans closer, popping her eyes wide. "Cecily," she whispers unnecessarily, elbowing me.

I nod down at the floor, remembering the school-picture version of Cecily with her rubber-band braces and her wide, sunny smile.

Above us, Kelly slouches against the counter, jiggling her foot, and I sit with my shoulder blades pressed against the built-in shelves, watching the back of her ballet flat slip off her heel and pop on again.

McGarahan keeps talking like he's forgotten I'm down here, and I keep being surprised at how when people aren't looking right at me, I can disappear.

"Look, you need to know that the crime scene . . . it's—" He stops and clears his throat. "I've just never seen anything like it."

"It's like if someone got killed in the middle of a flea market," says Boles from farther away, somewhere out on the floor.

For a second, I think I can't possibly have heard him right. Flea market. Flea market? No matter how I deconstruct the sentence, it's completely nonsensical.

Lillian, however, is suddenly wild, bouncing up and down, clutching at my arm. "We've got to get a look when they come in," she whispers, bony fingers digging into my skin. "We have to see."

I shake my head, trying not to look horrified. Even before

she died, Lillian was always getting excited about really dark things, so it's not like this is anything new. It's more like since she died, it's just gotten a whole lot worse.

Overhead, I can hear Kelly clicking the top of her clicky-top pen over and over again and then she stops. "Thanks," she tells McGarahan. "I'll look out for it."

After a few seconds, she takes a deep breath and reads off a case number. McGarahan checks it against his list and gives her the quantity. He tells her that one of the orders for today is a DUI with injuries. She asks him if she needs to print extra copies for the district attorney, and I wonder if that's just what happens when you grow up. If you learn how to agree to change the subject without ever saying anything out loud.

After the new police order is in and the old one's paid for, McGarahan and Boles head back out to their squad car to drive around Rossway and keep an eye on the boys at the skate park.

I tape the film to the plastic leader cards that carry it through the processor. Then Kelly runs the negatives through the scanner.

"Can you come sort for me?" she says, without looking away from the monitor. Her fingers strike the keyboard without stopping, adjusting the color balance faster than some people can type words.

Lillian watches the frames go by, leaning over Kelly's shoulder. "Nasty," she says, wrinkling her nose and gesturing for me to come look.

The shot is a close-up of a bruised mouth—an empty, bloody gap where two teeth used to be—and I flinch, screwing up my face, but we're both laughing a little.

Kelly spins in her chair and shoos me away, but not with any real seriousness. She runs off prints of scowling tattooed drug dealers and drunk, disorderly frat boys standing against a dirty wall outside one of the college bars.

I package the pictures carefully, making sure to touch only the edges, while Lillian studies them over my shoulder. She reaches to point things out sometimes, and it takes all my concentration not to bat her hand away, even though the sensible part of me knows there's no possible way she can do something as human as leaving fingerprints.

3: Charm

Music camp gets out at 2:00, and I make sure to be there before the teacher dismisses the class.

The day is blindingly hot. By the time I walk the three blocks to Harris Johnson, I'm sweating and my dress is sticking limply to my back and my legs like it's starting to wilt.

I'm already waiting next to the bike racks by the time the girls get outside. Pinky comes out first with her songbook and her saxophone, looking annoyed.

"Where's Ariel?"

"She had to stay. Mr. Tyler wanted to tell her all about her attitude."

The obvious thing is to ask what's wrong with Ariel's attitude. But I don't. Knowing would mean having to decide how bad it is and whether or not I need to tell on her. I figure I can wait. If Mr. Tyler calls our mom, I'll know it's serious.

When Ariel finally pushes through the double doors, she's already half incoherent, raging about how her music teacher is a total fascist.

She comes straight at me, mid-sentence, and I nod along,

unhooking her hair from the buckle on her clarinet case, trying to zip the pocket on her backpack so her sheet music doesn't go everywhere.

I duck around her to wrestle with the zipper, and when the doors swing open again, I almost run right into Finnegan Boone.

He's paying more attention than I am and steps back before we actually touch. I freeze with my hand on Ariel's backpack and we stand there looking at each other. I can't quite breathe. He is all shoulders.

"Watch it," he says, and his voice is low and husky.

He's wearing a plain wifebeater with nothing over it, which is against dress code, but it's been so hot lately that the teachers must not care anymore. I don't want to seem like I'm checking him out, but I can't help it. His summer-school books are tucked carelessly under one arm. They're all for classes I had two years ago.

It's been a while since I actually looked at him. In my head, I still remember him big and mean and sticky in elementary school. I remember him licking Lay's potato chips and throwing them at me.

The sun is crazy-hot and everything seems to come from far away. I can hear sirens and fire trucks out on Huxley Road, and a noisy bird in the ash tree above us.

His hair is standing up in crazy tufts like Johnny Rotten, bleached so blond it's almost white. The way the sun hits it makes the ends look translucent. When we were little, it used to be this dusty in-between color, not blond, but not really all that brown either. Then last semester near the end of March, for no apparent reason, he started bleaching it to within an inch of its life.

I remember because it was just after the two-month anniversary of Lillian's death—and the day I came very close to losing all my friends.

❆　❆　❆

Lillian was the one who'd started it. She'd been after me for weeks, telling me to stop moping, get happy, add more color. She kept saying I needed to start acting more like Hannah and less like one of the tragic emo kids who ate lunch out on the steps, so I was trying. That day, I had on a choppy lace-up tunic dress made out of one of her old oversize sweaters. She'd never wear them to school, but at sleepovers or on weekends, she lived in them. This one was printed all over with giant purple strawberries. The night before, I'd cut down the body and the sleeves, and sewed little bunches of sequins to the middles of all the berries, but it was still so obviously the same bright, obnoxious sweater she always used to wear. It was so clearly Lillian.

When I came up to our regular table at lunch and sat down, everyone stopped talking.

"Are you for freaking serious?" said Angelie, who'd worshipped Lillian when she was alive. "I mean, that's the one she got last year at Camelot. It's hers."

I nodded, trying to explain that I thought (knew) it was what Lillian would have wanted, but by then, Angelie wasn't even listening. She leaned closer, until her nose was almost

34

touching mine, and I could see the little hairs where her eyebrows grew too close together. "Do you think it's just okay? Do you think it's normal to go around cutting up dead people's clothes and wearing them?"

Over my shoulder, Lillian made a disgusted noise. I could feel her humming with a cool, skin-crawling static as she leaned to whisper in my ear. "God, those brows are horrific. Someone needs to get her, like, a pamphlet to encourage proper use of tweezers."

And I laughed, even though I knew that I shouldn't have, even though I knew it was a bad, bad thing to do.

Angelie was supremely not amused. "Is something funny?"

Well, yes. But when I opened my mouth, nothing came out and all the rest of them were just looking at me.

"Do you think maybe you should go see the counselor or something?" said Jessica, and I couldn't decide if she sounded like she was being nice or nicely vicious. "I mean, if you're having, like, some kind of psychotic episode."

And in that moment, I thought maybe I was. Maybe this was the part where I gave up everything and went to the counselor, admitted to myself that it wasn't normal, living with the ghost of your best friend.

I left my plastic tray and my hot lunch and my social studies notebook. I left everything except my coat, and instead of the counselor's office, I walked out of the building. It was a long, gray day and the sky was low and wet, spitting ice pellets like it couldn't decide if it should rain or snow.

I walked all the way across the south lawn toward the

football field, and sat alone on the bleachers. The field looked as big as an ocean and too green.

I thought about all the times we'd sat in the same place for football games or track meets or just hung around in the summer, and how we used to talk about what things would be like once we were in high school. I'd always imagined full-size lockers, better art classes. Lillian talked about boys. About parties and all the places we'd go once we got our driver's licenses, and then she stopped. After a while, the only thing she ever talked about was whether I thought her nonfat yogurt tasted like it had fat in it, and if no-calorie sweetener was made with real sugar, then where did the calories go? I thought about how I might be living with her ghost forever.

After a long time, the bell rang and I got up, but I didn't go inside. The thought of sitting through Earth Sciences made me feel like I was flaking apart into little pieces. Instead, I just climbed down the bleachers and started toward home.

I walked slowly, crossing the parking lot with the sleet in my hair and soaking through my jacket, until I was stopped in the bus lane by Mr. Harmon, the security guard.

He was wearing a clear plastic poncho and looking annoyed. "Are you supposed to be wandering around out here?"

The question hung there in the air between us, and suddenly my mind was blank.

He reached for my arm, talking louder, like I might be deaf. "Why are you here?"

I stood looking up at him, trying to think, because he was watching me like I was somehow so bad, and there were all these answers that he wasn't looking for. *I'm here because this is where my mom's family is from and after my parents got divorced, she kept the house. Because I was conceived and born and grew up. I'm breathing and my heart is beating and as much as it hurts—as much searing, monumental pain as it causes me—I have to exist.*

But there was a wall in my throat that kept the words in. I had a sudden uncomfortable image of something closing up inside me, slamming shut like a lid, and a memory of how last semester they explained diaphragms to us in health class, and I couldn't help it. The frantic, breathless feeling was coming up again and just like with Angelie, I started to laugh.

"Are you trying to be difficult?" Mr. Harmon said with his arms crossed over his chest, his Cracker Jack badge winking in the rain.

And that was a bad question, the kind adults only ask when they've already decided, but at least I knew the answer.

"No," I said, and my voice came out impudent and loud. I hadn't sounded loud in months. I was beginning to think I'd never sounded loud at all.

For a second, we just stood there. The rain was thin and constant.

"That's enough," Mr. Harmon said, but he didn't say enough of what. He put his hand on my arm and I didn't pull away.

The sky was so gray it was almost colorless.

And that is the story of how I got my first and only detention.

If something like that had happened even three months earlier, I would have been horrified, but by then, I just wanted to go someplace warm where I didn't have to talk or feel or think.

Detention was in the Language Arts wing, with a social studies teacher who never taught any of the college-track classes, some boys from the wrestling team, two ninth-grade girls with glam-rock haircuts, and Finny Boone.

I showed up late because I couldn't remember where Mr. Harmon had said to go, so I had to ask the ladies in the front office. My jacket was covered in a crust of ice and my hair was wet and sticking to my forehead.

The teacher was this short, stocky guy with an awkward beard. He sat at the front of the room looking bored, and let us sit wherever we wanted.

I picked the seat next to Finny because it was about as far from the wrestling boys as I could get, and also he was pretty much the only one in the room who was sitting still. I kept waiting for Lillian to show up so at least I'd have some company. But she didn't.

Finny was exactly the kind of boy I was just not allowed to look at. But I couldn't help myself. Even though I already knew, I was kind of surprised by how tall he was. Even squeezed into a desk, he was so clearly over six feet. It was the first time I'd been in the same room with him in a while, maybe since elementary school. I'd known his name and his face for pretty much my whole life, but it was different seeing him up close.

The thing about Finny was, we'd been at the same school since kindergarten, but we never really knew each other, and once they started sorting us into fast and slow classes, he was pretty much always in the slow ones. I kept being distracted by all these random details—all the things about him that were exactly the same as when we were little. The way the cuffs of his shirt were fraying away from the seams, and the tiny triangular scar on his chin. How his eyes were too light for his tan, but mostly how he was missing the pinkie finger on his left hand.

His expression didn't change, but I was sure he could feel me watching him, so after a minute or two, I slumped forward and put my head on the desk. With my jacket on and my hood up, I could peer out like someone in a cave.

Beside me, Finny was hunched on his elbows, digging at his cuticles with a safety pin, and I studied the missing finger. It was ugly and shocking, and I couldn't make myself stop staring. The skin around the joint and down the outside of his wrist was shiny and puckered, pale against the rest of him. There were all kinds of stories about what happened— garbage disposals and alligators—but no one knew for sure, because Finny never talked much.

A few rows over, Connor Price got out of his seat and crossed the room to flop down in the desk next to me. He used to go out with Lillian in junior high and now sometimes made out with Angelie and always smelled like Slim Jims and Axe body spray.

I thought he was going to comment on my strawberry sweaterdress or ask me why I'd been mean to Angelie at lunch, but instead he leaned across me and snapped his fingers at Finny. "Hey—hey! Jesus, what did you do to your hair, man?"

His voice was incredulous, but different from how Angelie had asked about the sweater. Connor sounded sincerely interested. Prepared to be impressed.

"It's Clorox," Finny said. Then he flipped his notebook over and didn't say anything else.

"Sick," said one of the rocker girls. But she said it in a voice that made it hard to tell whether she meant it as a bad thing or a good thing.

I stayed in my jacket-cave, looking out at Finny, noticing how red the skin was around his ears. Thinking how there were all kinds of bleaches and dyes that won't burn your scalp, but he'd picked the harshest thing, maybe just to prove that he could.

After a minute, Connor reached over and rested his hand on top of my hood. "Hey, is that Hannah under there?"

When I didn't answer, he poked me roughly between the shoulders, but I still didn't look up. I just closed my eyes and wished he'd stop touching me.

"What'd you do, Hannah? Write your name on the wrong line in math?"

I shook my head, keeping my face turned toward Finny.

"Aw, come on—don't be mean. What's with the silent treatment?"

On any other day, none of it would have even been a big deal, but right then, I was just so tired of acting fine and happy all the time. I was so unbearably sad, and it didn't matter that I'd known Connor since forever or that he wasn't even trying to be mean. All that mattered was how I couldn't stand to play this game with him, to be poked and prodded and teased, but I couldn't find the energy to make him stop.

Connor put his hand on my shoulder again, giving me another little shove. Then, on my other side, Finny stood up, and everyone in the room got quiet.

He was wearing work boots, gouged and scuffed, and I watched them, staring dully at how they left black smudges on the linoleum floor and then moved closer. He filled the aisle, leaning over my bent back. I could smell his deodorant and the bleach from his hair and I held very still.

For a minute nothing at all happened. Then there was a scraping sound as my desk went sliding sideways under me, and Connor gave this sort of yelp. "What the hell!"

I twisted around and looked up.

Above me was a big, complicated silhouette, blocking out the light. Finny had Connor by the collar of his shirt and was holding him so their foreheads were almost touching, but he didn't say anything. He just leaned over me while Connor yanked on Finny's wrist, trying to get loose.

"Hey, man! Jesus, what are you doing?"

With his hand on the back of Connor's neck, Finny held

Connor away from me, leaning close to his ear. "Don't be a douche," he said.

Then he opened his hand and let him go.

Connor thumped back down into his seat and Finny went back to digging at his cuticles.

I buried myself in my hood and put my head down on my arms so no one would see me crying.

❊   ❊   ❊

In front of Harris Johnson, the pavement is white-hot and the sun sits high and scorching over the roof of the school. Ariel's cheeks and forehead are already starting to turn red, and Pinky's squinting around like everything is too glaringly bright to look at.

Finny's still standing with his books held loosely by his side and his eyebrows raised, like he's waiting for something.

I understand in a hazy way that we're blocking the sidewalk, but he doesn't say anything, just sighs and steps around us, cutting across the grass toward the Qwik-Mart convenience store at the corner of Huxley and Coronado.

It's hard to stop looking at his wide, mostly bare back, and my heart is hammering out a loud, frantic drumbeat as I watch him stride across the parking lot and into the store.

The air is so hot and dry it's like opening the lid to the barbecue and leaning over the grill, a sudden updraft that can take your breath away. I step off the curb into the bus circle and feel around in my purse and then my pockets.

Ariel is making little panting noises, fanning herself with her sheet music. "Okay, that guy was weird."

"How bad were you?" I say, ignoring her remark and taking out a wad of crumpled dollars, flattening them one by one against the palm of my hand. "How bad were you in class?"

She gives me an indignant look. "I told you, I didn't do anything!"

"Okay, then I'll tell you what. It's way too hot out. Do you want a slushy before we go home?"

I almost stop to consider the fact that I'm only taking them to get slushies because Finny Boone has just disappeared into the Qwik-Mart and I kind of want to keep looking at his shoulders. That would be too awkward to think about, though, so I put it out of my head and follow the girls down the block toward the convenience store.

The parking lot is small and mostly empty, with a smashed beer bottle lying on the sidewalk by the pay phone, and weeds springing up in dry clumps where the cracks in the asphalt are wide enough to let them poke through. In places where the blacktop's been patched, the squiggly lines of road tar are soft from the heat. It sticks to the soles of my ballet flats as I cross the parking lot, like it's trying to suck them off my feet.

A couple of sunburned summer-school boys are leaning up against the front of the store, smoking and giving me unfriendly stares. I lead Pinky and Ariel past them, trying to look indifferent, like I don't even see them.

Inside, a wall of cold air hits me like a solid thing, making my face tingle. The whole store is jammed full of bumper stickers and magazines and candy, but the walls and the ceiling are bright fluorescent white, and suddenly I'm shivering even though thirty seconds ago all I wanted was to get out of the heat.

Pinky and Ariel head straight for the drink counter at the back, where you can get yourself slushies and fountain Coke and pink plastic straws.

I follow them through the narrow rows of shelves, keeping an eye out for Finny while still trying to look casual. He's near the back examining one of the endcap displays a couple aisles over from Pinky and Ariel.

When I come up to the drink counter, he glances away from a selection of fake Zippos like he's surprised to see me there. Behind him, a boy with worn-out jeans and a Lakers jersey is leaning down to dig through a cardboard display of Visine bottles and caffeine pills. I can't quite see his profile, but his ears stick out from his head, and he has a terrible unshaved strip along his jaw that looks like it sort of wants to be a goatee. Then he straightens up, turning to mutter something to Finny, and I recognize Nick Andelman.

Nick is bad news. Not like Brady Huff, who would grab girls around the waist when they walked by his table in the cafeteria last year and say things like, "Want to sit on my lap and talk about the next thing that pops up?" Not like that, but just bad enough to make you stay away from him in the halls. Bad in the stealing-Visine-and-NoDoz-from-the-Qwik-Mart way. He belongs in the same general category as Finny Boone, except that he would never try to do something nice for you if you were having a bad day.

Over by the slushy machine, Ariel is making a total mess with the Blue-Raspberry Blast, slopping it all over the counter. She and Pinky are trying to layer the different flavors and I know I should go and stop them, but right now I'm too busy appreciating Finny's arms.

He leans against the endcap, playing around with a lighter that has a pair of cartoon ravens painted on the side. Then, without breaking eye contact, he palms the lighter like he's daring me to say something.

His eyes are too green to look at, so I turn away and drop my gaze to his hands, then wish I'd looked someplace else. The lighter is tucked under his thumb. I can see just a silver stripe of metal peeking out, reflecting the harsh fluorescent lights. The place where his little finger should be is slick and pink, and I can't seem to stop staring.

Behind me, Lillian's voice floats down from somewhere near the ceiling. "Um, Hannah? He's shoplifting, in case you hadn't noticed."

I nod a tiny, disconnected nod and don't look away. The lighter is completely hidden in Finny's hand now. His expression is unreadable.

All I'm thinking suddenly is that it was such a bad idea to come in here just because he did. I can't even begin to explain what I expected to happen, but this isn't it.

Up at the counter, the store clerk is playing some kind of game on his phone, and the little blips and chimes and explosions are the loudest sounds in the store. There's a sudden chorus of electronic chirps, and Finny raises his eyebrows and then slips the lighter in his pocket, turning so the muscles in his neck and shoulders suddenly look much, much bigger.

"Let's get out of here," he says to Nick, sounding bored. He steps away from the shelf of lighters and brushes past me, even though it means taking the long way out. He walks straight out past the cashier, and the bell over the door makes a high, jangling noise behind him.

Nick starts to follow him, then sees me standing in the middle of the aisle with my mouth hanging open and my hands clasped against the front of my dress, staring at him.

"What are you looking at?" he says, even though I'm pretty clearly looking at the pocket where he stashed the NoDoz and the Visine and whatever else he's walking out of the store with.

"Nothing," I say, which we both know is a lie.

He grins and shakes his head, then steps closer, trapping me against the drink counter.

"Nothing," he says, like it's the funniest thing he's ever heard, or maybe the stupidest. His voice is deeper than most of the boys' in our grade, which wouldn't be so scary if he weren't two inches away, scuffing the toes of his sneakers against my ballet flats.

"You can't just take things because they're there," I say, sounding shy and tiny.

He doesn't answer, just gives me a mean, toothy smile and in one quick twitch, he reaches down and yanks my charm bracelet off my wrist. It's from Posy Boutique in the mall and has an Alice in Wonderland theme. Lillian gave it to me for my birthday two years ago and it's the only piece of jewelry I wear almost every day. The chain is heavy and silver-plated, but the clasp isn't the greatest, and as soon as he yanks, I can feel it let go. A metal jump ring hits the floor and bounces away, and I gasp, massaging my wrist without meaning to.

From the corner of my eye, I can see Pinky backing farther and farther away, like she wants to hide behind the wire sunglasses rack. Ariel just stands with her eyes very wide, holding her slushy cup in both hands, Blue-Raspberry Blast melting down over the rim and dripping onto the floor.

Nick gives me one scornful look and then starts for the door. The charm bracelet is still in his hand, its broken chain swinging sadly.

"Do something," whispers Lillian from the top of the slushy machine. "Don't just stand there!"

Her voice is like a bell, jolting me awake, and I shout after him. "Hey!" My voice sounds almost brave, but my face is hot and my legs feel weird and trembly. "Hey, come back. You can't just take people's stuff!"

The guy at the register glances up from his phone, looking around the store like he might sort of be thinking about doing something eventually. He starts to get up, but Nick just stalks past him and out into the parking lot.

Ariel is still standing with her mouth open and her hands dripping blue syrup. Pinky just peers at me from behind the tower of sunglasses like she's deciding if it's safe to come

47

out. I stand with my shoulders limp and my back against the counter. There's a raw half-circle of little red marks around my wrist where the chain dug in before it snapped.

What am I looking at?

Nothing.

4: Fashionable

"Look who decided to show up," Angelie says when I get to the Sno-Cone stand outside the mall.

She and Carmen are standing together in the shade, lounging against the wall by the main entrance. We were all supposed to meet at three to look at earrings and maybe see a movie, but because of the impulsive slushy decision, I'm late. And for what? The possibility of standing near Finny Boone? There's a stinging scrape around my left wrist where my Alice in Wonderland bracelet used to be.

Angelie steps away from the wall. "You're looking pink today." She gives me a long once-over, and I can't tell if she's talking about my face or just my dress. At least she doesn't say anything about how it looks like I got puked on by a rose garden.

"It's okay," says Carmen, who's wearing a lipgloss so red it looks like nail polish. "You're not the last one."

Carmen's sundress is almost as bright and outrageous as mine. It's hibiscus-orange with a ruffle around the bottom and a giant purple bow on the shoulder, and I wonder if Angelie gave her the same once-over I just got.

Lately Angelie's been acting nastier about a lot of things, and once or twice she's told me flat out that something I'm wearing is way too twee, even though for as long as we've been dressing like this, that's kind of been the whole point.

It was Lillian who decided, all the way back in eighth grade, that there was room for only one really enviable group in school, and we were going to be that group. Even before high school, she understood what it took to be popular. Not the sticky-sweet, sweaters-from-the-Gap kind of popular—where girls like Hilary Chase or Morgan Whitmeyer get all enthusiastic and involved and then run out and join cheerleading or student council or Future Business Leaders of America—but the real kind. The kind where when a band gets big or a movie comes out, everyone checks to see how you feel about it before they can decide if they like it, and if you come to class with neon crackle nail polish or colored eyeliner, they all have to dash over to Ulta right away and get it too, but they never forget that you wore it first.

That was what Lillian wanted—not the responsibility of running the committees or the clubs, or the boringness of us all buying the same plain cotton tank top in a variety of coordinating colors. Instead, we'd be the girls you could never confuse with anyone else. The girls who invented the colors and started the trends and rolled our eyes at anyone who tried to copy us, because no matter how much effort they put in, they just couldn't pull it off like we could. The girls everyone wanted to be, even if they denied it or pretended so hard that they didn't.

The biggest requirement of Lillian's fashion philosophy was to always wear it—whatever it was—like you meant it. Like no one in the world could inhabit that exact outfit but you. Today, though, Angelie's just wearing a striped tube top and cut-offs. Except for her cat-eye eyeliner and the way her thick, coffee-colored hair is pinned up in a complicated figure-eight braid, she looks normal. She could be anyone, and I wonder suddenly if maybe she only went along with the accessories and the outfits because Lillian said so, if maybe Lillian's idea of what popular should be was never really hers.

Jessica doesn't show up for another ten minutes. We spend the time hanging out on the little half wall by the entrance. When she finally coasts around the corner on her lavender Schwinn cruiser, Angelie sighs a huge, put-upon sigh and throws up her hands. Jessica just shrugs and locks her bike before starting for the entrance. I go in after them, wondering if this is how it's always going to be now.

The truth is, things haven't been the same since Lillian died, but mostly they haven't been all that different. Angelie still calls me almost every day. We still make plans for the weekend and spend the night at each other's houses. And even though these days we've pretty much stopped doing projects together and she occasionally ditches me to hang out with Connor, we're still friends. It's just like it always was. The kind of friends where you sometimes want to disappear.

The Deer Meadows Mall is the biggest one in Ludlow, with a movie theater and two escalators and a Cheesecake Factory. The air inside echoes like a canyon, and as we

51

walk down the middle of the main corridor, I have a little daydream about being home, burrowed in my bed with the pillowcase cool against my face, and the air bone-dry and freezing from the air conditioner.

I want to turn on my stereo and listen to songs about heartbreak on repeat. The mall is full of people from school, and even though I don't know most of them, I catch myself smiling automatically. The friendly expression is just a holdover from last year, when I was always smiling in the halls, always making an effort to look normal and happy. I want to be carefree, seem brighter. Mostly, I want to forget how Nick Andelman ripped the charm bracelet right off my wrist while I stood there and let him.

Carmen falls into step next to me, and I watch the way our skirts flutter against each other. The orange and the pink look nice together, like a garden party, and I'm just starting to feel lighter and more like myself when Lillian materializes on my other side, letting her arm thump down across my shoulders. I flinch without meaning to, then try to turn it into a little twirling skip, like a pirouette.

Angelie hears the soles of my shoes slapping on the tile and glances back. "Something wrong?"

When I shake my head, Lillian makes a high-pitched, incredulous noise, but Angelie just nods and starts for Claire's.

We're almost inside the store when Carmen stops me, catching me by the arm. "Hey, you do look kind of twitchy. Are you sure you're not upset about something?"

And, no, I'm not sure. The afternoon is still fresh like a slap, and Finny Boone is probably a sociopath. A big, lighter-stealing sociopath. But his eyes are steady and complicated, and I haven't really taken the time to notice boys since before Lillian died.

The day seems very long suddenly.

I consider telling Carmen that I just remembered something I'm supposed to do, that I have to go home. But her hand on my arm is light and warm. I can feel myself stepping away from the tense, helpless feeling, letting it go. Rising above it.

"I'm fine," I say.

At Claire's, we wander up and down the aisles, trying on barrettes and plastic bangles. Carmen wants to go to the pet store, but Angelie says the puppies make her sneeze.

"Untrue," Lillian says next to my ear, sounding bored. "Whenever she goes to your house, she never sneezes because of Joan."

I nod a little tiny nod, picking through a bin of on-sale lipglosses. Joan is my mom's ancient basset hound, and she spends most of her day following people around, waiting for them to give her food and shedding all over everything. Angelie is not Joan's biggest fan, but she'll usually condescend to pet her as long as she's had a bath. Lillian's right; the thing about the pet shop is just to annoy Carmen.

The lipgloss shades are mostly glittery neons—orange and fuchsia and green. I pick three of the craziest ones and head for the register.

When Angelie comes up to the counter with a handful of enamel jewelry, Jessica inspects her choices, then holds out a bunch of bangle bracelets from the same clearance bin. "Do you want to just give me yours and we can pay for them all together? There's an extra discount if you buy at least ten, and I have three more than you."

Angelie opens her eyes wide and gives Jessica a mock-offended look. "God, Jess—it's not a contest!"

Not a contest was this thing we started saying. Or, Lillian started saying it first and then it kind of trickled down to the rest of us. It was obviously a joke, making fun of the very idea that we would be so insecure and desperate that we actually had to compete with each other. And it was the perfect catchphrase because you could say it about anything—who could sing along to detergent commercials the loudest or whose hair was wetter after walking in the rain.

It took me a while to understand that there was this extra layer to it, this other thing happening underneath, and that maybe the second layer wasn't so harmless or so funny. That when Lillian said *not*, what she actually meant was *always*.

Angelie gives her handful of chunky plastic jewelry to Jessica and then lounges next to me leaning on the counter. I think she'll have something to say about the lipglosses, how they're for little kids, or that the colors are perfect for a disco-clown hooker. Instead, she reaches over and smacks Jessica on the butt.

"And, yikes! Do something about your pants! You're hanging your unmentionables out all over the place."

Jessica grabs her jeans, which are yellow and skinny and splattered with long streaks of rainbow fabric paint. She tries unsuccessfully to yank them up past the top of her thong, which is peeking a full inch above the waistband and printed with little pink and silver stars.

Angelie whistles and fans the air like she just touched something hot. "Damn! That is just too much ass for those jeans!"

And we all laugh—even Lillian, who's crouched ominously on top of the nail-polish display, watching our little group from over the top of a CLEARANCE sign. She's grinning with her head tipped back, even though if anyone had ever said something like that about her, she would have been mortified.

Angelie's phone buzzes frantically, and she grabs my arm and pulls, texting one-handed. "Come on, let's go over to the fountain. I have to meet Connor."

I start after her, but Lillian hangs back, swaying morosely by the false eyelashes. "What's the matter with you? Why do you always let her treat you that way? She's being a complete bitch."

I give her a jerky little shrug. It's true, at least a little, but I'm not sure what to do about it. It's not like Angelie's impatience or her bossiness even really matter all that much—and if we're going to talk about how friends should treat each other, then we'd have to start talking about Lillian. Because the thing is, yeah, Lillian never treated me the way Angelie does. She just treated everyone else that way.

When we reach the wishing fountain, Angelie drags Jessica and Carmen into the bathroom to help fix her figure-eight braid. She usually keeps her hair artfully messy, but now it's tangled and frizzing in tiny corkscrews around her face.

I know that I'm supposed to follow them, but Lillian's pacing circles around the oversize gumball machine in front of the play area, looking restless and distracted. Instead, I head down the steps to the fountain and sit in the shade of a huge potted rubber tree. The atrium is cool, and after a second, Lillian appears next to me before crawling back into the tangle of tropical plants.

She's rustling around in the planter, singing the chorus to "Fake Plastic Trees," and I'm sitting on the edge, trying not to nod along to the melody, when Nick Andelman comes slouching across the atrium.

The fact that I just saw him and now he's here in the mall isn't that weird, since pretty much everybody from Harris Johnson hangs out at Deer Meadows in the summer, but my heart is suddenly going a million miles a minute, and all I want is to vanish.

"Oh my God," says Lillian, poking her head out of the bushes and shoving me in the back. "That's the asshole who took your bracelet!"

He's smoking a cigarette, which is outrageous for a number of reasons, but mostly because we're in a shopping mall. As he passes, he drops the butt into the fountain.

Lillian is pushing harder now, fingers jabbing into my

back. "Go!" she says. "Go over there. Tell him you want your Alice bracelet back!"

I pull my feet up and scoot all the way back against the planter, shaking my head.

"Hey!" A boy's voice booms through the atrium suddenly, echoing against the skylight. A second later, Connor Price comes cutting across the little tropical area by the fountain, looking messy-haired and tan and sort of perfect. Either he's early to meet Angelie or she's late. Probably she's late.

Nick glances over his shoulder but doesn't stop. His expression is tight, like this interaction is the last thing he wants. He keeps walking, and I bury myself deeper into the shadow of the tree.

Connor comes up behind him and catches him by the back of his Lakers jersey. "What the hell do you think you're doing?" He jerks Nick around to face him. "That's massively not cool. You know that, right?"

Nick shrugs and pulls away. He's bigger than Connor but has this way of slumping his shoulders or ducking his head that makes him look sulky and thuggish. I have this sudden idea that maybe sometimes the people who are mean to you wind up on the other end of it more than you'd think. It doesn't really make me feel better, though.

Connor makes a big thing of checking his watch. "You're lucky," he says in a low, cool voice. "You're lucky I'm meeting someone and I don't have time for this. Otherwise, I would mess you up right now."

He raises his hand at Nick then, like he'll hit or push

57

him, but stops before he actually makes contact. "Do we understand each other?" he says, sounding like a guy in a movie, and not even a little bit like just a sixteen-year-old boy on the soccer team.

Nick pulls away, then glances across the atrium to where some of the other scowling, delinquent boys from Harris Johnson are standing around the statue of jazz musicians, scratching their names into the finish. I give them a quick look, but Finny isn't with them. Nick jerks his head at Connor. Then he turns and slouches away, looking at the floor.

Lillian laughs scornfully, peeking out from the rubber plant. "I'd like to see that same exact confrontation go down someplace without a closed-circuit camera and three security guards."

I know she's right, that Connor's just making a big show of being tough. I'm pretty sure he wouldn't be pushing Nick around if they were alone outside, with no one around to break it up if something happened.

He comes over to the fountain, glancing around the atrium, probably looking for Angelie. Behind me, Lillian makes a low, dismal noise and I know it's because of Connor. It's been a long time since they went out, but they were together for a while, from eighth grade till about the middle of freshman year. Then she got sick—or sicker, anyway—and it kind of fell apart. After a while, Connor started dating Angelie, and Lillian acted really hard like she didn't care—and Angelie acted really hard like it wasn't the greatest moment in her whole life because she'd finally beaten Lillian at something.

I swing my legs down from the planter and untangle myself from the rubber tree, trying to scoot away from it without getting my hair caught in the leaves.

When Connor sees me, he smiles and does a little salute. "Hey, Twinkie," he says, thumping down next to me on the edge of the planter.

"You have got to make him stop calling you that," Lillian whispers from right behind me. Her voice sounds bored, like she barely even knows him, but under that, there's an empty note. I'm practically sure that if I glance over my shoulder at her, she'll be watching him with wide, greedy eyes.

Connor leans back on his arms. "What were you doing back there in the bushes?"

I feel stupid, but I figure I might as well say it. Connor can sometimes be really obnoxious. He's not always a very good boyfriend to Angelie, and for the first few months after Lillian died, he was pretty hard to be around. But most of the time he's okay.

"I was hiding from Nick Andelman," I tell him, sounding only a tiny bit less ridiculous than I feel.

"That guy? He's a total loser. Why were you hiding from him?"

I sort of want to tell Connor everything, explain about the bracelet, but instead I just shrug.

When Angelie exits the bathroom, newly brushed and braided, she comes bounding down the steps to the fountain and kisses him on the cheek. She gives me a look and I scoot away from him, even though he's the one who sat down next to me.

The two of them decide to go see one of those loud, summer action movies they've been advertising constantly, even at the gas station and Taco Bell, but the rest of us opt out. Carmen and I both hate movies about explosions. We say good-bye to Angelie and Connor and then head down the walkway to Bathing Beauty so that Jessica can get some more Harvest Peach body spray, which comes in a round orange bottle and smells exactly like peach schnapps.

As we pass the food court, I slip my arm through Carmen's and try not to search the crowd for Finny. I know I shouldn't be looking for him, but I can't help it. I keep picturing him standing over me in the Quik-Mart every time I let my mind wander.

On my other side, Lillian's mood has darkened abruptly. She's glaring at the clusters of afternoon shoppers with their french fries and their floppy slices of pizza. "Don't waste your time swooning over him, Hannah. He's just a big dumb animal who hangs out with bracelet thieves."

I don't answer, but I have the stark, uneasy feeling I always get when she does this, like she's just seen straight down into my soul. The magic of ghosts is that she always seems to know what I'm thinking, and even when she was alive, Lillian was a little bit of a mind reader.

"God, you're such a weenie sometimes," she says as we wander through the fragrance section at Bathing Beauty. "If you had any self-respect, you would have gone up to Nick and told him to give it back."

I twist away and pretend to be very interested in an elaborate pyramid of pastel bath bombs, but she steps in front of me, making me look at her.

"Seriously, Hannah. When are you going to stop letting everyone in the whole entire world walk all over you?"

I turn my back on her. In the long mirror behind the counter, I look strange and secretive, like I'm trying to keep my face under control. Behind me, Lillian is watching, waiting for some kind of reaction.

"Fine," she snaps, but the way she says it makes it clear that this isn't over. It isn't fine.

When she swings her fist at the table, it's fast and ferocious. I don't expect her to make contact, but as soon as she brings her arm down, there's a sound like pond-ice cracking, and the whole display goes crashing to the floor.

Bottles hit the tile in an avalanche. Plastic cracks and lids fly off, splattering pink and blue bath products everywhere. I stand with my hands clasped tightly under my chin and cupcake-scented bath gel dripping down the front of my dress.

Sometimes Lillian tries to throw or break things, but even when she concentrates, she hardly ever actually moves them. When I turn to face her, she has the strangest look— not shocked, not sorry, but defiant.

Jessica comes hurrying over to me, picking her way around broken bottles, doing her best to avoid the spilled gel, which is all over the floor and splashed up the sides of the shelves. "God, Hannah, are you okay?"

I nod, glancing at the woman behind the counter, wondering if I'm going to get in trouble, but the table is in pieces on the floor with its legs splayed out like a flattened bug, and this is clearly not my fault.

"That's it," Lillian says, shaking her head and turning away. "Just keep telling yourself that."

5: The Ghost

It's almost seven by the time I get home. As soon as I let myself in, I'm hit by the smell of garlic and peppers, and my mom calls from the kitchen that dinner will be ready in twenty minutes and can I please set the table?

"Sure," I yell back from the front hall. "Just let me change first." The top of my head feels burned, and there's bubble bath all over my dress.

Upstairs, Lillian is already waiting in my room, balancing precariously on the footboard of my bed. Outside, the sun is low. The air is starting to look blue.

I want to lie on my floor and listen to Imogen Heap or The Sundays, but I smell like a soapy, chemical cupcake, and I should really go help in the kitchen. Anyway, I know if I turn on the stereo, Lillian will get all excited and remind me that she's the whole reason I even know about whatever band I'm playing. She'll clap her hands and dance around like she owns it, because she was always doing that—acting like a song or story or poem was so important. Like she was the first person to ever know about it. Like it didn't exist before the second she heard it for the first time.

She hops down from the footboard and begins to pace, striding back and forth across the room. "You need to get cleaned up," she says in a distracted voice. "You're a mess."

The way she moves is frantic and jerky, like a nervous bird. Completely exhausting.

She's wearing the powder-blue flannel pajamas she died in, and her hair is loose and straggly and unbrushed. Her feet make no sound as she crosses the floorboards and the little braided rug. Sometimes I catch myself wondering all these strange, perplexing things, like if she ever wishes for a change of clothes, and whether time and distance mean anything to ghosts. If she can even feel the ground under her.

I gesture to my soapy dress. "Yeah? Well, whose fault is that? I didn't make the mess."

She doesn't answer, just gives me a tiny shrug, like she might be half sorry.

After watching her pace for a few seconds, I sit down and take off my shoes. The AC clicks off with a sharp mechanical sound and then there's silence.

I can hear my mom and Decker downstairs in the kitchen, laughing about paella and for a minute, I just sit there in the dimness, listening to them sound happy.

Lillian folds her arms over her chest but doesn't stop pacing. "God, could an afternoon with Angelie be any more gruesome? I don't know why you even do this to yourself. When she talked Jessica into getting that feathered headband, I actually wanted to shoot myself."

"Don't," I say. "Don't joke about things like that. Anyway,

you used to hang out with Angelie all the time. We've always hung out with Angelie. She's my friend."

"Oh, I forgot. Hannah doesn't like to live in real life. Hannah just wants to pretend that we all live in happy fairy-land, where everyone is super–best friends and no one is a heinous bitch and nothing bad is ever going to happen. Yeah, well. Maybe you should ask Cecily about that."

I've been waiting for this. Ever since the breaking-news story and Lillian's little tangent about ghosts the other night, I've been wondering when we'd get into the topic of Cecily Miles—all the gory details.

Lillian sighs and flops down in my desk chair. "What do you think the police are doing right now? Do you think they'll call in the FBI?"

"Come on," I say. "It's not exactly a freak occurrence or anything. I mean, do you know how many people die in Ludlow every year? This is just the kind of thing that happens in cities."

That's not really true, though. The only other time anything this bad has happened was almost a year and a half ago, to a girl named Monica Harris. She was in our civics class, and she died the winter of freshman year, the Saturday before Valentine's Day. One of the city garbage collectors found her out in the parking lot behind the Bowl-A-Rama in her pink polyester jacket, beaten dead with a piece of two-by-four and her own ice skates.

It was one of those shocking nightmare things, and af-terward, I wove floral wreaths for the makeshift memorial by the bowing alley and tried not to think about it too much. For the next few months, though, it was all anyone at school could talk about.

✳   ✳   ✳

When Lillian first got the idea to contact Monica Harris from the dead, it was like just another part of this same bad running joke that people had started spreading around. That Monica would come back and haunt you. I said absolutely, positively not—no way. The whole thing was awful. It was stupid. It wouldn't work.

Lillian kept after it, though, teasing me about ghosts whenever I slept over, waking me up in the middle of the night with the sheet over her head. And when that didn't work, she threatened to do the séance with Carmen and Angelie instead.

I think she always knew I'd do it, though. And in the end, I did.

Neither of us had a Ouija board, but Lillian had read this article about how you could make one the way they did in the 1800s, with a card table and a drinking glass. My mom had a whole set of vintage barware from the seventies, up on the top shelf in the front closet where she kept extra merchandise for the store. The corners of the box were held together with Scotch tape, and I worried it would be full of spiders, or that my mom would be able to tell we'd been messing around with her inventory, but Lillian just picked through the box and found the smallest, fanciest glass and took it up to my room.

We did the séance on a Wednesday, because Lillian said

Wednesday was the best day for contacting the dead. I made a board with a permanent marker and a square of leftover plywood and put a piece of clear shelf paper over it because Lillian said it had to be slippery. Then we sat on my floor with the plywood between us, and she lit her mom's aromatherapy candles in a circle around us, just like the instructions said in an article she found online.

"Spirits," she said in a whisper, with the fancy little glass turned upside down in the middle of the board. "We call on you to help us contact Monica Harris. Spirits, are you with us tonight?"

She'd barely finished talking when the glass jerked hard and skated along the edge of the board in a long arc. The way it moved so effortlessly made a cold shudder run right down my spine. The shelf paper wasn't that slippery.

"Stop," I said. "Stop doing that."

Lillian shook her head. "I'm not moving it." Her eyes were big and she didn't look like she was lying, but by then she was so good at lying about everything that it made it hard to believe her.

She scooted closer, staring at the board. "Am I talking to Monica Harris?"

At first the glass just sat there. Then, in one long, lazy swoop, it drifted to the top corner of the plywood, where I'd printed the word *yes*.

"Okay," Lillian whispered, almost like I was gone and she was saying it to herself. "Okay. Monica, can you tell us how you died?"

We sat perfectly still, and I watched without breathing as the glass slid down again and hit the *H*, then circled briefly before gliding across to the *E* and stopping.

"*He?*" whispered Lillian, staring hard at the board. "Who's *he?*"

But then the glass moved again, sliding to the *A* and then just as quickly to *R*, and finally coming to rest on *T*.

Heart.

"What does that mean?" I said. My voice sounded thin and tiny.

The glass was already moving again and I took my hands away. I couldn't help it. The feeling of it gliding around under my fingers was just too creepy.

Lillian gave me an outraged look but didn't say anything. She sat with her hands over the glass, but it didn't really look like she was touching it at all anymore. Maybe a little, but it didn't seem that way. I could have sworn I saw the glow of candlelight in the gap between her fingertips and the bottom of the glass.

I sat perfectly still, watching the board with goose bumps coming out on my arms.

The glass looped across the rows of letters, spelling out *P-A-P-E-R*. Then, without pausing, it circled its way back to *H-E-A-R-T*.

After that, the glass wouldn't spell anything else. We tried for another half hour, but it was no good. It just sat in the middle of the board, motionless. Silent.

As soon as Lillian went home, I put the cordial glass back

in the closet and threw the board in the Dumpster behind my house.

✳   ✳   ✳

After a minute, I shut myself in the closet and change into one of my old wrap dresses, then sit down at my dressing table, and switch on the lamp. The light makes everything look warm and ghostly, but it never seems to do that to Lillian. She's always more solid at night.

I get out my hairbrush and wish for her—the real Lillian, and not the worst, most selfish parts of her. I wish for a warm, true best friend, one who didn't die.

She stands behind me, reflected in the mirror. The shape of her shoulders when she cups her elbows is fragile, but real enough, almost like I could reach out my arms and hug her. Only, I know that if I do, she'll feel like ice against my skin, too freezing to touch, and even when she was alive, all I'd be holding on to was her bones.

Sometimes girls online or at school called it Ana, like a real actual person, someone you could play Yahtzee with or talk to on the phone. But because Lillian never liked to do what everyone else was doing, she called it Trevor, after this Christian Bale character in a movie about a guy who never sleeps or eats. A guy who looks like the walking dead. Even then, I guess she knew what she was up against.

I toss my hair back over my shoulders and start brushing. It bothers me, remembering all these random little things, like they're part of a book or a TV movie, or happened to someone else. Like it isn't really real somehow. But I know better.

69

My best friend gave up a life and a future for something else, and the indisputable proof is standing right behind me.

"I couldn't help it," she says close to my ear, always so good at knowing exactly what I'm thinking. "I didn't have a choice."

I yank the brush through my hair, feeling the bristles dig at my scalp. The string of paper lights tacked around the outside of the mirror makes my face look dreamy and all the wrong colors.

I hate that she says *choice* like it wasn't one. Like it was something that just happened, some natural phenomenon or twist of fate, instead of something she actually did. And maybe, when everyone is always competing to have the most ironic thing to say and wear the most unique outfit and be the most special, maybe it starts to feel like you don't have a choice. Because the truth is that if everyone's special all the time, then really, no one's special, so maybe all that's left is just to be perfect, because at least that's something you can measure.

Or anyway, these are the things that I think about. Because when you hang out with Angelie Baker, it's like even just existing starts to be a contest all the time, every day, and I always thought that because Lillian was the brightest and the wildest, she was somehow exempt.

"It wasn't Angelie's fault," she says behind me, leaning her elbows on the back of my chair. "Don't give her that much credit."

I glance at her reflection. Beside her, my own face looks pink-cheeked and kind of startled.

"It was more like this obsessive little part of me I couldn't shut out," she says. "I could hear it all the time, whenever I was alone, reminding me how I was worthless and stupid, that nothing would ever be okay if I couldn't get myself under control, because who wants a person with no self-control? Who wants a fat, stupid pig? I wasn't good enough to have what everybody else did."

Her mouth is close to my ear, like she's telling me a secret, but it's ugly and self-satisfied, the kind of secret you throw around like a live grenade any chance you get, and I can feel the anger—the absolute fury—welling up in my chest. "Well, you didn't have to listen!"

Lillian grabs me, fingers digging into my neck. "Yes," she says in a deadly voice. Her face is terrible and gaunt. "I did."

I spin around with the brush in my hand, and I would hit her if I thought it would make a difference or if I could justify beating at a ghost. The fact that she's here telling me about some kind of relentless, judgmental voice she couldn't ignore when she lurks around everywhere and says mean things to *me* all the time is just pretty much hilarious. "No, you didn't. Get off me!"

Lillian skips back and clasps her arms over her chest to shield herself, but she's smiling. "Aw, you're so cute when you're mad."

The way she says it is warm and cozy, like I am not significant enough to be mad. Not significant enough to be anything but this scared little bunny hiding in the rubber tree just because Nick Andelman walked by.

Suddenly, I'm on my feet. "I said, leave me alone!"

We stand facing each other and I clench my hands into fists, squeezing the hairbrush. I want to throw it at her. The distance between us seems to hum, and my room is so quiet and still that for a second, I'm not even sure if I'm breathing.

"Hannah." The voice is low, coming from just outside my window. "Hey, is everything okay?"

I turn around and almost scream.

Finny Boone is crouched in the cottonwood outside my window, blurry through the screen. The clearest, most visible part of him is his white undershirt, and the second is his Clorox-blond hair. Everything else is in shadows.

I move toward him cautiously, still holding the hairbrush in front of me. "Why are you here?"

He's resting his palm against the screen, steadying himself. I have a sudden idea that if he overbalances and falls through the window into my room, Decker will kill him. The shape of his mangled hand is intriguing. The fingers that are left look weirdly delicate. It was clearly a nice hand, before whatever happened.

"You were shouting," he says, and I have the same hot rush of panic I always feel when there's a chance someone's just caught me talking to Lillian. Like I've just made a huge, unforgivable mistake and someone is seeing straight into my head.

I move closer, still clutching the hairbrush. "Why are you here, though, at my house?"

He lets out his breath like he's been holding it. "I, uh,

72

I brought your bracelet back. It's on the steps. You should bring it in, though. So no one takes it."

Behind me, I can feel Lillian moving closer. The air around me seems to buzz with icy static and I must look sort of petrified, because right away he starts shaking his head, a white-blond glow outside my window. "I didn't mean to scare you."

"You didn't scare me. I mean, I was startled. Just . . . why are you in my tree?"

He shrugs, but his face is blurred by the screen and I can't see his expression. "I heard you from down in the yard. I just thought you sounded like maybe something was wrong."

I concentrate on my voice before I answer, keeping my back very straight and my face calm and innocent and curious. "Why would something be wrong?"

"I don't know. Last year—" He sounds awkward and starts over. "Last year, you started looking sad."

The hairbrush feels heavy in my hand, turning into a stone. Behind me, Lillian is standing so close I can almost feel the chill of her in my own blood, like our skins are running together, getting all mixed up. "I'm okay."

He doesn't say anything, but suddenly I like so much that he climbed up here just to check on me. I reach toward the window, almost meaning to touch his hand. As soon as my fingers brush the screen, though, he jerks away.

"See you around," he says.

I listen to him rustle down through the branches until he's gone.

73

Then I cross to the bed and sink down onto the rug, pulling the sheet with me. On the floor, with the sheet over me, I sit with my knees pulled up and my head on my arms. My heart is beating in huge spasms, but under the sheet is safe, like I'm the ghost and Lillian's the real live girl.

"Hannity," she says, from somewhere above me. "Are you really all squishy over Finny Boone? He's a total delinquent."

I don't answer. The word *delinquent* is sort of right. Finny is a troublemaker and a lighter-thief, and probably a lot of other things, but those parts aren't everything. He's also the boy who cared enough to bring my bracelet back, and once, when I was very sad, he stood up out of his seat and pulled Connor Price off me.

Lillian reaches down and twitches the sheet away. The shadows around her eyes are deep purple. "You really, truly like Finny Boone? Oh my God, I thought you had better judgment."

Her voice is mocking, and I flop down so I'm lying at her feet. Me and her, staring at each other in the dim rainbow light.

I'm choking on all the things I never could say when she was alive, at first because she was always Lillian and I was just Hannah and then later, when Trevor got bad, because I was supposed to be strong and supportive—because I didn't want to do anything to make it worse. This whole list of bad, forbidden things: Never say, *Be reasonable.* Never say, *You're too thin.* Never say, *Eat a goddamned Twinkie* and *I'm not stupid, Lillian! Chewing up food and spitting it*

74

into your napkin isn't fooling anyone! Why do you have to control everything? So you don't run the universe. So what? So the world is big and scary and chaotic. You know what? Deal with it. I do.

I never said those things, and when they bloomed in my head like huge, toxic flowers, I pushed them down again. I did everything I was supposed to. I nodded and listened and never bullied her. I went to her house after school and made crochet arm warmers and shared pieces of my bagels and my granola bars, because if it was mine, then it wasn't the same as her eating it.

I did everything I was supposed to, which is such a lie. Whatever thoughtful, comforting things I said, whatever effort I made, it wasn't enough. She died anyway.

And if I go downstairs now, Decker will be in the kitchen making paella, and Ariel will be standing on the corduroy ottoman and singing "Mamma Mia" and "Girl Anachronism" for our mother. There will be a broken Alice in Wonderland bracelet waiting out on the steps, because Finny Boone might be big and quiet, but he isn't stupid, and I spent the last four months of tenth grade looking sad.

Lillian is blocking the door, standing over me, with her cadaver's jaw and her sunken, bloodshot eyes. I take a deep breath and yank my sheet out of her hand. With the fabric draped over my head, the light looks dim and I can barely see Lillian at all.

I open the door and walk right past her.

6: Paper Heart

On Tuesday morning, I wake up late and can't remember if there's something I'm supposed to be doing. The sunlight makes a crisp yellow square on the wall.

I'm lying there with my chin on the edge of the mattress and my pillow wadded up under me when Ariel comes tip-toeing in, holding her hands behind her back. "I have something for you."

I roll over but don't raise my head. "What is it?"

She turns her palms up to show empty hands and smiles slyly. Then she jumps on me, hugging me around the neck and pressing her face into the top of my shoulder.

I laugh because I can't help it. We wrestle together, rolling around until I'm flat on my stomach with the comforter wrapped around my legs and the sheets in a mess on the floor.

Ariel is lying flopped across my back. "When you get dressed, you should wear your big boots," she says, playing with my hair.

"Is that right?"

She nods and flips over so she's staring up at the ceiling, still holding on to my hair. "We need you to look menacing."

"Ow, don't pull. What are you talking about, menacing?"

She thumps down next to me and pushes her face close to mine. "So when you walk me and Pinky to school, no one will come and snatch us."

I have a drowsy feeling that my mom has put this idea into her head. It's not the kind of thing Ariel would come up with on her own, and she doesn't even look particularly worried about it, but then, Ariel never looks worried about anything.

We lie side by side, staring past each other. I think I see Lillian watching from the closet, but when I turn my head, she's gone. Morning is the only time when Lillian is really truly ghostly. Practically nonexistent.

"You have to get up," Ariel says into the silence. "Pinky's almost here."

"That's right, Hannah." The voice that comes drifting out of the closet is a ghost voice, the way Lillian in the morning is always a ghost Lillian; the sun shines through her, making her seem pale and faraway. "You just need to figure out how to look menacing."

I lie transfixed, staring into the closet like a bird staring helplessly at a snake.

"Get up," Ariel says again, pulling at my arm. "Or we're going to be late."

"I am. I will." The way I say it is just a little off, not bright enough somehow, and I take a deep breath, trying to channel Old Hannah, who always had an easy laugh and something whimsical to say. "I was just watching how the sun looks on the wall. When you squint, it looks like a window to a secret yellow place—like a fairyland," I say, shooting Lillian a dark look, even though I can barely see her anymore.

Ariel lets me go, turning to see. "Really?"

"Yeah, try it."

She lies with her cheek resting between my shoulder blades. "It does," she says, and the tone of her voice sounds like she's humoring me, but it doesn't matter. The weight of her head is sort of nice, and for a second, it's just the two of us, lying there together, looking at that bright yellow square.

When I come downstairs ten minutes later, Decker is sitting at the kitchen table, sorting through the mail.

"What are you doing still home?" I ask, taking down a bowl and a box of cereal. We have five kinds, but three of them are cornflakes.

"Money day," he says, which means he'll spend most of today driving around in his truck with the air conditioner on, harassing contractors to pay him.

As I pour myself some shredded wheat, he gives me a long, doubtful look but doesn't say anything. I'm wearing a sleeveless minidress made out of a heavy-metal T-shirt from the thrift store, which is the most menacing thing I own. The dress is black, with SLAYER angled across the front in pointy silver-glitter letters. It would probably be more menacing if the scalloped trim around the neckline and the armholes weren't pink. Decker just looks at me, and I can't tell if his fixed stare is because of the outfit or something else.

His eyes are too serious. If it were the outfit, he'd just say something.

"What?" I ask, trying to sound unconcerned, like he's not freaking me out.

Decker shrugs and shakes his head. He's picking at his arm, touching his four-color sleeve tattoo. "Nothing. Just you be careful out there, okay?" Then he pushes back his chair. "I'll take off pretty soon here, get back maybe around two. Three at the latest."

The way he says all this has a false easiness to it, and it occurs to me that maybe my mom has been after him too, reminding him to remind us of how the world is actually dangerous.

Out in the hall, the doorbell rings, and Decker goes to let Pinky in.

❊　❊　❊

"We should do some new portraits before school starts," Kelly says when I come into work. "I could set up some really dramatic lighting, and maybe do some fun makeup."

"Yes, let's," I say, lacing my fingers together and propping my chin on my hands, elbows stuck out in imitation of a 1950s pinup pose.

Over by the register, Lillian mimics me, flopping herself down on the counter with her arms splayed out, elbows jutting. I make sure to keep my eyes focused somewhere to the right of her, like I'm not looking at anything.

Kelly loves high-concept shoots, but the truth is that it's been a while since I've liked having my picture taken. It always makes me feel like I'm being magicked into someone else, and then I don't even know how I look anymore.

❆ ❆ ❆

Some days I'm pretty, and some days I'm not, and once, for three hours and forty-five minutes, I was beautiful. But that was a long time ago, at the eighth grade dance, and I wore a blue dress that I'd made from a McCall pattern after I fixed the serger, and Jason Forrester really, really liked me. I mean, he liked me so much that it wasn't just hypothetical. I could actually tell.

I let Ariel put my hair up in a fancy braided bun that she'd just invented, and I didn't even mind that it was kind of lopsided or that the ends stuck out, because it looked almost intentionally messy. It looked the way girls' hair looks in magazines sometimes—like their lives are so wild and glamorous that their hair is constantly getting tousled. I wore makeup, and everyone kept looking at me in this confused, startled way—like they'd never known before that I could surprise them.

And I know it's what you're supposed to want, but it scared me.

Lillian laughed because I was so awkward, and because usually she was the one who made people stare. She was the beauty, with her sweet fairy-tale face and her long black hair. And then, not.

I was no one, barely even a real girl. I'd had to alter the pattern to make up for the fact that my waist was 22 inches and my bust was 26.

Even shoes and blouses were a problem, and shopping for swimsuits was embarrassing, but Lillian never made fun of me. She already wore a real underwire bra and the kind of jeans that you don't buy in the kids' section. She said I was lucky. That I was so delicate and tiny. *Like a pixie*, she said, but I knew that 26 inches wasn't something to want. That's not even the size of a real person.

The blue dress was the best thing I'd ever made, covered in pleats and flounces, with a tulle overskirt. My mom helped me with the flounces because the fabric was fragile and stretchy, which made measuring tricky, but I did everything else myself.

Before the dance, we got ready at my house, but we went to Lillian's to meet our dates. I never minded that. I knew it was because she didn't have a sister to be loud and sticky and mess things up or a dog to shed all over everyone, and because my house wasn't as nice as hers. And that was just how it was.

"Lillian," her mother said when we stood in front of the gas fireplace for pictures. "Honestly, honey. I don't know if you should be wearing those kinds of dresses anymore. You've just got a little too much going on in the chest area to be wearing spaghetti straps. Don't you want to wear your black one?"

As if Lillian hadn't just spent four hours trying on every single dress she owned, looking for the one that didn't make her look fat. She was smart and stubborn, but her mother was the voice of authority. Mrs. Wald was so well-meaning and so picky, and she was always right.

In her room, Lillian sat slumped at her ruffled vanity with

the oval mirror in front of her and the black dress spread out on top of her quilt, but she didn't change right away. She just looked at herself, and I sat on the edge of her bed and didn't remind her that Connor and Jason were waiting for us.

"You can wear my bow," I said, running my fingers over the black dress. "It will look better with the flower pattern than it does on me."

Lillian just stared into the mirror.

I didn't know what to say. I wanted to tell her that her mother didn't mean she wasn't okay just the way she was. She had this expression on her face like she'd lost at something, and I thought, *How awful to never be allowed to fail.* I took the bow out of my hair and saw that she was crying a little.

"It's okay," I said. "It wasn't true about the straps. You look nice."

She just shook her head and cried harder.

"If you don't stop," I said, "you're going to wreck your makeup."

And she pinned her hair back from her face with the bow and stopped crying, but it was already too late. All her happiness was gone. Her face looked numb and empty, like all the joy and the excitement had run out of her.

We went back upstairs, and Lillian's mom drove us to the school. We went inside and stood in the cafeteria along with everyone else. And maybe Jason Forrester liked me, but he was too nervous and awkward to stand next to me with the music blasting through the speakers and Lillian acting like anyone who came near us needed to be shot.

I didn't care. I didn't even really know how to slow dance, even if he had gotten around to asking me. I was waiting for Lillian, watching to see what she would do, always ready to let her show me the way.

Connor didn't ask her to dance, though, and neither did anyone else. I thought maybe it was because of how Lillian had basically ignored him in the car the whole way over, and because she looked ready to set fire to anyone who got close, but she thought it was because she was fat.

"You can dance with me," I said.

She shook her head, avoiding my eyes. "That's stupid. I mean, we're not little kids anymore."

Over by the refreshment table, Connor was standing with Jason and Max Sodermeyer, flicking the roasted peanuts from the pretzel mix at all the couples shuffling past.

"Lyle," I said, reaching for her, holding out my arms. "Dance with me."

I thought she would turn away, but then she reached for me too, collapsing into me like a building coming down.

We stood in the corner of the gym, with the reflections from the mirrorball trickling over us in silver coins of light. I put my arms around her waist and held on, held tight like we were magical girls in a story, or like I had a big sister. She rested her head on my shoulder, and I knew she was crying, but I didn't say anything. The song was one from an old TV show. It was happier and brighter than the moment, but I didn't care that the soundtrack to our evening was bouncy and all wrong. I was just glad to be with her.

Even when things weren't okay at all anymore, and she got sad and sick and awful, I was always just so glad to be with her.

Eighth grade was a long time ago, but it's what I want to remember.

I was pretty and skinny.

Lillian was beautiful.

❊ ❊ ❊

When officers Boles and McGarahan come in at lunchtime, Kelly beats me to the counter to write up the order.

"What's up?" she says, reaching for the forms. Her smile looks warm and friendly, but her hands are nervous, skittering across the counter.

McGarahan is watching her in a long, meaningful way, like if he stares hard enough, she'll understand without his actually saying anything.

"We've got the film for the Miles homicide," says Boles, who tends to lose patience with things like etiquette and beating around the bush. He gives her five rolls of film and two sets of special instructions.

The whole time, McGarahan keeps up this constant stream of conversation, like if he just keeps talking, everything will be fine.

After they leave, Kelly sits down to print the order, and I do my best to stay busy. I sweep the main aisle and the floor behind the register—all the places that aren't anywhere near the printer.

Lillian is just as restless, pacing back and forth between

the counter and the door, while Kelly works on the order. She's clicking her way through the second roll when her face changes.

I put down the broom and go into the back.

In the little office, I sit on the edge of the counter and stare at the workers' compensation poster on the wall, thinking about Cecily. I think of the version of her that I saw on TV—the wide, goofy smile, and the way she will never get her braces off. The counter is cold against the backs of my legs. Lillian sits next to me, hunched over with her hands clasped between her knees.

After a minute, she leans into me, resting her shoulder against mine like she used to when I was upset about something. "What are you doing back here?"

"Nothing," I say, without looking away from the workers' comp poster. It shows a guy lifting with his back, red arrows of pain shooting out from his spine.

"You can't keep acting like this," Lillian says, and for the first time in months, it's like she's actually trying to be nice. "Tragedy isn't this evil thing that came from outer space. It's just there, you know. Along with everything else."

I don't answer. The fact is, she can say that because she's not the one who lost everything.

"That's not true," she says softly. "You know that's not true."

When Kelly comes into the office, I think that maybe she's come back to get me, but when she sees me sitting on the counter, she looks surprised. She's carrying the police photos in their brown paper bag and then she does something really strange. For the first time ever, she doesn't just tuck them under the front counter with the rest of the orders. Instead, she locks them in the little floor safe, like they're an ugly creature that might get out.

"You could look," Lillian says in my ear, "if you wanted. It won't hurt you. If you look, maybe you'll feel braver."

I nod, but I don't feel brave. I feel like we're playing the worst game of Truth or Dare in the history of the world. Lillian is right there next to me, though. After a second, she reaches for my hand and squeezes it.

When Kelly goes back out to help Connor Price's mother choose negatives for enlargements, I slip down from the counter.

It's not like the safe combination is a secret or anything. Kelly keeps it on a tiny piece of scratch paper taped under the edge of the desk in case she forgets. She even has me open it sometimes, when she needs extra quarters for the register.

Still, it takes me two tries before I actually manage to twist the dial the right number of turns.

With shaky hands, I take out the stack of envelopes and sort through the order. I used to be honest. Not underhanded, not a sneak. I never would have looked at the crime-scene photos when Kelly said not to. But Lillian's right, it's no good pretending the tragedies aren't happening, and I have to believe I'm brave enough to know the bad things. Anyway, this isn't the same as taking something. I'm not vandalizing lawn ornaments or stealing candy from the gas station or cheating on a test. I'm just looking.

I hold the pictures in the palm of my hand, flipping through two traffic accidents and a B and E before I get to the final set. Cecily is lying just below the little cement dam at the west end of Muncy Park.

She's wearing a blue sundress. The kind with a smock front, where the straps tie in little bows at the tops of the shoulders. I can tell just by the way the skirt is crumpled that it's probably made of cotton, and it feels wrong to be noticing these things when I should be noticing other things instead.

Her face is shockingly white—dead white—and there are dark finger-shaped bruises all over one shoulder. In the blue evening light, the bruises look black. Almost as black as the blood that's splashed in the weedy grass around her.

She's lying faceup with her legs twisted awkwardly and her arms out to her sides. Even though the crime-scene photographer took the shot from twelve feet away, it's not too hard to see how she died. The blood all seems to be coming from one side of her head, like maybe she was hit with something big and heavy.

None of this is the most shocking part, though. The real, actual worst part is the thing that Boles mentioned the other day. *Flea market.* When he said it, the words didn't even add up to anything in my head, but now I understand.

The body of Cecily Miles is the drabbest thing in the picture. All around her, arranged in no particular order, marked with yellow police markers and reaching all the way to the corners of the photo, is a collection of toys. Most of them are tiny and cheap, like party favors. There's a little airplane made of pink plastic, barely two inches long, and a sparkly rubber ball, like the kind you get out of a bin at the dollar store, and too many others to count. Threaded through the surrounding bushes and tied in a crazy web above her is a tangle of rainbow craft string.

"Oh," says Lillian in a tight, shaky voice. "Oh, Hannah—Hannah, look." She's leaning in over my shoulder, pointing with a trembling finger.

But I already see it. Lying against the back of Cecily's outstretched hand is a red heart, cut from construction paper and glued carefully to the center of a lacy white doily. It's a strange, eerie thing to see lying in the grass, in the middle of summer, in the shadow of a dead body, but that's not what makes the horror come bubbling up from the bottom of my memory.

"You remember?" Lillian whispers. The tightness in her voice makes her sound like she's begging. "Remember, Hannah?"

I nod so slowly it feels like I'm underwater, thumbing through the rest of the prints until I get to a close-up. The valentine is big and bright red, but you can tell from the unevenness of the scallops and the crooked way the pattern doesn't line up that the doily is handmade, cut out with scissors or maybe a utility knife. The tile floor is cold under me, and I feel wobbly and full of needles and pins, like maybe I'm going to faint.

Together, we crouch on the floor of the office, in front of the open safe.

"Remember?" Lillian says again, in a desperate, strangled voice. "The spirit board and the message?"

"*You* did that!" I mean to sound impatient and kind of bored, but it comes out much too loud.

I wince and clap my hand over my mouth. Out in the front of the store, Kelly and Mrs. Price both stop talking. There's nothing but the sound of the machines, and I sit very still. Then Mrs. Price says something I can't hear, and Kelly laughs and everything is normal again.

I shove the pictures back in their paper bag and lower my voice to a whisper, glaring at Lillian. "You did that. It doesn't mean anything."

She shakes her head, raising one hand and keeping her back very straight. "Hannah, I swear to you, I didn't move that glass."

I sit staring down at the package of photos in my hand, not really seeing them. "That's not possible, okay?"

"What's a better explanation, then? That I was trying to play a prank on you and I accidentally broke a murder case that hadn't happened yet? That I psychically tapped into some freaky collective unconsciousness? Look, whatever—*whoever*—wanted us to know about the heart, it was someone else."

I put the pictures back in the safe and close the door, making sure not to let it slam.

Someone killed a girl one winter—left her dead like a worn-out toy, all powder-pink ski jacket and bloody hair—and then they killed another, tucking her in a nest of the

89

cheapest party favors ten dollars can buy.

This is not one of those dismal everyday tragedies that Lillian talked about, those bad things that just happen.

This is something black and monstrous.

It's so much worse.

7: Rabbit Hole

The rest of the week is like a strange alternate reality where everything keeps chugging along like always.

It's one thing to know—know, with a crazy, impossible knowing—that someone in my city is out there killing girls, but it's another to actually be able to talk to anyone about it. So I don't. I walk Ariel to school and I go to work and I paint my toenails, and I act like nothing is wrong.

Since I saw the crime-scene pictures of Cecily Miles, though, that raggedy homemade valentine has mostly been all I've thought about. I'm almost sure I'd be having nightmares, except that it's been really hard to sleep.

I've started wearing my Alice bracelet all the time. I never take it off, even though the chain sometimes pinches my wrist and a lot of the charms are kind of sharp. I don't care. The weight of it against my skin is comforting, and it's nice to have something solid to remind me of Lillian. I never told her, but the Queen of Hearts charm always reminded me of her, even when she was alive. The way that all ways were Lillian's ways, and how in the story the queen is unpredictable and kind of scary, but even when she throws a tantrum or threatens to cut off Alice's head, she never really means it.

Sometimes Lillian got mean or moody, or snapped at me to stand up for myself, reminding me that she wasn't going to protect me from every cranky teacher and varsity jerk forever. But mostly? She liked me exactly how I was, and I liked her right back.

I wrap my fingers around the charm and hold on until I fall asleep.

On Monday night, when I went downstairs for dinner, the bracelet was lying on the porch where Finny said it would be, arranged in a careful circle on the welcome mat. It wasn't in great shape, but I fixed it so it's wearable at least. The chain was still in one piece, but the jump ring holding the clasp had to be replaced. The Cheshire cat's tail is broken, and some of the enamel is scratched off the card guard. The white rabbit is just plain gone.

Now, it's four o'clock in the afternoon on Friday, and the house is empty except for me. Ariel's at the pool with the Orteros, and there's a note from my mom on the refrigerator door saying she's taking Joan to get her shots. Decker is out at one of the new housing developments on the east side of town, putting up drywall.

I can remember so many days when all I wanted was to be alone. Hating how crowded and noisy the house was, wanting so badly to have the place to myself. Now, though, I don't really want to be by myself.

No matter how loud I turn up the stereo and dance around, I can't shut out the list of random words that keeps popping into my head: *bone* and *blood* and *bludgeon*. When I close my eyes, I see Cecily. I see Monica Harris, who I did an English project with one time and then never thought of again until she was dead.

Lillian's sitting on my dresser, rocking from side to side in time to the beat of my dance party, while I bounce on my mattress and scream along. After my legs get tired and my throat starts to hurt, I stop jumping and turn off the music. The air feels suddenly still, like the silence right after a thunderclap.

"Okay," Lillian says finally. "This can't be how you spend the rest of your life. Come on, what are you doing, Hannah? I'm supposed to be the obsessive one."

I sit on the edge of my bed, breathing hard with the raw, screaming feeling still sitting in the back of my throat. I know she's right. It's strange to have Lillian be the voice of reason and me the one who can't relax or sit still or act normal.

"How do you stop obsessing?" I whisper, pulling at the little tufts of fleece on my bedspread.

Lillian laughs and rolls her eyes. "Do I look like I know the answer to that? I always just locked on to the target and then followed it all the way down."

I nod and stop ruining the bedspread. Then I get up and dig through the pink footlocker at the end of my bed until I find my yearbook from freshman year.

It's weird to look at a picture of someone and know that they're not even in the world anymore. You are never going to run into them in the beauty aisle at Rite Aid or pass them on the street. They've gone past the point of no return. They've winked out.

In her class photo, Monica looks almost unbearably happy. Her teeth are small and straight, but there's something in her smile that reminds me of Cecily—at least, the photo of Cecily they keep showing on the news.

For a freshman, Monica is in a lot of the candid shots. She was in a ton of clubs and activities, which is one of the surest ways to get your picture in the yearbook, but still I can't help thinking that maybe they included more than they normally would because she's dead.

On the front page of the fall sports section, there's a picture of her with Taylor Wetherall and Izzy Marks at the first football game of the year, wearing matching sweatshirts with their hair up in pigtails and GO, FIGHT, WIN written on their cheeks in greasepaint. It's the kind of undisguised enthusiasm that Lillian always considered dorky, but I don't even know if that's fair. They look really happy.

Lillian has climbed down off the dresser and is crouched on the floor next to me. She watches me flip through the book, leaning over my shoulder to study a black-and-white photo of Monica looking responsible and serious as she represents Turkey during a debate for Mock UN. "God, she was a piece of work. Do you think Cecily was even one-third as annoying?"

"They seem like they were both really sweet," I say, running my finger along the caption underneath. *International drama sparks lively discussion.*

Lillian rolls her eyes and makes a dry, scornful noise. "That's one word for it."

I don't answer or tell her to be nice. I'm thinking about smiling Monica, about smiling Cecily and the awful scattering of plastic toys lying in the grass around her. The valentine that is the only thing tying them together, and I'm not even sure it's a real thing.

I glance over at Lillian. "When Monica died, it was in the newspapers for a while, right? All the interviews and details about the investigation and everything?"

I expect her to say, *How should I know*, but instead she nods, looking almost awkward.

"Well, I think we should try to find copies of that stuff, check the details, see if there's anything about a heart, or Valentine's Day, or what her head wound was like, anything that could connect her to Cecily. The library would have all that, wouldn't it?"

Lillian sits very still, like she's bracing herself for something. It takes a minute before she answers. "Or you could go get it from my house. I have a scrapbook in my room."

I sit with the yearbook open on my knees, staring at her like she's blurry around the edges and I'm trying to make her come into focus. "Sorry, a what?"

"It was just this thing," she says, sounding defensive, talking very fast. "I was really bothered that someone could just die like that, with no warning. I just—I sort of kept a record of all the important things, plus a bunch of little details, dates and stuff. So it's all there. You just have to go and get it."

"Are you insane? I'm just supposed to ring the doorbell and ask your mom if I can go downstairs and get your secret dead-girl scrapbook out of your room?"

Lillian gives me a disdainful look. "Don't be stupid. Anyway, she's at work right now."

✻   ✻   ✻

Lillian's house is big and eggshell-white, and right across the street from Muncy Park.

When she was alive, Lillian and I would sometimes climb out her window late at night and run across the street to the playground. We'd swing on the tire swing or lie on the grass by the baseball diamonds, even though Lillian's curfew was eleven o'clock and the park was supposed to be closed to the public after dark.

I haven't been on this side of Muncy Park since before she died, and it's weird to me that her street doesn't look any different from the way it looked six months ago. The trees and bushes all have leaves now and the daylilies are in bloom, but otherwise it's exactly the same.

I have to climb in through her bedroom window, which is in the front, barely hidden behind a row of snowball bushes. I cross the lawn, trying to look inconspicuous and like I belong there. The neighborhood is deserted, though. It's still before five, so most of the neighbors aren't home yet.

Her bedroom is in the basement, which means that in theory, all I have to do is open the window and crawl in. The window is the sliding kind that locks with a metal spring latch, and even though I don't think it's very likely, I'm a little worried that someone will have noticed the lock doesn't exactly do what it's supposed to and gotten it fixed.

The thing is, Lillian's mother caught her sneaking out. Lillian's mother caught her sneaking out more than once. The first time, she got all worked up and yelled and threatened to take away her cell phone, but yelling at Lillian has never really had much of an impact.

After a while, it got so that any time Mrs. Wald woke up and found Lillian gone, she'd go through the house and make sure everything was locked, so if Lillian wanted back in, she'd have to ring the doorbell. It was supposed to be this tactic of parental control, but Mrs. Wald underestimated exactly how much Lillian hated being told what to do.

Lillian's solution was simple. She took apart the window latch with a screwdriver and put it back together so the little metal lever always looked like it was in the locked position, when really, it didn't lock at all. The fact that someone might be able to break into her house didn't even faze her. Ludlow was safe enough—safe enough to walk around the park in the middle of the night, safe enough to leave her window unlocked so she would always be able to get back in. But now that sense of security is gone, and it makes me wonder if it was ever safe at all.

I have to slide through the window on my stomach, which is precariously awkward, and for a second, I'm scared I'm going to fall through and land on my head on the floor. Her bed is still pushed against the wall, though, right under the window. When I drop down onto it, the impact sends a puff of dust billowing up around me, and I have to press my hands over my face and close my eyes to keep from sneezing.

Being in Lillian's room is like being in a wax museum or someplace just as eerie.

It's so dark that at first my eyes can't focus, and the air seems oddly damp, like I'm standing under a swamp cooler. The bed is still half made, the quilt hanging down over the mattress at an angle so one corner of it touches the floor. Her Emilie Autumn poster is still tacked up on the wall, but her computer and most of her books are gone. The closet is empty, but her basketball trophies from elementary school are still on the little shelf above her desk.

When I swing myself off the bed, Lillian is standing in the middle of the room, looking around like we're in the wrong place. "What happened to all my stuff?" she whispers.

I cross to the bookshelf, which is mostly bare except for a few figure-skating programs and a framed picture of Lillian with her dad. Things the Salvation Army probably wouldn't want.

"Maybe your mom got rid of it," I whisper, picking up a glass paperweight with a tiny seahorse suspended in the center. "Almost everything's gone."

I'm suddenly so sure that we came here for nothing and the scrapbook has gone into the donation box or the trash with the rest of her stuff, but Lillian shakes her head and motions me over to her bed.

It's a huge oak cabin bed, with a carved headboard and built-in drawers underneath. The scrapbook is in the one closest to the wall, shoved all the way in the back. It's a three-ring photo album, with a lumpy handmade paper cover, cream-colored with real rose petals and dried ferns mixed in with the pulp. It would look elegant, like something for a wedding, but Lillian has drawn all over it with a marker, making the dried flowers look spiky and ominous.

Inside, the book is filled with articles cut out of the *Ludlow Herald* and printed from various online news sites. The last item in the book is a one-page follow-up article from December, ten months after Monica's body was found. After that, the rest of the pages are blank.

I sit on the carpet with the book open in my lap. In the margins, Lillian has added all these little notes and comments, mostly cross-referencing people and places.

It's detailed and methodical, but that part doesn't really surprise me; Lillian was always writing things down. After she was sick, it got worse. She started keeping this little purple notebook full of numbers—how many steps she'd walked, pounds she'd lost, calories, carbs, grams of sugar she'd eaten. Breaths she'd taken.

No, the shocking part of the scrapbook is the absolute gruesomeness of it.

"This must have taken forever," I say, touching a bold five-pointed star that she's scrawled next to the clipping of Monica's obituary. "How come you never told me about it?"

Lillian laughs, and it's not as harsh or as mean as it could be. "You would have just said I was being creepy and then changed the subject."

I nod, because it's probably even true. The book is one of the creepiest things I've ever seen.

Suddenly, from upstairs, there's a faint metallic jingling, barely audible, but I freeze, listening. It's the sound of a key in the front door. The door opens, then closes again, and the ceiling echoes with the sound of footsteps overhead.

"It's cool," Lillian says, leaning over the scrapbook. "Just don't make any noise. It's not like she's going to come down here or anything."

I'm pretty sure she's right, but I get up and close the door anyway, before picking up the book and heading for the window. Lillian was a lot taller than me, and I'm not sure how to get myself back into the yard.

I'm trying to figure out the best way to climb out, when upstairs, another door opens and I can hear Mrs. Wald talking to someone. And then comes the sound of frantic, scrabbling feet. I recognize it immediately. Our dog, Joan, does the same noisy, ecstatic dance any time you shake the Milk-Bone box.

There's an explosion of barking right outside Lillian's door—the huge, booming kind of barking that only comes from something the size of a pony—and Lillian gasps and makes a grab for me, pushing me toward the window.

I turn to stare at her. "Your mom got a dog?"

She opens her eyes wide and gives me a hard shove. "I didn't know!"

I scramble for the window, trying to boost myself up through the opening, but it's too high and I can barely even get my head level with the flowerbed.

My heart is pounding in my throat, and now I can hear Lillian's mom on the stairs, yelling for the dog to be quiet. The storm of barking doesn't even slow down.

"Shut up!" she yells, and this time I can tell she's right outside the door.

I toss the scrapbook out into the yard and swing one foot on top of the headboard. Then, with my toe braced on one of the carved wooden roses, I shove myself face-first into the snowball bushes in front of the house, rolling over and pulling my legs up.

Behind me, the barking is suddenly much, much louder, and I lie flat, desperate not to make any noise. I can just see the top of Mrs. Wald's head as she comes into the room, and while she's staring in the direction of the closet, I slide the window shut, then snatch the scrapbook up and run.

I pelt across the street into the park without checking for traffic—past the soccer fields and the playground, past the white plywood concession stand. I cut straight across the bike path and into the wooded nature area, where everything is underbrush and tall grass, and the only paths are narrow dirt trails that wind aimlessly along the edge of the river, all the way through town.

The rational part of me knows that there's no one behind me, that Mrs. Wald didn't even see me, but I tighten my grip on the scrapbook and keep running, following the paths that lead toward Sherwood Street and home.

It's too hot to run for long, though, and I'm so far back in the trees that I can't even see Lillian's neighborhood behind me anymore. After a few more yards, I slow to a walk, heading in the direction of the nearest bridge.

As I start down the shallow embankment toward the river, a huge, unearthly bang echoes through the trees, sending storms of birds flapping into the sky above me. I try to catch my balance, but my ballet flats are slick and I slide the rest of the way down on my butt, landing at the bottom in a tangle of honeysuckle bushes.

Everything is quiet.

The leaves are cool against my face and arms, and under the bushes the air smells sweet like fresh wet dirt and sugar. Mosquitoes are everywhere, whining around me in a cloud, but at first I don't even wave them away. I just lie in the shade of the bushes, gasping, trying to catch my breath. The force of the explosion still echoes in my ears, making my head feel numb and fuzzy. I stay very still, listening, but it doesn't come again. I try to remember if I've ever heard a car backfire and if it sounded like that. If thunder ever happens when there are no clouds.

When I finally sit up, my hair is sticking to the back of my neck. I brush the dust and twigs off myself but don't crawl out from under the bushes. The honeysuckle flowers are baby-yellow with a flush of pink around the edges of the petals. My skirt is a mess, covered in dirt and streaked with grass stains from Lillian's front yard.

I'm sitting with the scrapbook in my lap and my head tipped back, staring up at the little gaps of sky that show between the honeysuckle branches, when from somewhere close by there's the heavy, plodding sound of footsteps crunching through the underbrush.

In a panic, I curl over Lillian's scrapbook and close my eyes, like if I concentrate hard enough, I can disappear. All I can think of is how running into the park was insanely, incredibly stupid, that there's a killer loose in the city—maybe even in my neighborhood—and there is no way my red tulip-print skirt won't be totally obvious through the leaves. I don't move. I don't breathe. Everything is perfectly quiet. No crickets or grasshoppers, no birds. All I can hear is the river.

The silence goes on and on, and I stay perfectly still, waiting for a squirrel to chatter down at me or a thrush to sing. Then, when the silence gets too long and I can't stand it anymore, I take a deep breath and raise my head.

Finny Boone is standing over me. His shoes are muddy and he's got a package of Black Cat firecrackers sticking out of his front pocket, which at least solves the mystery of the booming explosion. In his good hand, he's holding the stolen Qwik-Mart lighter.

"Are you okay?" he says.

I stare up at him with the scrapbook clutched against my chest. It takes me a few tries before I manage the word "Yes."

For a second, he doesn't do anything. Then he nods. He doesn't look at me like I've completely lost my mind. He doesn't ask me what I'm doing in the middle of the park, in a honeysuckle bush, with a stolen photo album full of morbid newspaper clippings.

"Haven't you been watching the news?" he says. "You shouldn't be out here alone."

❋ ❋ ❋

Finny waits with his back to me, staring off in the direction of the river, while I fight my way out of the bush and yank my skirt straight.

It's still early, and the sun is just starting to sink down over the tops of the trees. The air is hot, and all around us, the little hollow is full of shadows.

There are bridges all along the length of the park, and I start toward the closest one, which will take me across to the other side of the park and to Sherwood Street.

"Hey," Finny says as I step around him onto the path. "Wait up."

"Why?"

"I'm coming with you," he says.

It's weird walking through the park with him. All I can think of is how much I don't really know him, even though during the school year I see him in the halls almost every day, and he lives on my side of the park, and we've been in the same district since first grade.

At the river, Finny steps down the slope above the bridge and I start to follow him, but my shoes are useless, slipping and sliding on the packed dirt. I almost have a repeat of my tumble into the honeysuckle, but he holds out his hand to steady me and I have to grab it or else I'll go right into the water. His fingers are warm and solid in mine, and I think how it's surprising and kind of cool that he will just offer his hand to another person, even someone sweaty and red-faced and covered in leaves.

When we get to the edge of the park, I kind of expect him to leave me to walk the rest of the way alone, but he doesn't. He just turns in the direction of my house like it's something we've already agreed on.

"You don't have to walk the whole way with me," I say. "I'll be fine. It isn't that far."

Finny gives me a bored look and shakes his head. "It's far enough. Seriously, you can't be walking around out here without someone to watch out for you." Then he smiles. "And I don't want to brag or anything, but I'm kind of scary-looking."

It takes me a second to realize that he might actually be making a joke. I didn't even know he was the kind of person who made jokes. He is kind of scary-looking, though.

We walk in silence, winding our way through my neighborhood. The sun is setting now, and it's sort of . . . nice not to talk. Usually, I have this whole parade of things I could be saying—how *Spirited Away* is a really good movie and what kind of Jolly Ranchers I like and whether or not the new statue in front of the bank is ugly. But most of those things aren't that important, and sometimes when I talk all I'm really doing is filling up the silence. The streets are empty and still, and it's funny to think that I've never walked anywhere alone at night with a boy, and now I am.

"Hey," Finny says when we're almost to the little flag-stone walkway that leads up to my front porch. He sounds careful, like he's trying to get a poem or a motto right, only he's not sure he knows all the words.

I glance up at him, waiting for the rest. The way he's scuffing his shoes along the pavement seems almost nervous, and I can't help thinking that right now, if he wanted to move closer or reach for my hand again, there's a part of me that would really, really be okay with that.

"Do you remember in Mrs. Winslow's class?" His voice is low and flat. It takes me by surprise. Mrs. Winslow was our teacher in elementary school.

"Sure. What about it?"

He doesn't answer right away. His hand skims the brittle crest of his hair, like he's trying to make it lie flat. "She had that whole thing about birthdays."

"Oh. I guess?"

But she did. She had this special birthday calendar on the wall behind her desk. When your day had a star on it, you got to come up and pick a prize out of a cardboard box in her desk, and your parents could bring cookies or cupcakes, and everyone would sing. The way you could tell who was popular was by whose parents sent them to school with fancy store-bought cupcakes piled high with frosting, and whose sent weird homemade ones, wilting in their paper wrappers. Or else, who got sent with nothing, which happened sometimes too.

"One person gave me a birthday card," he says in a flat matter-of-fact way that makes me walk faster and squeeze the scrapbook against my chest.

It was just a piece of construction paper folded in half, but I spent a long time on it, making sure all the words were spelled right and the letters were straight. It said HAPPY BIRTHDAY in army-green marker, with the vowels outlined in orange and a squished-looking drawing of a truck underneath, because he liked trucks.

He stops walking and turns to face me, standing with his feet apart and his shoulders squared, so he's taking up most of the sidewalk. "Why did you do that? You didn't even like me." The way he says it is like he's just telling me the truth, but his voice sounds low and empty suddenly, all wrong. Maybe sad isn't the right word, but he's something.

I wish so desperately that the answer was better. That in third grade, I was kind and thoughtful or didn't want him to feel left out, but that wasn't why I made him the card. It just hadn't occurred to me that there was any reason I wouldn't.

Finny sighs and starts walking again. "Never mind. I don't even know why you'd remember. Anyway, it was a long time ago."

The way he says it is so similar to the way Lillian always acts, like she has to remind me of the past, as though I will have somehow actually forgotten, that I laugh even though it really isn't funny.

Finny gives me a quick, defensive look, like I might be laughing at him. "What?"

"Nothing. You just sound like my friend, is all."

Out of habit, I glance around the empty street for her, but she's nowhere.

8: Serial

When I open the front door, Lillian's waiting for me in the hall, perched on top of a cardboard box of hand-embroidered linens from the fifties.

I start to go upstairs to change out of my ruined skirt, but she holds up a hand to stop me.

"No time," she whispers. "Quick, it's all over the news."

In the living room, Ariel is standing in the exact center of the antique rug, staring at the screen. I'm about to come up behind her and tweak her ear, when the stiffness of her back catches my attention and I stop.

"They found another one," she says, glancing over her shoulder. "Just above that big culvert at Muncy, where the water comes in."

News anchor Ron Coleman is shuffling his papers around on the desk. When he raises his head, the look he gives the camera is heartfelt and sober. "Police are investigating what authorities now suspect is the second in a pair of related murders. The victim was found earlier today and has been identified as thirteen-year-old Hailey Martinsen, a student at Lincoln Middle School."

The photo they show is of a pretty, brown-eyed girl. Now deceased.

Ariel and I stand transfixed as they play a grainy video of some elementary school kids singing a math-themed parody song to the tune of a babyish pop song that Ariel and her friends like. All the kids in the video are blurred out except for one grinning dark-haired girl in the middle. She's younger than in her school picture, and the circle of focus floats around her in a halo, following as she dances to the beat.

Ariel turns slowly on the spot, revolving like a windup toy. The way she looks at me is lit up with something almost like excitement. "I did that project," she says in a breathless voice. "Last year. Me and Pinky and Katie did. We did ours on integers."

The anchor comes on again, reminding us that the body of Cecily Miles was discovered in Muncy Nature Park just this past Saturday. Reminding us that the park is close to a hundred square acres and that until the killer is caught, no one should be walking there alone.

The segment is followed by special correspondent Cora Butcher interviewing one of the detectives. "Is it true," she says, waving her microphone in his face, "that the way this second crime scene was staged is highly suggestive of evidence found around the body of the first victim?"

The detective tells her that this is an open investigation and he isn't free to comment. Then the news switches over to a story about the recent rise in petty crime, clips of police and local store owners talking about vandalism and an upsurge in shoplifting, and finishing with another segment on communicable blood diseases and the dead birds.

Ariel's standing with her arms stiff at her sides, and it's weird to see her so still.

"Go turn down the thermostat," I say, not quite daring to touch her. I want to shake her hard, just to make her move. "Why is it so hot in here?"

"The air conditioner's broken," she tells me, glancing up at me in a flat, distracted way.

The look on her face is the strangest kind of vacant, and she doesn't ask me why there's dirt all over the front of my skirt or why I'm carrying a wedding album.

When I turn to leave the room, Lillian is standing in the doorway. She's cupping her elbows in her hands, and when she meets my eyes, her expression is stricken. "That's our killer again already. That just happened today."

I nod, trying to get a grip on the fact that I was in the park at the same time that the killer was in the park, and now Hailey Martinsen is dead in the park, almost exactly a week from the death of Cecily Miles. My thoughts are fast and circular, like ponies on a merry-go-round I can't get down from.

In my room, Lillian stalks over to crouch on the edge of the bed. Her face is turned away from me, and her fingers are sunk deep in the fabric of my comforter.

I sit down in the middle of my rug, still holding Lillian's scrapbook. Right now, I don't want to open it. The thing is, there are just going to be more articles, more girls to go inside.

I'll have to open it eventually, whether I want to or not, and so for a few minutes, I only sit there holding it in my lap.

Lillian scoots to the edge of the bed, looking down at me over the side. "Aren't you going to read any of the articles? It's what you wanted, right?"

I lie on my back and study the ceiling, which is covered in smears of glitter glue and stick-on stars. The way Lillian says it is hungry, like she's waiting for something to be revealed, and I wonder if maybe that's the real difference between us—that when she pulls back the curtain and stares into the blackness behind it, it's just one more way of testing herself. Like some game you can never win, because even if you face all the shocking realities and the horrors of the world, once you've seen that kind of awfulness, you can never un-see it. You have to carry it around with you forever.

She stands up in the middle of the jumbled mattress and then begins to pace, walking briskly from the bed to the desk to the dresser. Perched on the bookshelf, she seems impossibly tall, towering over me. Then she crouches down and clasps her hands.

"Why do you think he does it?" she says, picking at her bloodless cuticles. She's hunched over like a giant bird, hair hanging down on either side of her face, making a kind of hood.

I stare up at the ceiling. "That's the big question. I mean, if they knew that, they'd be able to catch him, right? Do you think he put all those toys around her the way he did with Cecily?"

111

Lillian sits up straight and cups her chin in her hands. "The way they wouldn't talk about the crime scene means it probably looks a whole lot like the other one, which means he's got a thing about the ritual—an obsession. He'll need to keep indulging it now. He'll keep going till they catch him."

"Jesus." I squeeze my eyes shut and cover my face with my hands. "What kind of person even does something like this?"

I mean it rhetorically, but when Lillian answers, she sounds serious and thoughtful. "He'd be someone angry, maybe. Someone who wants to feel like he's got power, because maybe the rest of the time, he's at the mercy of someone else?"

"Why do you keep saying *he*?" I whisper, letting my hands fall.

"Oh, come on. If a woman kills a lot of people, it's almost always for money or self-preservation. This, though . . . This is for fun."

I shake my head, still staring at the ceiling. "Psycho. How do these girls not see that he's psycho?"

"Appealing and dangerous can sometimes look like the same thing," Lillian says, touching her jutting collarbone.

"What's that supposed to mean?"

Lillian sighs and looks away. "Nothing. It's just that sometimes it's hard to tell the difference. I mean, look at you. Someone's out there killing girls, and you're running around with Finny Boone—this total reject who steals from the Quik-Mart. I mean, don't you think it's kind of reckless?"

But the idea of Lillian Wald—self-destructor extraordinaire—telling anyone else about reckless behavior is totally laughable.

I want to remind her about the time she took that bottle of Sour Apple Pucker from her mom's liquor cabinet and we drank it in the back of her garage, and the time she snuck out alone to catch the midnight bus to see her dad even though it was twenty degrees out and she didn't have permission, and that time she talked me into breaking into her mom's house to steal a makeshift shrine to a murder victim. And that time she didn't eat for so long that she died.

❊ ❊ ❊

My room is sweltering. When Decker got home, he spent forty-five minutes out in the backyard trying to fix the air conditioner, but it's frozen over, covered in a thick crust of ice.

Lillian is humming to herself, stretched out on top of my bookcase like she doesn't mind the heat, and of course she doesn't. Even when she was alive, she could never seem to get warm. The tune she's humming is thin and tight with anxiety. It's the opposite of carefree.

The obvious explanation for her mood would be the new murder, but somehow I don't think that's all of it.

It was hard seeing Mrs. Wald today. After the funeral, I never called her or went to visit, even though I'd been coming over for years, almost every day. And now, on some insane secret mission, I've broken into her house, risking all kinds of trouble, when the truth is she probably would have just let me in if I'd asked. Knowing that makes me feel guilty, but even now it seems like there was no other way. I don't think I could have faced her.

It would have been just like it was after the funeral. She would have hugged me stiffly. Invited me in to sit in the living room with her, and I wouldn't have had any idea what to say.

When we were little, Lillian even used to get along with her mom. Kind of. They weren't always arguing at least. Back then, all Lillian wanted was just to make her mom happy.

Then she started dieting, got more interested in track than school or clothes or boys. And after a while, being sick was the only thing that mattered at all.

"Why did you get so weird about food?" I say, moving my head against the pillow.

"I wasn't. I wasn't being weird. I was just . . ." Then she stops. Even though I can't see her face from down here, I know she's pressing her lips together. "It was a place to put the awful stuff. A box for everything about myself that I didn't like."

I have a box like that, but it's a real one, covered in cutout pictures of lips and mouths, all printed on slick magazine paper, all gaping wide open and full of teeth. I put disappointing quizzes and bad history reports in it. I put the sixteenth-birthday card I made for Lillian in the box, and the evaluation the guidance counselor gave me to take home to my mom.

"Why?" I say, so quietly that it comes out sounding like a tiny, tired sigh.

"Nobody wants to be mediocre."

Her shadow on the ceiling is monstrous, a witch in profile.

"Your mom didn't ever say anything or get worried about you?"

"Not when it might have made a difference."

And I know it's the truth. I was there, after all. But the idea is so foreign, and until recently, my mother has been a never-ending voice of anxiety, always coming right at me with sunscreen and Band-Aids and night-lights. "How could she just stand there and let you do that to yourself?"

Lillian turns her head sideways and smiles, showing all her teeth. "Well, it was my problem, right? My own shit to deal with."

The way she says it is nasty and final. She doesn't say anything else, and after a minute, I roll over and reach for the lamp.

The broken air conditioner seems more broken in the dark, and the heat comes in waves, throbbing like a bad tooth.

Someone has stolen the trees outside my room and replaced them with bones—the kind that throw long shadows on the wall, reaching in through the butter-yellow curtains until morning.

If I were younger, I would think of ghostly hands. Hailey Martinsen, reaching in from the afterlife, fumbling through my things until at last she finds the way back to the real world. But what a joke. Lillian found her way in, found the secret passage months ago, and now her skeleton grin is just normal.

After two, when I still can't sleep, I flail around in the

tangled nest of covers and then throw all the blankets onto the floor. The air is dry and suffocating.

I'm lying on my back with the window open and my T-shirt hiked halfway up to leave my stomach bare, when there's a low rustle and Lillian climbs onto the bed and hunches there, crouching over me. The air around me is suddenly freezing.

"You get to need it," she says. "That's the thing. You start out so strong, in perfect order, controlling everything, and then you get to need it."

Lying there in the dark, I know that no matter how deeply I imagine needing something, I'll never understand.

My body is . . . my body. In the past four years, it hasn't changed much. My hipbones are wider, but other than that, it's practically the same one I had in seventh grade.

Except for the way I want to press it against Finny. The thought of him is electric, beating in my chest like a birthday wish, dark and warm and secret.

"Did you ever think about boys?" I say, staring up into the dark.

The shape of Lillian looms over me. If she were a live girl, I'd be able to hear her breathing.

"There wasn't room," she whispers, and her voice is unbelievably sad. "At first, after Connor, I was just waiting. I was going to get a new boyfriend soon—as soon as I was prettier or better, more perfect. But after a while, there was no room for anything else. If I thought about kissing, or sex, I just started feeling ugly, too awful for anything good."

116

Above her, the galaxy of stick-on stars stands out in pale specks, but the glow is faint, losing all the light the stickers soaked up during the daytime. I never really used to get too philosophical about things like existence and free will and mortality, but since the murders started, I keep thinking more and more about how hideous it is that someone can just take your entire life away from you, at any second. You won't have a choice.

"And it was still worth it?" I whisper to Lillian in the dark. "Not to have the laughing and swimming pools and movies and the kissing? How could you just give all that up?"

"Because you want to have a real, normal life and be okay, but even more, you want to be beyond it and not want anything. You're always thinking two different things."

So am I. The pattern alternates between *Lillian died from a bad disease* and *Why the hell didn't she just decide to get better?*

9: Circus

In the span of a weekend, everything has changed. By Monday, there are public service announcements running on TV every hour, telling parents to keep their kids inside as much as possible and to watch their neighborhoods for anything suspicious.

I spend half of Saturday afternoon on the phone with Angelie, talking about the murders and how crazy everything is, how our parents are dealing with it and what new rules we each have to follow.

"This whole thing is just so out of control," she says with a weird little shudder in her voice. "I mean, I was so freaked out when I heard about that second girl. Weren't you so freaked out to hear about it?"

I nod into the phone. The way she says it is loud, almost theatrical, and I want to tell her that it's not a contest, but it wouldn't be the right thing to say. Because maybe for the first time since Lillian started that whole stupid thing two years ago, it would actually be true.

My mom is nearly hysterical over the fact that there's been a second murder, and there's a very tense twenty-minute period after breakfast where she decides that I'm not allowed to go out after seven, or go farther than the end of the street, or spend the night at anyone's house.

Even after Decker takes her into the kitchen and talks to her in a soothing voice for so long that they're both late for work, she still seems like she might be on the verge of a meltdown. I have to make a million promises not to get in anyone's car or go anywhere secluded or talk to strangers, just so she'll let me walk the three blocks from Harris Johnson to Quality Photo without making Jessica or Angelie come with me.

When I get to the shop, Kelly is sitting at the counter with her calculator out, glaring down at the price schedule. She doesn't even glance up until I'm right in front of her, and when she finally does, she squeaks and drops her pen.

"Sorry," I say, propping my elbows on top of the register. "I didn't mean to startle you."

"Trust me," she says, raising an eyebrow. "Nothing startling about you, except for maybe that dress."

I'm wearing a yellow sundress with a little white petticoat underneath. The dress is vintage, worn soft at the hem, and the petticoat flares out just enough to give the whole silhouette a slightly fifties look. I tilt my head and drop a curtsy, holding out the hem of my skirt. Admittedly, the fabric is very bright.

Kelly sets down the calculator, then spins on the stool, looking into my face. "Hannah, I want you and Ariel to be really safe, okay?" She says it like someone's squeezing her throat, but she's determined to get the words out anyway. Kelly has never been a sentimentalist.

"Yeah, I know. My mom already gave me a whole speech."

"Still, you should listen to her." Kelly clears her throat and mumbles the next part down at the counter without looking at me. "I worry about you guys."

"We're fine," I say, sounding bright and airy. The back of my dress pinches me when I breathe in, the zipper teeth digging into my skin.

And even as I say it, I'm thinking that we're not. *We're not fine. Nothing is fine.* I'm thinking, *This isn't how Ludlow is supposed to be*, that the whole awfulness of this is not safe or right or fair, just ugly.

When Boles and McGarahan come in with their bag of film, Boles dumps the whole thing out and begins to pick through it, separating out three rolls and setting them aside. "We need these ones ready this afternoon—as soon as you can get them. It's our dead girl number two."

McGarahan gives him a warning look and shakes his head. He glances at me, but carefully, like he's trying to do it without me seeing. I don't bother to tell him that I already know. It was all over the news all weekend. Everyone already knows.

"My God." Kelly shakes her head and takes a little step back, like by leaning away from the bag of film, she can avoid the ghostly touch of a dead girl. "I can't get over this. It's just crazy."

McGarahan nods, looking anxious, younger than he

usually does. He leans closer, speaking in a low voice just under his breath, but I can hear every word. "We won't know anything for a few more days. We're still waiting on forensics, but everything's pretty consistent. We're almost definitely looking at a serial killer."

Behind the counter, Lillian jabs me and I don't flinch. I twist my hair around one finger to make a limp curl. I try to keep my expression mildly curious, but it keeps feeling horrified instead.

McGarahan turns to me. "You know," he says, in that way grown-ups do when they have something crucial to say, but they don't want to scare you by letting you see how important it is. "I'm sure your parents already told you to be careful about talking to strangers and not to go places alone, right?"

I nod, peeling a stray piece of tape off the counter. The number of times I've been told this in the past twenty-four hours is beginning to rival the number of days the thermometer at the bank has broken a hundred. Days when the sun sits over the city, blindingly white and baking everything to a hard, brittle crust. The nights when I let Lillian's ghost in bed with me, because maybe she's cloud and vapor and not really real, but the dry chill of her next to me is still better than empty silence and brutal, unrelenting heat.

Officer McGarahan's eyes are full of a deep, troubling concern. It scratches my throat like sand. "Look, just be careful. There's someone dangerous out there, and it's not smart to go thinking that because you're young, it's the same as being immortal."

I open the junk drawer for a rubber band and look up at Officer McGarahan. His face is steady and sad, like he's seen it all before. Like he's thinking of some other dead girl—one he couldn't save with his friendly neighborhood warnings. The unsuspecting victim.

Lillian was always so good at treating everything like a test, like some kind of game where the prize was shiny and untouchable. Perfection. She wanted me to back off, butt out, stop trying to control her life. And she wanted me to save her.

There are all kinds of things in the world that can happen to a person. Terrible, unpredictable things. Suddenly, the world seems very random, full of freak accidents—killers and bird viruses and pinch points.

Maybe she thought she was immortal, but I don't.

❋ ❋ ❋

Kelly spends the rest of the morning pacing back and forth between the printer and the door. Every time she sits down to work on an order, she gets maybe three frames in and then jumps right back up again. I don't know if she's doing it on purpose, but it's nerve-racking.

I'm beginning to think there's no way I'll ever have a chance to slip into the back and get a look at the photos of Hailey Martinsen before I have to pick Ariel up from band, but then Mrs. Price comes in with Connor to pick up her enlargements.

I don't like Mrs. Price, because she has this way of treating everyone like they are much, much stupider than she is, and once she yelled at me for touching her prints without gloves on. Also, every time I've been over to the Prices' house, which is easily fifteen times in the past three years, she always looks at me like she's never seen me before and I don't belong in her living room.

Or maybe that's just how she feels about anything she didn't put there herself. Her whole house is full of Tiffany floor lamps and velvet upholstery and faux-Victorian bookends shaped like cupids, and is always featured in the Ludlow Home Decorating Tour, which is something she never gets tired of mentioning.

Today, she goes straight up to the counter without even glancing at me, but Connor comes over to the sink, where I'm washing a big stack of plastic leader cards. "What up, Twinkie?"

I shake the water off the card and set it on a towel. "Not a lot. I'm just here till I have to go pick up Ariel from band. What are you doing here?"

Connor makes a face and lets his shoulders slump. "I need to get a new set of screw-ins for my cleats, but my mom didn't want me to go by myself, so now we're running errands."

At the counter, Mrs. Price is flipping through her order. "You printed this one blurry," she tells Kelly, holding up an eight-by-ten.

Kelly's standing with her elbows propped on the shelf behind the register, and the look she gives Mrs. Price is frighteningly patient. "No, I didn't."

Mrs. Price pinches the enlargement between two fingers

and holds it out, giving it a little shake. "Are you really going to look at this and tell me it's not blurry?"

Kelly takes it from her and makes a big thing of examining it. "Yep, that's blurry all right."

"Then you're going to reprint it free of charge."

"No, I'm actually not."

"It's not a machine error," I say before I can help myself. The way Kelly just announces things without explaining always makes me feel so agitated, like I need to jump in and translate for her. "Matilda Braun uses an optical lens, but it's stationary. As long as the lens is clean, there's no way for it to be us."

Mrs. Price turns on me with a fierce, uncomprehending stare. "I just looked through fifteen perfectly clear shots, so don't tell me that it's not your machines."

"Mom," Connor says, looking kind of mortified. "God, calm down."

"Don't you dare talk to Hannah like that," Kelly says, snatching up the photo. "I was standing right next to you last week when you picked out your enlargements on that light table, and you told me that you had to have this shot. And when I said that all the exposures of your giant, tacky-ass mantelpiece were soft, you told me you couldn't see anything wrong with them. Well this? This is that thing you couldn't see."

Mrs. Price is leaning forward, eyes narrowed. Sometimes, mostly when she smiles, she looks a little like Connor. Right now, though, the resemblance is nonexistent.

"Let me explain something to you, missy. I don't have to bring my business here. I don't have to put up with your language or your disrespect or your laughable customer service. Although honestly? I don't know why I'm even surprised that you have no idea how to run a business, considering this is coming from someone who has children working in their store!"

Connor snorts into his hand and gives me an incredulous look, like *Can you even believe this?* "Mom, she's not 'children.' Hannah's in my same grade at school."

With her face arranged in a perfect icy mask, Kelly takes me by the shoulders and turns me toward the back. "Hannah, why don't you go straighten up the supply cupboard?"

I give Connor a little wave and head for the back.

As soon as I step into the office, I find Lillian standing in the shadow of the supply cupboard, looking gaunt.

"Quick," she says, motioning me toward the desk. I cross the room and crouch down to open the safe.

The homicide close-ups are in the third envelope. I stand with my hand resting on the desktop, almost like I need to catch my balance. The way my head feels is light and dizzy, like this is all taking place in my imagination. Just some dream I'm having, and soon I'll wake up and go downstairs and everything will be fine.

But it isn't a dream and nothing is fine. I can feel the shock at the base of my skull, throbbing to the hum of the air conditioner.

Hailey is one of those girls that everyone just liked

without even knowing why or having to think about it. You can see it, even as she's lying in the tall grass above the culvert. Even with her T-shirt torn and her hair bloody and tangled. Her absolute goodness is everywhere, right down to the orange polish chipping off her fingernails and the spray of freckles on one cheek.

Around her, lying in the grass like spilled candy or Easter eggs, are the toys. The pattern seems to be random, just like with the things that littered the ground around Cecily Miles.

I immediately notice an assortment of candy—squares of Bazooka gum and red-and-white striped Starlight mints. Then a rubber pencil topper shaped like a slice of watermelon, liquor store keychains and plastic whistles and a Hello Kitty compact with a broken latch. I spend a long time squinting at one of the close-up shots, trying to figure out what I'm looking at. I finally have to turn the print upside down before I recognize the thin, twisted shape. A purple crazy straw.

The riveting thing, though, is the valentine. It's placed carefully, propped against the curve of Hailey's shoulder. It's bigger than the one that was lying near Cecily's hand, and more complicated, made of two interlocking hearts and decorated with little clusters of concentric circles, alternating pink and red. The scalloped lace around the edges is dusted with a sprinkling of pearl-colored glitter, and in the close-ups I can see where the glitter landed unevenly and the glue beaded up, making lumps along one side.

126

I stand with my back against the counter, flipping through the entire set, then going back to the beginning, looking over all the evidence a second time. Every time I get another look at Hailey's face, I have a painful, electrified feeling in my chest.

I keep thinking Lillian will at least say something, but she just stands against the supply cabinet with her hands cupped over her bony shoulders and her teeth working at her bottom lip.

I don't know what to do or what I should be looking for. I can make out twenty-eight different police markers in the grass right around the body, and there are another five or so scattered farther in the weeds, denoting objects, but I can't tell what they are.

"This is trash," I whisper, glancing at Lillian. "It's, like, party favors from third grade and the world's crappiest candy. I mean, what is this?"

Lillian doesn't answer. She's chewing distractedly on her pajama cuff, watching my finger as it hovers over the photo, following the trail of police markers. I squint down at the photo and shake my head. There's a thought squirming in the back of my mind, but it's tangled up with all these other thoughts and I can't quite make it come into focus.

Lillian's still chewing her cuff, but she isn't looking at the photos anymore. She glances up and starts to speak, but just then there's a scuffling noise from the doorway, and she opens her eyes wide and points frantically behind me.

I whip around, expecting Kelly, and almost gasp out loud

with relief. Connor is leaning around the doorway to the office, peering at me curiously. Quickly, I jam the photos back into their envelope, then shove the whole stack of orders inside the safe and close it.

Connor gives me a look of mild surprise. "Wow, what were those?" Then he grins, wiggling his eyebrows. "Wait, were you looking at something dirty? I bet you were—I bet you've got something completely filthy in there. Come on, let me see."

"Pervert," Lillian says, folding her arms across her chest and staring at the ceiling, but she's biting her cheek like she's trying not to smile. And I know that for all her disdainful comments and her eye-rolling, there's still this tiny, sentimental part of her that never really stopped liking him.

I shake my head, then motion Connor into the office so I can whisper. "It wasn't anything like that. It's just . . . We print the police photos, but I'm not supposed to look at them, so I was . . . That's what I was doing."

If I ever admitted something like that to Angelie, she'd probably tell me I was disturbed, but Connor looks frankly impressed. "You get to see the crime-scene photos? How come you never told me you get to see crime-scene photos? I thought your whole job was just to put up with unreasonable, high-maintenance ladies like my mom. That's actually cool."

I shrug and try to casually steer him back toward the front of the store, hoping he won't ask me to show him the pictures, because then I'd have to tell him no. It's one thing to sneak a quick look when I'm alone in the office, but it would be totally unforgivable to show them to my friends. Except Lillian, but that's different because she doesn't really count.

Connor looks back over his shoulder like he's going to ask, but just then, there's the hurried scraping sound of Mrs. Price gathering up her things, and Kelly says, "Thanks for choosing Quality Photo. Come again," in a bright, clipped voice.

Connor claps his hand on my shoulder and gives me a shove. "Looks like the Price family five-ring circus is on the move. Next stop: Silver Spring Cleaners, and if her slacks aren't ready, look out! Because that show is going to be super-spectacular."

As he leaves the room, I think I catch a wistful look wash over Lillian's face, just from the corner of my eye. But by the time I turn toward her, her expression is back to normal.

"God, I hate her!" Kelly shouts as soon as Connor and his mom are out of the store. "How did that wretched, wretched woman ever even find someone to procreate with?"

I still have to finish washing the leader cards, but I don't go back out to the sink right away. There's a word going round and round in my head, tripping all over itself, and the word is *circus*. I stand perfectly still, staring into space and trying to work out why that word is stuck in my brain, because it's not the right one, but it's sort of close in that maddening way that's right on the tip of your tongue.

Lillian is standing by the supply closet, hugging herself.

"Not a circus," she says softly, almost like she's talking in her sleep. "More like a trashy neighborhood carnival. Or a tragic, seedy shrine to something."

And suddenly, the thing I've been trying to find words for slips into place, and I freeze in the doorway with my hand pressed flat against the wall.

All those cheap toys and broken party favors? Not a carnival, not a circus. It's bigger than that. They might look like trash, but what they stand for is childhood.

10: Raw

The sun is beating down by the time I leave to walk over to Harris Johnson, so bright and hot it makes my eyes ache. I have the unsettling idea that I can actually feel the heat thudding up from the pavement like a deep, constant drumbeat.

The bank clock on Evans says it's 102 degrees Fahrenheit and 1:37 PM. My lipgloss feels slick and sticky on my mouth, like it might be melting. I'm way too early to meet Pinky and Ariel, but it's better than being late. Since the discovery of Hailey Martinsen, the school has put out a new flurry of safety bulletins, and none of the kids are allowed to leave unless someone's there to pick them up.

I probably should have stayed and finished out my shift, but I had to get out of the shop. After Connor and Mrs. Price left, I went out to the front of the store like nothing had happened. I washed the rest of the cards, rinsed them carefully, and clipped them on the wire rack to dry. I did it without moving too fast or too slow, without attracting attention, and if Kelly noticed anything weird about my behavior, she ignored it, or maybe just chalked it up to Mrs. Price shouting at me and calling me a child. When I asked to leave early to go pick up the girls, she acted like it was the best idea I'd ever had. Then she hugged me, which isn't something Kelly does, and reminded me twice to be careful.

I walk the three blocks to the school slowly, like if I'm not careful of every step, every tiny movement, I will lose my grip on gravity and go flying up into the stratosphere.

It takes almost the whole walk to stop feeling like the world is tilting every which way, and I have to focus on each breath, telling myself I'm fine, that I won't come unstuck from the earth, because the staggering heat will hold me down. That the soles of my flimsy, cloth ballet flats are heavy, unmovable. I imagine myself sinking into the ground, anchored there by fabric and rubber and gravity. I'm here. I'm okay.

But as soon as I come around the corner of the school, the vague, floating feeling rushes back in, making me hold out my hands like I need to catch my balance.

Finny Boone is standing by the east doors, looking tall and brown and Clorox blond. He adjusts his grip on his books when he sees me and pushes himself away from the wall, looking off somewhere over my head.

I stop on the sidewalk a few feet away and stare up. I haven't seen him since Friday, when I broke into Lillian's room and he found me in the park and walked me home and touched my hand. I have an awkward feeling that I should say something, but I don't know what.

The thing that finally pops out is so inane I almost wince. "Aren't you supposed to be in class?"

He still doesn't look at me. "We had a test. They let us out early."

I don't ask why he hasn't gone home. I'm scared that if I ask, he'll tell me. He might say that he stayed to wait for me, and that scares me—but so does the thought that he doesn't even care that I'm here and is waiting for something else.

For maybe five seconds, we just stand facing each other but not making eye contact, looking around the parking lot at all these places that aren't each other. The sun glares down overhead, and I'm already starting to burn across the tops of my shoulders where the straps of my dress keep slipping sideways.

I tuck my bangs back into my beaded headband and make myself look at him, taking in his blank expression, his massive shoulders, and his white shirt. The way his shoes are breaking apart at the seams, like his feet are still growing.

I lace my fingers together, thinking that this is where I could use some friendly guidance from Lillian, some vague inkling of what to do now. This is where Angelie would deliver a wide, Crest-commercial smile and play flirtatiously with her cocktail rings. The part where Lillian would work her magic, punch her number into his phone, and give herself some clever nickname in the contacts. All my friends are so much better at knowing how to talk to boys.

I stand in front of him, trying to figure out how to look friendly or normal and where to put my hands. I never used to have to think about any of that—it just came naturally. It seems ridiculous suddenly that people have hands and no place to put them.

Finally, I gesture to his stack of books, which is bristling with loose papers. "Careful, you're losing one of your worksheets."

Finny raises his eyebrows and right away, I wish I hadn't said anything. The sentence hangs, and I have this idea that it's because the air is so insufferably hot. There is no room for a conversation to move.

"Thanks," he says, then yanks the worksheet from between the pages of *Foundations of English* and jams it in the trash.

The gesture is unexpected and weirdly refreshing, but he must think I'm staring at him for some other reason, because he takes a deep breath and says, "I'm sorry, okay? About the other day, with Nick. That was really shitty, what he did."

I shake my head and smile so easily it's almost automatic. "It's fine. It wasn't a big deal or anything."

He doesn't answer. The way he's looking at me is oddly gentle, like he's seeing all this bad, uncomfortable stuff inside my head, all the things I've tried so hard to ignore.

Then he clenches his jaw and looks away. "So, are you ever going to act like something actually matters?"

"What are you talking about?"

"You," he says. "You're always acting so smiley and happy, even when you shouldn't. You're like the pretend plastic doll of you. What Nick did, taking your bracelet? That was a shitty thing. At least admit that—say it. Otherwise, you're just letting bad stuff happen and then acting like you don't care."

I stare up at him, this big, scorched-brown boy squinting down at me, telling me that I should stop smiling just to smile, or start keeping a list of all the things that suck about the world. That if I don't, I'm some huge, unrelenting fake.

I want to make him see, but I don't know how to say any of the things that matter. That I have to be this way. That before, it was just the easiest way to deal with home and school and everything. And now, it's the only way to live with being haunted constantly by the deadest dead girl— one who was dead months before she actually died. And yes, things might be black and messy on the inside, and yes, this town might actually be dangerous and I'm holding a scrapbook full of all the gory details. But when I put on my lacy dresses and give the world a little shrug, at least I know exactly how I look. Bright, small, sparkly. I look perfect.

When I don't say anything, Finny throws up his hands and shakes his head. "Whatever. Act happy if you want, but know that it's not going to make the shitty stuff better."

I just look at him.

Then I turn my back on him and start toward the parking lot. I head for the shade under the cottonwood trees, where it's green and cool, far from him and anything that might hurt me.

I step off the curb without looking, dazzled by the heat and the blinding midday sun. Some idiot has left his bike sticking out of the rack, and I hit the back wheel with the toe of my shoe and go straight over, landing on the sidewalk on my hands and knees.

The pain bursts into focus, sharp and real, so intense it almost knocks the breath out of me. I don't stand up right away, just stay there on my hands and knees, feeling the impact shudder up my arms. I picture it like silver stars, raining down around me like fireworks.

Then a shadow falls over me.

When Finny bends and scoops me up, I go rigid but don't pull away. He sets me on my feet with surprising care, holding me steady.

"Easy," he says from behind me, and I stumble back a little so that my ponytail skims his chest. "Looks like you cut yourself pretty good."

When I look down, my knee is a torn-up mess. As I watch, blood springs up in drops. It looks like the surface of water for pasta just starting to boil.

"Are you okay?" Finny says in a low voice. His hand is big and warm on my waist, not holding on but just resting there, like I might tip over.

"It hurts," I gasp, staring down at the bleeding place.

He doesn't say something mean, like what did I expect? He doesn't even ask why I sound so surprised. He just lets me go and takes my arm, leading me off the pavement and into the grass.

Blood is running down my shin and into my shoe. I keep waiting for him to say something because that's what normal people do, but he just stands over me, studying my face.

"Here," he says, but he doesn't say where, just takes me by the arm and tugs me gently toward the bike rack.

It's half empty and cluttered with old Schwinns and beat-up BMX's. The metal rods that hold the bikes are bent and rusted, but the outside part—the frame—is made of poured concrete, with straight sides and a flat top where some of the potheads like to sit and wait for their friends after school. Without a word, he takes me by the waist and sets me up on the cement bike rack like I'm some package or box that needs to be put somewhere. Like it's nothing.

For a second, I just sit there with my feet dangling, looking at him. I can tell my mouth is moving, opening and shutting in little gasps, but no sound comes out.

He bends over my knee, brushing the raw center of the scrape with his fingertips, and at first I think he's wiping up the blood, but that doesn't prepare me for the sharp, electric pain.

"What are you doing?" I whisper, trying not to wince.

He doesn't answer right away, just tosses a few chips of something small and lumpy onto the sidewalk, and I see that he's picking out all the little pieces of gravel and broken soda bottle.

"You need to clean this out," he says, wiping his fingers on his jeans.

I nod slowly, staring at the little white scar on his chin. *Peroxide*, I tell myself like I'm memorizing a word in another language. *Peroxide. When I get home, I'm going to use peroxide*.

And then we're looking at each other, and it's a look that goes on and on, stretching across space and time. Across galaxies.

Finny doesn't speak or look away. He smiles, and the shape of his expression is uneven, like his eyes are smiling more than his mouth is. And then, for no reason, he touches my cheek.

The feeling is shocking and it occurs to me that no one has ever done that, touched my cheek like it's unavoidable, like his hand belonged there. His palm feels rough, and I reach up and run my fingers over the back of his wrist. It's strangely comfortable to touch the place where his finger used to be. It feels right. Not like a hand is supposed to feel, but like how Finny's hand feels. He tenses when my fingers brush the mangled place, holding very still, but he lets me keep touching it. His eyes are fixed on mine, and the look on his face is very complicated, like he's saying a lot of things at once. His mouth is open a little, and his hair looks translucent and brittle in the sun.

"Are you waiting for someone to come and get you?" I whisper. I sound small and thirsty.

He doesn't answer. Instead, he bends his head and kisses me, just once, then lets me go. When Connor would kiss Angelie in the halls last spring, he did it like he was trying to suck the chocolate off the outside of a Klondike bar. It could last hours.

This is more like seeing a star fall—thrilling and soundless and then over.

"Why did you do that?" I say when he straightens, surprised at how conversational my voice sounds. I don't know if I mean *Why did you start?* or *Why did you stop?*

Finny's mouth is open a little, and I wonder if we're about

138

to get into the reasons for things, or if this is one of those awkward moments that we never talk about and spend the rest of high school pretending didn't happen.

Instead, he leans down and kisses me again. It's slower this time, and he moves like he's learning me, the way I did with his hand. His tongue brushes the curve of my bottom lip, grazing the hollow underneath, and something leaps and fidgets in my chest. It's like a bright silver shock, running through my whole body, and I want him to never stop. But the other thing is that I think I need him to stop right now because my eyes are dry and hot, and if he doesn't stop, I might start crying.

When I pull away, it's with a huge, shuddering relief. I turn toward the treetops and the sun, staring up at the glossy canopy of leaves so Finny can't see the tears in my eyes. When did June turn into July? When did I become one of those girls who makes out with delinquents?

He rests his hand under my chin and turns me very gently back to face him. His touch is so light that it's barely a touch at all. It would be so easy to pull away.

When I finally look up into his face, he raises his eyebrows but doesn't say anything.

"I'm sorry," I tell him, but I have no idea why I'm apologizing.

"For what?"

"I—just . . . I'm sorry."

He shrugs. He looks like kissing me without warning was totally natural. Totally planned.

"What happened to your hand?" I say, and my voice sounds wobbly, like I'm trying not to cry.

He glances out into the street and shrugs. "Dog."

"What kind of dog?"

"A real shit-house bastard of a dog."

I laugh, which is probably about the least acceptable response for the situation. "Connor Price said it was an alligator."

Finny grins and shakes his head. "Connor's kind of a tool, though."

And I laugh again, sounding nervous and breathless. "Yeah, I know." Then I decide that's not really fair. "Well, he used to be, anyway. He's kind of better now."

I wonder if Finny's going to argue, but he just nods. "People do that sometimes. Change."

He smiles, and his mouth looks rueful and heart-fluttering at the same time. The thought crosses my mind that this whole day cannot possibly be happening.

Behind us, the doors fly open and Ariel comes storming out in a flurry of chatter and noise, dragging Pinky behind her. As soon as she sees us together at the bike rack, though, she stops.

Finny is standing very close—so close he's almost between my knees—and as soon as Ariel starts toward us, he takes a step back.

"What happened to you?" she says, eyeing Finny like she suspects him of scraping the skin off himself. "Why are you bleeding?"

"I tripped." It's funny, but I feel less stupid now that I'm sitting up on the bike rack, with the soft, dry sound of cottonwoods rustling over me and I can still kind of taste Finny's gum.

Ariel looks up at him, narrowing her eyes. "Okay, but what's he doing here?"

"Nothing," I say, slipping down from the bike rack and moving past him to sweep her hair back into the headband again. "He helped me clean up my knee, and now he's just leaving."

Finny glances at me, looking mildly surprised, but I am not about to tell my twelve-year-old sister that the gigantic delinquent we saw stealing impulse items from the Qwik-Mart the other day totally just kissed me. And that I kissed him back.

Ariel moves closer, clutching the clarinet case against her chest. "Did you?" she says. "Help her, I mean?"

Finny nods, looking unsure of himself, and for the first time, kind of awkward.

I think that Ariel will ask the most obvious question— *how?*—but instead, she wrinkles her nose and scowls up at him. "Why is there blood on your hand?"

I answer for him, fast and bright. "There was some glass in my cut and he took it out."

Ariel looks up at him, cradling her clarinet. She stares hard, and I brace myself to hear all her thoughts on whether or not I should be allowing him to put his unsterilized fingers all over my abrasion. But she just watches him, eyes moving

141

over his features, taking in the shape of his jaw, the bleached hair. The way his ends are almost white, but the roots are coming in dark.

She opens her mouth and then she does something very strange. She closes it again.

Now that Ariel has proven there's no danger, Pinky comes picking her way across the grass and hugs me around the waist. "I'm not coming over today," she says against my shirt.

"Why not?"

She turns and points to where Mrs. Ortero's station wagon has just pulled up and is waiting by the curb.

"Okay, that's fine."

Pinky gives me a one-armed good-bye squeeze, refusing to look at Finny. Then she lets me go and starts off toward her mom's car. I expect Ariel to wave and then demand to go home, but instead she wobbles back and forth like she's being pulled in a million different directions.

"What?" I say. "What are you standing there for?"

"I'm going with Pinky," she says, looking unsettlingly like our mom.

Her voice is serious and she's still eyeing Finny as if he can't be trusted, or I can't be trusted with him. Like, *Are you going to be okay by yourself, Hannah?*

"You should probably come too," she says after a long pause, and I realize her concern has nothing to do with Finny after all. What's on her mind right now is my mom's decree that we're not supposed to walk home alone.

"Come where?"

"Mrs. Ortero's taking us to the pool."

The public pool is basically the most disgusting place in all of Ludlow. It's always packed, the cement lounging area is a billion degrees, and instead of water, the pool's mostly just full of screaming kids and soggy Band-Aids and pee. I haven't been there since eighth grade, when Lillian and Angelie and I all made a pledge to never, ever set foot in it again, under penalty of death.

"I don't have my suit," I say, then stop and look at her. "Neither do you."

But Ariel just shrugs. "I'll wear one of Pinky's."

The way the two of them can just trade everything is so unfamiliar, and swimsuits are not the kind of thing I ever shared with Lillian, even when we were little. Maybe we were only four months apart, but even in elementary school, we were never close to the same size.

"Okay, then you just go and have fun," I tell her. "I'll see you at home."

Ariel shakes her head. "We're not supposed to split up," she says. "You promised Mom."

"Ariel, I just walked all the way over here from the shop by myself. It's fine."

Ariel nods but doesn't look convinced. She keeps sneaking glances at Finny.

"I'll be okay," I say, giving her a look that's supposed to be reassuring. "I promise. He's not going to hurt me."

The best thing about Ariel being twelve is that I can

almost always get my way, because she still believes whatever I tell her—even the things I'm not so sure about. She gives me one last doubtful look. Then she climbs into Mrs. Ortero's station wagon and leaves me there on the sidewalk next to Finny, where the afternoon sunlight bakes the pavement, and everything is hotter than it was just seconds ago.

11: At Finny's

For a long time, Finny and I just stand there. It's one of those excruciating silences where you can't focus on anything else. The ones that feel so fatal and weigh so much you think you'll go deaf from the pressure.

Then Finny scrapes his textbooks off the top of the bike rack and turns to face me.

I wish I still talked, because then I'd have something to say. I know I need to break the silence, but something is wedged in my throat, and anyway, it's too embarrassing to say what I'm actually thinking, which is that no one's been this nice to me in a while.

I have a sinking feeling that this is it. He's going to go and leave me standing here like an idiot, with blood drying on my shin and soaking into the edge of my shoe.

"You really need to clean that up," he says, glancing at my knee. "Before it scabs over."

I nod and look down at the red, stinging mess but don't actually move. The sun is so hot that my skin feels like it's humming.

Any minute, he's going to ask me why I told my sister he

wasn't dangerous—why I'm still standing here with him in the crushing heat, with the tops of my collarbones turning pink, and sweat running down between my shoulders—and I don't even know what I'd say. Any question he asks is going to be impossible to answer.

"Come over," he says suddenly, and he says it in a voice I can't quite figure out. Like he's offering a compromise or telling me a secret. "It's only a couple blocks."

Immediately, there's this storm of noise in my head, telling me that's a bad idea. I can hear all these different voices: Kelly, Decker and my mom, Officer McGarahan. Responsible, grown-up people who know better, saying that I can't. *There's a killer hunting girls*, and *How well do you even really know Finny?* Even if the last week hadn't happened and the whole summer were different, I could never go over to his actual house. It would be too weird, too awkward.

But under all that loud, unhelpful noise is this other voice—the one that understands the big things. It reminds me that I've known Finny almost my whole life. That if he were one of the boys from my housing development, I wouldn't think twice, and when Lillian was alive, we were always going over to Connor's or Tyler Campbell's or Austin Dean's, even though we didn't really know them that much better. And I never even really liked any of them all that much.

Finny hitches up his books and starts for the intersection, then glances back over his shoulder like he's waiting. I feel my pulse get faster and thank God that he doesn't expect me to say anything.

Finny lives over on Wabash Street, where the driveways are weedy and narrow, and rows of houses are just starting to fade into rows of warehouses.

As we turn off the sidewalk and start toward the front porch, the screen door bangs open and we're met by a little woman with a round, cheerful face and dark, curly hair. She's carrying a wooden stepladder and a huge, drooping spider plant in a hanging basket.

Finny hurries up the steps and takes the stepladder from her, then situates the plant on a little metal hook at the edge of the porch roof. She hugs him, standing on tiptoe with her arms around him, and when he smiles, it's a different smile from any of his other ones.

When Finny slides past her into the house, I hesitate. I know how I must look—sticky and hot, with a bright yellow dress that's drooping from the heat, and a gash on my knee.

She doesn't seem bothered, though, just smiles and holds out her hand. "I'm Jolene," she says. "Finn's aunt."

I climb up onto the porch to shake hands. Hers is small and warm, and when she gestures me inside, I follow her.

The front hall is narrow, with paper-yellow walls and dusty wood floors. At this end of Wabash Street, all the houses were built a hundred years ago, and all the floor plans are small and dark and cramped.

There are drifts of bright plastic blocks scattered down the hall toward the back of the house like breadcrumbs in a fairy tale.

I'm just starting to relax, glad to be inside and out of the sun, when I see Lillian standing very still in the shadow of the coat rack, grinning at me like there's no place she'd rather be than lurking around the front hall in other people's houses.

Jolene sees me looking in the direction of the scattered toys and sighs, kicking a few of them under the hall table. "Sorry about the mess. We used to make an effort to keep the clutter under control, but I've just accepted that it's useless." The way she says it is easy but disconnected. It's the tone of someone who is used to having entire conversations all by herself.

I pick up one of the blocks, pointedly ignoring Lillian. "Do you have a baby?"

Jolene shakes her head, then stops shaking and nods instead. "Sometimes," she says. There's a weird sadness in her voice, but she smiles anyway and keeps talking like nothing's wrong.

"I knew it would be a commitment, but I couldn't just sit back and watch anymore, and there were so many kids with no place to go." She glances at Finny, who's standing just inside the door to the kitchen. "I said, what the hell, you know? If these other people can do foster care, then so can I. It seemed ridiculous to do social work and still not be around when they needed it the most. I guess it seemed hypocritical."

Behind her, Finny is watching my face, like he's waiting for a reaction. I try to figure out what he's thinking, but he looks how he always does. Unreadable.

Jolene turns and smiles at him. "Finn, can you run out to the garage and put those picnic chairs on the back porch?"

He nods and ducks past us, leaving me there with his bright, fast-moving aunt, and the lurking ghost of my best friend.

Jolene buzzes into the kitchen, which is low-ceilinged but well-lit, with big windows and white lacy curtains. It seems completely unbelievable that Finny is in this room every day. It looks much too cozy, like something that belongs to a little old lady, not to this bright, busy woman and her huge, defiant boy.

I realize I'm standing very near the table, and step away without thinking. The way the tablecloth hangs down halfway to the floor gives me a bad feeling. I keep expecting Lillian to pop out at me, grabbing for my ankles, trying to make me jump.

"Would you like something to drink?" Jolene says.

"No, thank you," I tell her, and immediately wish I'd said yes.

Yes would mean something to pass the time until Finny gets back. It would help me take my mind off the fact that Lillian is haunting my entire life.

Also, something about being alone in the kitchen with Jolene feels unnerving, like she's seeing too much of me before I'm ready. It occurs to me that maybe she has to be able to do that in order to live in the same house as Finny, because he never talks.

"Hannah," Lillian says in a ferocious whisper, peering around the doorframe and then flouncing across the kitchen and climbing up onto the table. "What are you doing here? This is crazy. It's not okay! Go home, right now."

I don't respond, but I can feel my cheeks get hot. The fact that she's telling me what to do and what counts as crazy is pretty much hilarious.

She flops down hard on her back on the tablecloth, and dust puffs up around her, twinkling in the yellow shaft of sunlight. Her skin looks yellow too, ugly with liver damage. "Okay, look—yes, sometimes it can seem really tempting to do something you know you shouldn't. I get it, believe me. I know all about that."

I raise my eyebrows at her, just for a millisecond, as if to say, *But?*

"But this is way too much of something you shouldn't! God, not him. He's a total waste. I mean it—he's not even cute. And he made you cry. In fifth grade, don't you remember?"

I do remember, like an old TV show or a movie I used to watch. Something you can relive any time the notion takes you; just stick it in the player.

The snow was weeks old, crusty with ice, and when he scrubbed my face with it, the crystals were so sharp they made me bleed.

I felt stupid for crying, stupid for caring. Stupid for being small enough that Finny Boone could hold me down in the snow with one hand. I blamed him a long time, only thinking of how much it hurt, and being completely humiliated that he could overpower me.

But now, the memory runs over and over, playing out like a punishment. What had I been doing in the minutes before he tried to whitewash my face off?

I'd been standing in the recess yard with Lillian and Jessica and Angelie, and we'd been whispering to each other in shrill, gleeful tones, cackling like a bunch of little witches. We'd been talking about something pointless—flavored lipgloss or the best kind of gummy candy—when Finny went by.

Even back then, he was already bigger than everyone else, and none of his clothes fit right. His jeans were too short and his coat was so big that the shoulder seams slumped halfway down his arms. The only thing that wasn't too big or too small were his sneakers, which were dingy, white canvas with rubber soles. Not the right kind of thing for snow.

"Nice shoes," Lillian said, and I hadn't said anything.

But I'd laughed this high-pitched, witchy laugh, and looked right at him. Mostly, I remember feeling vital and untouchable, like I was free and separate from him. I would never be him, and because of that, I would never be lonely or laughed at, and I would never have to worry about anything.

And that was why I couldn't stop crying. I was so ashamed of myself for being awful, and for the fact that he could see it, see the meanness in my expression or hear it in my laugh. He'd done the most logical thing and tried to scrape it off me.

❅   ❅   ❅

Lillian lies stiffly on the table, arms straight at her sides, head turned so she can watch me. "You can't possibly like him, Hannah. He made you cry."

I stare back at her, not moving or blinking or anything. The only thing I can come up with is indisputably true, and I'm not going to say it. That yeah, maybe he made me cry. But so did she.

When Finny comes back from the garage, he looks rumpled, and there are huge dust smears down the front of his shirt. "They're on the porch," he says.

Jolene gives his arm a squeeze. "Thanks, I'll go out and hose them off later."

I stand in the kitchen watching them and feeling like an intruder, like they're putting on a show for me—not the fake, lying kind, but just trying to figure out who they are and how to show it in front of someone else.

Finny glances over at me. Then he jerks his head, indicating my scraped knee and motioning for me to jump up on the counter. I balance next to the sink, leaning out of the way while Finny reaches around me to turn on the faucet.

He holds a paper towel under the water and then uses it to mop up my bloody knee. He works his way around the edges, dabbing gently with just the corner. His other hand is resting against my shin, and I'm concentrating on the feeling of it, the way his fingers reach around almost to the back of my calf, when something moves in the corner of my vision, reflected in the glass cabinets. Right away, I just assume it's Lillian and don't think anything about it.

But it can't be her, because Lillian's still lying on the table, and the shape in the glass is small and wispy and has much lighter hair. It's faint, hard to make out in the wash of sunlight that fills the kitchen, but its appearance makes something tighten in my throat. I sit very still.

Finny's still bent over my knee, rinsing the scrape with handfuls of lukewarm water. I stare past him at the reflection in the glass, so indistinct that I might be imagining it.

Then, a stray cloud drifts across the sun and in the dimness that follows, the reflection darkens, becoming sharp and clear and horribly familiar. I'm looking at a pale, round-cheeked girl with shoulder-length brown hair and a small, pointy nose and silver braces, smiling at me with blood running slowly down the side of her face. Her eyes, which were cloudy blue in the crime-scene photos, are still cloudy blue, but now they're lively and alert and looking right at me.

It's Cecily Miles.

All the breath goes out of me and my hands move on their own, fluttering at the air. My mouth is open in the shape of a soft little *oh*.

"Stings?" Finny says, turning off the water and leaning to look into my face.

I nod in a series of little jerks, trying to make my hands stay still. The cloud moves over, and the kitchen brightens.

Lillian is standing in the center of the table now, the top of her head almost touching the ceiling. The cabinet still reflects the sunlit kitchen, but the bloody reflection of Cecily Miles is gone.

"Don't you need to put something on it to disinfect the cut?" My voice sounds unnaturally high-pitched and I fidget on the edge of the counter, trying to seem normal.

153

Finny shakes his head, opening the cupboard under the sink and dropping the paper towel in the trash. "Something that shallow, anything you put on will just burn like hell, and it won't heal any faster."

Jolene comes back in just then, carrying what looks like a box of old clothes. "Hey, Finn, can you get the hide-away bed set up in your room this afternoon? It doesn't have to be right this minute."

Finny glances up from the sink, where he's scrubbing his hands. "Nah, I can do it now."

Without a word, he helps me down from the counter, then leads the way down the hall toward the back of the house. I follow him, keeping one hand out, trailing my fingers along the wall. My heart is beating so hard the inside of my ribcage actually hurts, but on the surface, I'm trying hard to look normal.

Finny's room is small and ankle-deep in a stew of clothes, very few of which are folded. I have no idea how he ever knows if anything's clean.

His closet is half buried in a drift of crumpled jeans and skate magazines, and he forces the door open, shoving a variety pack of Black Cat firecrackers out of the way with his foot.

"She's my real aunt," he says with his back to me. "Just so you know."

"Okay."

The tone of his voice is like he expects a fight, like he's challenging me to disagree, and I want to tell him that I don't care one way or the other. That her blood-relative status

154

makes no difference as long as she loves him. And she does. She wears it, beaming it around like a neon sign.

Finny drags a folding cot out from under his bed and wrestles it over against the opposite wall, kicking his laundry out of the way.

After the cot is up, he crosses to his closet and yanks his dusty beater over his head, keeping his back to me. He's sturdy and brown, with muscles that ripple in huge slabs under his skin. The way he just peeled off his shirt in front of me is kind of shocking. Most of the boys I know would never just undress like that in front of a girl they barely knew. They wouldn't just let you see them.

But then, most of the boys I know wouldn't scoop a girl off the sidewalk or take her home or blot her knee with a paper towel. Finny just peels out of the shirt like it's nothing. Like he already knows exactly what he looks like.

"Yikes," Lillian whispers in my ear, propping her cold, pointy chin on my shoulder. "That is a lot of boy."

I nod, trying not to watch too closely as he makes a production of going through his closet and then the dresser, digging around for a clean shirt. On his left shoulder, the skin is marked by four round scars in a row down his back, each a deep, glossy pink.

I sit down on the edge of his bed, even though he hasn't told me I could. There are free-weights of various sizes just lying around, mixed in with the fireworks and the crumpled jeans. It makes sense, I guess. Even boys as tall and as broad-shouldered as Finny don't get that big by accident.

When he has his shirt on, he kicks his way through the drifts of clothes and magazines and sits down next to me. The weight of him makes the mattress sag, and I slide sideways into the depression so that our hips are touching.

His hand is resting palm-down on the top of his knee. When I take it in mine, he goes still but doesn't pull away.

"What happened?" I ask, touching the smooth, abbreviated stump of his little finger. "For real."

The question seems important suddenly, because the truth is, something did happen. There are so many stories about Finny's mangled hand.

"It really was a dog," he says, and his expression goes flat and out of focus, like he's off somewhere, stuck someplace and it's not pretty. "This mutt of my dad's. Part bull terrier, part chow. This mean, hard-edge devil of a dog."

I nod, lacing my fingers between his. The way he says it is simple and casual: *A dog did this. The end.* But that's only one tiny piece of the story, because the real problem is that the dog belonged to someone who didn't care much about keeping it away from his kid.

I let my eyes move to where the slick, pink marks are hidden under his shirt. "Did it bite your shoulder?"

He sits very close, watching me. "No," he says. "Those are cigarette burns."

He says it in a voice that tells me not to feel bad for asking. He meant me to see his shoulder. He told me about it by taking off his shirt. His story was there in the way he pawed through his closet, apparent in how he never turned his bad side away or looked awkward.

I wish he would talk to me, but instead he just sits there on the bed, staring into my face with his nose very close to mine. The look goes on and on, and my lips move, but no sound comes out. I want to say something smart and cool, but instead there are just the shapes of all these different words. *But why?* and *That's awful* and *I'm sorry.*

For a long time, we sit facing each other, like we are each waiting for the other to know what to do. I don't know how to proceed, but suddenly I have this deep, consoling certainty that I'm not here because of those reasons that Lillian said. Not because I'm looking for something jagged and hazardous to fall on. The way Finny watches me is nice, and not just in the way it can sometimes feel nice to be watched by someone you might like.

The way he watches me is kind.

Lillian is circling the room, making a big thing of picking her way through the mess, making sure I see how dramatically disgusted she is by the state of his things.

"Do you skate?" I say, as she gestures to a copy of *Grind* with one derisive toe.

Finny shakes his head. "Not really. Not enough to count."

"Then why do you have all the magazines?"

Right away, I think I've said something wrong, that the question is too difficult or too personal. Then he leans back, clasping his hands behind his head. "They're not mine. You know Dustin Sykes?"

157

From over by the dresser, Lillian laughs a shrill, unpleasant laugh. Dustin Sykes used to be in our grade. Then he was in the grade behind us. Now I think he's in Lehigh, which is the boys' detention center out at the edge of Park County.

"Is he your friend?"

Finny smiles, shaking his head. "Nah, that guy's an asshole. He was here this spring, though. He wound up with protective services 'cause his dad was using him for a punching bag."

"But then he moved out?"

For the first time, Finny looks helpless and kind of uncomfortable. "That's not really how it works. After a few weeks, he got turfed back home, and things went back to normal. Whatever. I mean, he's not like my brother or anything."

He reaches over and touches my bracelet, tugging gently on the chain, running his fingertips along the row of charms. The movement makes them jingle against each other, a small shimmering sound, like a lullaby coming from someplace. For the first time since I looked at the pictures of Hailey Martinsen this afternoon, the vague sense that I might be dreaming finally starts to wear off.

"Thank you," I say suddenly, and it comes out sounding way too formal.

Finny squints at me. "For what?"

"Bringing my bracelet back. You didn't have to."

He laughs and shakes his head. "No, I really did. That was way out of line, even for Nick."

"How did you get it back?"

Finny shrugs. "When he came outside, he was all snort-ing and laughing about how he took it, so I said for him to hand it over."

"And he just let you have it?"

Finny gives me an ironic look. "Well, not quite. At first we had a little bit of an issue."

I have a feeling that the issue involved someone getting punched, which would explain why the bracelet kind of looks like it spent some time in a garbage disposal, but I don't ask. "Wasn't he mad at you?"

Finny throws his head back and laughs. "Do I give a shit? He can fucking deal with it! I told him that maybe he's free to act like a total dick any other time, but not to girls and little kids. Not when he's with me."

The edge in his voice is new and unexpectedly hard, like he talking about something that disgusts him.

"Why do you even hang out with Nick, then? I mean, it doesn't seem like you like him, so why were you—" I almost say why were you shoplifting together, but I stop myself before I get to that part. "Why were you hanging out with him in the Qwik-Mart?"

Finny shrugs, looking resigned. "He was around." Then he ducks his head, and his face softens. "And Jolene would have wanted me to. She always likes for me to hang out with those guys sometimes, to show how just because they're not here anymore, we didn't forget about them. He's another one like Dustin."

"So, he lived with you?"

"For maybe two months in ninth grade. He wound up in Lehigh for a while last year, but since then he's kind of been staying out of trouble. Or at least, trouble bad enough to get someone sent to Lehigh."

I shake my head, trying to picture Finny doing something bad enough to get sent to the detention center. "It doesn't seem like you guys really have a lot in common."

Finny laughs, but not like anything is all that funny. "Don't you ever just have those days where even if you don't really like someone, you might as well hang out with them because right then, it's better than being alone?"

I have a sinking feeling that I would know a lot more about what he's saying if I didn't spend the greater part of every day with Angelie or Carmen or the ghost of my best friend. I am pretty much never alone.

As if to prove her constant presence beyond any shadow of a doubt, Lillian makes a disgusted noise, and I glance around. She's standing in the doorway of his closet, peering down at a pair of ancient gym shoes and looking appalled.

"Come on," she says, wrinkling her nose. "Please, let's go. If your mom gets home before you do, she's going to freak out, and anyway, it is just way too gross in here."

"I should probably go home," I say, but I don't stand up just yet.

Finny nods and squeezes my hand. He's smiling, but it's a small, disappointed smile, like this is about what he expected.

"You could call me, though," I say. "If you wanted."

"Okay."

His hand is warm and I hold on, looking down at the floor. There are crumpled school assignments and stray clothes lying everywhere, but I don't even care, and it's nice knowing that right now, at least for this second, I'm someplace I actually want to be.

12: The Scrapbook

The rest of the week passes in a hot, high-octane blur, fast and silent, skimming along like clouds in a time-lapse photo.

Even at two o'clock, when I go to get the girls from school, the streets seem unnaturally quiet, like everyone's waiting for the apocalypse to come, or like the whole city is holding its breath.

Mostly, I've been staying in the house. My mom is weird about me going any farther than the photo shop, or even going into the backyard by myself if it's after dark. Angelie calls a few times, but she's stuck inside too, so we pass the time playing I Spy with all the stuff in our rooms, and texting back and forth with Carmen and Jessica and Connor.

Finny doesn't call at all, which makes something tug in the center of my chest, but it's also kind of a relief. I want to see him again and hold his hand and maybe make out a little, but the thing is, if he comes over, then Decker and my mom will have to meet him. And maybe Decker has tattoos all over his arms and shaves his head with a BIC razor. And maybe when I was little, my mom had five tiny silver studs in each ear and wore a motorcycle jacket, but now she wears blouses from Stein Mart and drives a Prius. And maybe I just don't think they're going to be overly excited about a boy who shoplifts from the gas station and is in all the slow classes at school.

It took a while, but the police have finally given an official statement, letting the press in on the bizarre nature of the crime scenes. It's awful to have seen the actual details myself—this ugly, secret mix of blood and cheap colored plastic—and now every newscaster and reporter in Ludlow is talking about the Valentine Killer like he's some kind of major figure or celebrity.

Every headline, breaking bulletin, and news feature seems to be basking in the horror.

It would be so tempting to put the awful things out of my mind. Tempting to ignore the way the cop cars crawl the streets, and the way the TV never, ever stops talking about the fact that two girls are dead.

Except I can't ignore it because every time they talk about two girls, all I can think is that they should be talking about three, and because twice after getting out of the shower, I thought I saw a brown-haired shape reflected behind me in the door of the medicine cabinet. Each time, though, it disappeared. There and gone so fast that by the time I wiped the condensation off the glass, I was half sure I'd imagined it.

The air conditioner is still broken.

I find a few old blog posts and online write-ups about the Monica Harris murder, but Lillian's scrapbook is the only account of what happened that feels truly honest. I read it through again and again, looking for some piece of insight or tiny detail that might link Monica to the other two girls. For the first time, I kind of understand how Lillian could be so obsessed with numbers and facts. There's this constant nagging feeling that if I can just collect the right information, keep adding one more piece and then one more, the whole picture will fall seamlessly into place.

The clippings all start to look the same, though, and it's hard to know what counts and what just gets shuffled off to the side somewhere. Monica was the middle sister in a family of three girls. Cecily had an older brother who's majoring in business at UCLA, and Hailey was an only child. They had different friends, different hobbies. They didn't go to the same church or live in the same neighborhood or play on the same sports teams. They went swimming and had birthday parties. They all liked little kids and animals and sleepovers with their friends, but who doesn't?

We don't get the paper at my house, but sometimes people drop them in the recycling bin behind the photo shop, and so every day, I pick through the jumble of bottles and cans, looking for a stray copy of the *Ludlow Herald*.

On Thursday, when I was coming back inside with a crumpled Local section, Kelly finally said something. "Hannah, if you really want one, I will buy you a paper. You don't have to dig in the trash."

But it sort of seems better this way, like when I fish a paper out of the bin and search through it, looking for clues, this is how it's supposed to be. Like this whole grisly mess is just some kind of complicated story told in glimpses and in found objects, and if I follow the clues the way I'm supposed to, I just might find the pieces that matter.

I've missed most of the early newspaper coverage of Cecily Miles, but it's not hard to find the text-only versions in the library database, plus the *Herald* runs community portraits and supplementary pieces almost every day. I collect as many as I can, along with the features and interviews and letters to the editor.

I make a two-page profile of Hailey Martinsen, complete with her age and description and her interests and the nice things people have said about her. I draw exclamation points around all the adjectives and cut out a photo that I got online from one of the dismally pastel memorial sites that keep popping up. It's a different one from the birthday photo they keep showing on the news. In it, she's got her arms around the neck of a bronze statue of a horse and is pressing her cheek to the metal curve of its muzzle. She's wearing a lavender dress and smiling in a wide, impish way that reminds me so much of Ariel that it makes something flutter in my throat every time I look at it.

It's Friday afternoon, and my room is so hot I think I might pass out. I keep opening the windows and then, when that doesn't help at all, getting up and closing them again.

Lillian is lying on her stomach across my bed, watching as I kneel over the scrapbook, pasting in an article from yesterday's paper about neighborhood safety. Ariel and Pinky are downstairs somewhere, freezing lemonade for ice pops or playing cards or standing in front of the refrigerator with the door wide open.

The newspaper is limp from the heat and from how much I've handled it. I reposition the clipping, pasting it down with the glue stick. In the margins of the book, I've drawn lines between pages and paragraphs, circling words like *happy* and *generous*. The same words keep coming up over and over: *helpful, well-liked, lively, outgoing*.

"You look confused," Lillian remarks, watching as I run my finger over the corners of the clipping, pressing it flat.

"It's just, these articles don't add up to anything," I say, staring down at *vibrant*. It's just that it's 110 degrees in my room, and my brain feels scrambled.

Lillian nods very slowly, and in that moment, everything about her seems to get thinner, more transparent, like she's thinking so hard that it takes away from her appearing solid in my bedroom.

"Here's the thing," she says finally. "*None* of what we know really adds up. This is someone who clearly has no problem with homicide, right? In fact, it would be pretty safe to say he's a fan. But then he's also someone who goes out of his way to collect plastic piñata stuffers and make doilies. Doesn't that seem a little weird to you?"

"Well, but he's crazy, though. I mean, he pretty much has to be, and it doesn't always make sense, what a crazy person does."

"Maybe," Lillian says. Slowly, like she's tasting it. "But we can't go confusing psychopathic with unhinged. This is someone who is totally in control of his actions."

166

I have the sneaking suspicion that while she's not exactly wrong, she's not quite right either. I keep thinking that there has to be some other place between sane and crazy, some mysterious territory that rests in the middle.

Lillian crosses the room and settles herself on top of my dresser, where she hunches forward so that her shoulder blades jut through her pajama shirt, and cups her chin in her hand. "Okay, so things we know: We know he doesn't hoard his victims, or else these girls would have been missing for days or even weeks before they were found. No, this guy kills them quickly, within a few hours. He bludgeons them and arranges the bodies in the grass. Private but not hidden. He wants to show them off."

I nod, and in that moment, I can almost see it—the killer, kneeling over Cecily or Hailey, turning her arms and legs, straightening her clothes. Sprinkling the body with toy airplanes.

"The toys and candy," I say, staring down into Hailey's smiling face, remembering the little flash of insight that came to me in the shop the other day—that these are the remnants of childhood. "It's how he defines these girls."

Lillian scowls down at the floor, squinting hard, like she's trying to see further. "Maybe we're going about this from the wrong angle. Maybe we need to start thinking more about what it means to die while you're still a kid."

And then we're quiet. Me looking at her, her looking at the floor. Her eyes are unfocused, like she's looking off somewhere into the distance, and I don't know what she's thinking.

I'm thinking that my best friend killed herself so slow it

was almost like a magic trick, and other people let her do it. That there's got to be a point somewhere in this. There's guilt or blame, and it's all over our hands. Even mine, or maybe especially. I wonder why she never seems to blame me, when sometimes I think I blame her so much because it's easier than blaming myself.

Lillian is still watching the floor, with her hands braced on the edge of the dresser and her elbows locked, when the doorbell rings.

She gives me a long, resigned look, drumming her heels against the front of my sock drawer. "Don't get that. You know who it is."

But her voice is strange, like there's something somewhere inside her that wants to smile. It reminds me of the way she looked at Connor in the shop the other day, like someone wishing on a star or a dandelion clock or a stray eyelash. Wishing for happiness. For someone to love her.

The bell rings again, chiming through the house. Lillian's mouth is working, like she's trying to figure out the right expression for the moment. It doesn't come, but her eyes are soft and she shrugs as if to say, *This is it, the thing you want. If you go down there right now, you can have it.*

I don't wait for her to tell me again.

❊ ❊ ❊

Downstairs, Ariel and Pinky are standing in the front hall, ten feet back from the front door.

I come up behind them and they both jump. "Why didn't you answer it?"

Ariel stares back at me over her shoulder, looking scandalized. "Because there is a murderer out there, and Decker's not home."

She's right—of course she's right—but we're standing in our own front hall, with the door between us and the rest of the world, and the sun shining high and glaring outside. It seems safe enough.

"Who's there?" I say, just to be sure, calling it over the top of Ariel's head.

"Me," answers a low, steady voice that I immediately recognize as Finny's. And maybe I had no reason to doubt Lillian, who—since she became a ghost, anyway—only really says things that are true. But I'm still relieved.

I go to step around Ariel, but she lunges at me and grabs at my arm. "Hannah, don't! It might be a stranger."

I shake my head and turn the deadbolt. "It's not a stranger."

When I open the door, he's waiting on the porch, leaning against the porch railing with his hands in his pockets.

"Hi," I say, and even to myself, I sound kind of breathless. There's a long, expectant pause, but I don't invite him in. I'm suddenly way too aware of how my house is nothing like his.

He doesn't say hi back. Instead, he pushes himself away from the railing and comes up close, hooking his pointer finger with mine. "Can you come out for a while?"

I look up at him, amazed at how he can always act like he belongs anywhere, like showing up on someone's porch when there's a killer on the loose is just the most normal thing.

I hook my own finger in return and squeeze. "I don't know. I'm not really supposed to."

Finny gives me a small, conspiratorial smile and raises his eyebrows. "Do you always do what you're supposed to?"

The way he says it is like it's supposed to be a joke, but I've been breaking the rules more than he knows. My room is starting to feel like a hellish, baking cage, and my head is stuffed full of all these different words that describe kind, friendly girls, and I feel a rush of desperation, like if I don't get out of the house, I'll go crazy.

"Keep me safe?" I say, giving him a sly, sideways glance, smiling in a way that I know makes me look ironic and innocent at the same time.

He steps closer, staring down at me in the shade of the porch. "Always."

Ariel is standing with her back against the newel post at the bottom of the stairs, biting her bottom lip. I know I should stay, that I shouldn't leave her and Pinky home alone, that my mom would say I'm not supposed to go out by myself. But I'm not by myself, and maybe Finny's big and rough and unpredictable, but he's also the boy who walked me home after he found me out in the woods alone. He's the one who helped me up off the sidewalk, kissed me in the bus circle, and cleaned the blood off my knee.

"Do you like jumping?" he says, sounding perfectly reasonable, like this is not a weird question.

"Yes," I say after a beat, even though I can't actually say I know what he's talking about. I don't know about jumping, but I really like being with him.

"Come on," he says, reaching for my hand. "I know a place."

13: The Rope

We cross Ashby Road along a narrow blacktop bike path that runs under the train tracks. Beneath the bridge is littered with empty cans and cigarette butts, and the sides are spray-painted in a whole mess of bright, dirty colors.

It's already after four, and the sun is high and pale, scraping its way slowly across the sky toward the west. The day is still unbearably hot, but the shadows are starting to get longer.

Even before we're close enough to see it, I can hear the Coureur de Bois River. It runs directly through town, and most of it's bordered by parks and bike paths. People ride up and down the paths, or kayak in the deep parts. There's a shallow sandy spot by the Muncy playground where little kids splash around and catch crawdads and minnows in plastic buckets.

Most of the river is public space, but the stretch of bank above the dam and just below it is fenced-off with a spiral of barbed wire along the top. Halfway down a little hill and overgrown with bindweed is a narrow gate that almost blends in with the rest of the chain-link. It's posted CITY

PROPERTY, NO TRESPASSING, but the lock is broken, and when Finny shoves the gate open, the hinges screech like a dying bird.

The river is lower than it was in the spring or early summer, but just above the dam, the water slows up against the cement lip deep enough that you can't see the bottom.

Finny leads the way along a narrow dirt path worn hard and flat in the grass.

The shrill, grinding cry of the grasshoppers in the weeds makes me think of rusty harmonicas, of silver pinwheels spinning.

We follow the path until we come to a huge cottonwood tree. Finny stops under it, smiling like he's just presented me with something glorious.

"What are we doing here?"

He looks up, pointing to a thick rope knotted around one of the upper branches, and all I can think is how amazing it is that someone actually climbed up there to tie it.

Finny turns and gazes out toward the river. The rope dangles limply, draped over one of the lower branches to keep it out of the water, but I can see that if one of us were to unhook it, it would swing directly over the river.

"Won't we get wet?"

He shrugs. "Well, yeah. But do you actually mind?"

I shake my head a little too frantically, trying to figure out if, under his easy manner, there's any indication that he expects me to strip down. That I'm supposed to take off my T-shirt dress and swing off the rope in just my bra and underwear.

But Finny doesn't seem to be using the excuse of swimming in the river as a ploy to get me undressed. He grabs the rope in both hands, pulling himself up onto a low, heavy branch, and now I understand that wet clothes are just a normal part of the activity. With the end of the rope twisted around one wrist, he climbs higher. It's nice watching him climb. I like the way his arms move, the muscles tensing and pulling as he hauls himself up into the branches.

He plummets from the tree, arcing out over the river. He waits until the very top of his swing before letting go and then it's just the white-haired shape of him falling through air in a wild dive toward the water. When he hits, the splash is tremendous and frothy white. The rope tail is so long that it dangles in the water, trailing back and forth in the current.

He stays down a long time, and the seconds stretch out, heart-stopping as I stand on the bank, waiting for him to break the surface. When he finally comes up for air, it's in a huge, exuberant burst, water spraying away from his spread arms.

Finny splashes in the current, catching hold of the rope and then wading up onto the bank with it, water pouring off his shoulders and running down his arms. He shakes his head in a huge spray, like a dog, sending icy drops spattering against my face and my bare arms. The chill of it feels good in the dry, broiling heat.

He hands me the rope, helping me wind the end around

my wrist. It's rough against my skin, and makes me think of being tied up somewhere, even though there's no evidence that any of the girls were restrained. Before I can help myself, I think of choking, but Finny doesn't seem to see it on my face. He smiles at me and gives me a little shove toward the tree.

When I climb up to the jumping place, the air feels cooler as I make my way out over the river. The rope is thick and rough in my hands, fibers sticking into my palms. I stand balanced on the curve of the branch, looking down into the water. The bark is worn smooth from so many feet stepping in the exact same places.

"Do it," Finny says below me. "What are you waiting for?"

I glance down at him standing on the bank, dripping wet and grinning up at me with his jeans hanging soaked and heavy on his hips.

I want more than anything to let go of the rope, to climb back down and kiss him, right now, with the wet fabric of his shirt sticking to his back and the sunlight streaming through the trees. But he's watching me, waiting to see what I'll do. If I'm going to chicken out or if I'm brave enough to jump.

I tug the rope once, just to feel the sturdiness of the knot, and then I grip it in both hands and step off into space. At first, there's nothing but the clear, empty sensation of falling, falling. I'm plunging away from the horror and the blinding sun, the scrapbook full of dead girls, the claustrophobic cocoon of my room, and the heat.

Then the rope jerks taut in my hands, and I'm carried up, sailing over the river like a dandelion seed.

"Let go!" Finny shouts from the bank. He's laughing up at me, waving his arms for me to do it.

Suddenly, letting go seems like a wonderful idea, a terrible idea, and when I do, the feeling is like nothing I've ever felt. I'm rising up, up, and then, for one breathless second, I am perfectly still. For that glittering moment, I stay suspended in space, caught in the wash of hot dry air and sunlight before gravity takes me and I plummet.

The water is freezing. I hit the surface, and the current sucks me straight down to the bottom of the river. It's pure runoff, and even the heat of hundred-degree days hasn't done much to warm it up. There's a rush of gritty sand under my fingers, and my skin feels brittle, like it might crack into pieces. There's a pressure in my chest, huge and aching, and I kick my legs once and strike for the surface.

I come up gasping, and as soon as my head breaks the surface, I yelp shrilly into the still, silent air, trying to catch my breath.

Finny is still up on the bank, hugging his ribs, laughing with his bleach-white hair plastered against his forehead and falling down in his eyes, and his shirt stuck to his chest. "How's the water?"

I start to paddle for the bank, still gasping for breath. My ribcage feels so cold that my lungs don't want to work. I'm just struggling up the riverbed into shallower water when I stub my toe on a jutting shelf of rock and almost fall. I stop and look down, trying to see where to put my feet.

And then I scream.

Floating in the current just below the surface is the body of Hailey Martinsen. She's stretched on her back, with her hands folded on her chest. She's wearing a pale green tank top, and there are leaves stuck to her cheeks and tangled in her hair.

As I stare into her bloodless face, inches from mine, she opens dark, filmy eyes and rolls her head to look at me. She moves her mouth like she wants to say something, but all that comes out is a storm of tiny bubbles. With terrible slowness, she reaches out a hand. Her chipped orange nail polish is obscenely bright, even in the shade of the trees.

Then she catches hold of me, fingers closing around my wrist, and I scream again, louder and more panicked, twisting my arm out of her hand, kicking and shrieking away from her.

And then Finny's in the water with me, splashing against the current. He catches me around the waist and lifts me off my feet, pulling me back toward the bank. "What's wrong? What happened?"

The apparition of Hailey, with her dark, staring eyes and pale face, is gone. My teeth are chattering so hard I can barely speak.

I cling to Finny even though the water only comes up to my chest, trying to come up with something plausible. "I think—it was a fish—a fish touched my leg."

The look Finny gives me is confused and just a little worried, but he doesn't tell me I'm making a big deal over nothing, and he doesn't take his hands away from my waist.

"Hey!" The voice is harsh, rising over the sound of the river. "Hey, you're going to need to step away from her right now."

I raise my head, twisting in Finny's arms. Standing above us on the far side of the bank is Officer Boles.

At first I hardly even recognize him without the yellow backdrop of the photo shop behind him. Mostly, I don't recognize the way his hand rests on the grip of his gun.

"Step away," he says again, looking down at us with his fingers still skimming his holster.

After a second, Finny lets me go and takes a step back toward the bank, keeping his hands held carefully above the water. I have to flail wildly to catch my balance against the current. My sneakers keep slipping on the algae-covered rocks, and my legs are so weak and shaky I'm afraid I'll fall.

Boles stares down at me, looking rattled. "Hannah, are you okay?"

I gasp out a pitiful yes, fighting to stay on my feet. The river swirls around me and tugs at my shirt. My hair is loose around my shoulders, getting tangled in my clothes.

There's another voice calling to Boles from farther up the hill, and a disturbance in the tall weeds behind him, and Officer McGarahan comes crashing out of the underbrush.

"What's going on? Who screamed?" He peers over the bank at me, looking anxious. Then his gaze moves past me to land on Finny. "Hannah," he says, crouching down and holding out his hand. "I need you to get out of the water, sweetie."

I understand, with an icy burst of clarity, that I have two choices. I can move toward them, or away. The third option is to stay where I am, but the water is freezing and if I see Hailey's body again, I think I might start screaming and never stop.

Boles and McGarahan are both standing on the edge of the bank, waiting for me.

There's a moment that seems to go on for so long that my scalp starts to hurt. Then I turn and stumble over the rocks to the far side of the river, where Finny is standing under the cottonwood tree, looking hunched and awkward.

I haul myself out of the water, wading up onto the bank with my shoes squelching and my hair hanging in my face. I realize that everyone can see the outline of my bra through my dress, which didn't seem like such a big deal when it was just going to be Finny, but now that I'm standing on the bank across the river from two police officers, it seems horribly inappropriate.

I turn to face them, hugging myself as hard as I can. "He wasn't hurting me. I just screamed because . . . because of something else. What are you even doing here?"

Boles starts to say something, but McGarahan sighs and rakes his hands through his hair, shaking his head. "You know why. The park's not safe these days."

And he's right—I knew before I asked. It's the right time of day and the right kind of place for a murder.

"Just get out of here and go home," he says. "And you." His gaze shifts to Finny and it's not friendly or patient at all anymore. "You make sure she gets there. If she doesn't, I'll hear about it."

Boles sighs and shakes his head. I can almost see his earlier intensity fading out of him, replaced by something more like anger. "Kid," he says to Finny, "I don't know what you think you're doing, but you know you're not allowed to come in here. There are places on the river that you're allowed to be. This is not one of them."

Finny speaks for the first time, crossing his arms over his chest and squaring his shoulders. "Am I in trouble?" he says, watching Boles with a tight, wary expression, measuring him.

Without even thinking, I move closer to him.

Boles presses his fingers against his eyelids as if something hurts inside his head. "Not today. But you need to stay away from places like the river. There's a killer running around. Don't you kids understand how serious this is?"

❋　❋　❋

Finny walks me home, his soaked jeans leaving a trail of splotches in the dust on the path.

I'm still shaking, shivering convulsively, and whenever I close my eyes, I feel the freezing shock of Hailey's fingers around my wrist. I want Finny to reach over and hold my hand, but right now he seems scared to touch me.

As we start down the little hill that leads to the main bike path, there's a harsh, barking sound ahead of us, like a metal hinge screeching against itself.

Finny stops, freezing in the weeds with his shoulders rigid

and his chin up. I follow his gaze, staring down into the little hollow of shadowy grass under a big cottonwood tree, where a magpie is hopping around at the bottom of the hill.

I shade my eyes, squinting down into the hollow. I can just make out a heap of random objects and a tangle of brightly colored ribbons, half hidden in the grass. My whole skin suddenly feels tight, like I might freeze solid. The understanding, the inevitable conclusion, is that they're scattered around a body.

As we get closer, though, I see that they're not. It's a memorial, like the one we made for Monica behind the bowling alley last year. The trampled patch of grass under the cottonwood tree is clustered with tiny teddy bears and fake flowers, Mylar balloons and homemade cards. Leaning crookedly against the tree trunk is a big Styrofoam wreath covered in roses and decorated with a picture of Hailey, smiling for the camera and wearing a silver party hat. It's the same picture they used on the evening news the day they broke the story.

The magpie is hopping excitedly back and forth, tugging at a silver best-friends necklace hanging from the top of the wreath.

In the photo, Hailey is glossy-haired and pink-cheeked, but in my mind that image is superimposed over the white, bloodless face staring up at me out of the water.

"You okay?" Finny asks, moving next to me for the first time since we left the river.

"This is so messed up," I say, hugging myself so I won't

shiver. My voice sounds hopeless and stunned. I wonder if I'm about to start crying.

Finny makes a low, wordless sound. He shoves the wreath gently with his foot, and the bird flies away. Then he takes me gently by the shoulder and turns me away from the little shrine. His hand is a little unsteady, like he might be shaking.

"They didn't have to talk to you like that," I say, touching a silk tiger lily with the toe of my shoe. "They didn't have to act like you were a criminal."

"Whatever," he says, staring down at the flattened grass. "It's not like they've ever talked to me any other way." Then he lets his head drop forward and his shoulders slump, giving me a strange, rueful smile. He looks exhausted. "If you want to know the truth, I think maybe the only reason I'm not sitting in the back of a cop car right now is because you came over to me instead of them."

"They'd really have arrested you just for being there? If it mattered so much, wouldn't somebody just come take down the rope swing? Or at least fix the gate?"

Finny shakes his head. "Not about that. About me, being there with you, the two of us. It's weird—they've been everywhere all week. I mean, every day now, they're picking up guys for stupid shit like jaywalking or messing around in the fountain. Asking all these questions, like asking Nick if he's ever owned a baseball bat, or Alex Vega if he likes to walk through that little field by the culvert, which is totally crazy because everybody walks through the field by the culvert."

I nod and realize that I'm squeezing my own wrist for no good reason. Even Lillian and I used to walk over there after school with Angelie sometimes to pick irises and talk about boys, or when we were younger, we'd play in the narrow strip of meadow below the culvert. It's only a few hundred feet from the bike path, and there was an elm tree growing sideways over an old fence that made a perfect little playhouse. Now, though, it's not a place for secrets or tea parties. Now it's just the spot where Cecily Miles's body was found.

"Do you think they're right, that a kid could have done these things?"

Finny stares down at the ground like he's never really thought about it before, but he's sure thinking about it now.

"No," he says finally. "At least, not the kind of guys I know."

The way he says it is matter-of-fact. In his voice is the difference between all the petty, destructive things that boys do, and this.

At the base of the tree, the magpie is back, yanking violently at the little silver necklace.

14: The Hammock

We walk along the wide, quiet street that curves around the park. It's not really that late, not dark yet, but the sun is almost down, making everything look dim and hazy. The air feels dry, buzzing over my skin, prickling on my bare arms.

We don't talk much, but I'm getting used to that. Used to the way Finny doesn't feel obligated to fill up the silence and how I don't really mind it. It's nice being around someone without always having to think about who you're supposed to be and what you're supposed to do and think and say. It's nice to just concentrate on being the person you are— whoever you are.

The walk around the park is slow and winding, and when we get to my house, Finny tries to lead me up onto the porch.

"Not yet," I say.

The lights are all on, looking warm and welcoming, and if I go inside, all I'll have to look forward to is Lillian and dark, disquieting questions with no answers, and maybe a lecture from my mom about going out without asking permission first. The house will be bright and hot and suffocating, and who knows what other specters of dead girls will be waiting for me in the corners of my room when I turn out the light.

"Please," I say, holding out my hand. "Come with me."

After a long moment, he nods and lets me lead him around back, through the side gate.

In the dark, secret place under the cottonwoods, I sit on the edge of the hammock, careful not to overbalance. I still don't say anything, and then Finny sits down next to me, holding us steady with his foot.

He's inches away, looking down into my face, but I can barely see him in the dusky shadow of the tree. His hair is a light spot above me, and his undershirt glows white.

I slide my fingers under the edge of his shirt, feeling for the cluster of round burns. Under my fingers, the scars are slick and oddly soft.

Finny leans down like he might kiss me, but instead he just sighs and rests his cheek against mine. It feels warm and soft and a little bit rough, like maybe he already shaves even though it doesn't really look like it. When he presses his forehead against mine, I clasp my hands at the back of his neck and close my eyes. I think that if I just hold very still and listen hard, I might be able to read his mind, to find out how he feels about the way I'm feeling for the scars.

For a long time we stay like that with our heads pressed together, our arms around each other.

"It's okay," he whispers. "You don't have to feel sorry for me."

I nod and stick my nose in the little depression at the base of his throat. His shirt is still damp and murky-smelling from the river, but his skin smells like summer—dust and sweat and the green smell of trees. The scent of it is breathable and warm. When I reach for his bad hand, all his muscles go rigid.

"It's not okay," I whisper, and I don't just mean his cigarette burns or his hand, but all the catastrophes and the tragedies and the bad, brutal things that happen all the time and everything that makes Finny so quiet. Every awful thing that's ever happened in the world.

He just slips his arms around me and holds on, taking me around the waist and pulling me into his lap. The hammock rocks under us, and we are very close against each other.

When he finally speaks, whispering into the dark, the words are gentle, like he's comforting me. "It's something that happened, that's all."

I want to know why the world is like this, but I don't think that even in his most nuanced silences he'd be able to tell me. When he kisses me, the shaky hopeless feeling that's been hanging over me for months seems distant and smaller.

"Does it hurt?" I say, cupping my palm around the base of his remaining fingers.

He shakes his head and leans back in the hammock, pulling me with him so I'm lying on top of him and our faces are very close.

Finny's chest against mine is broad and hard and solid, but comforting, too.

"Why don't you want to go in your house?" he whispers, his breath warm against the edge of my ear.

I shake my head, not knowing how to tell him or what I want to say. "It's just stuffy and hot, and I'm so sick of being stuck in my room. It's hard not to think about Lillian in there."

Saying it out loud is stranger than I thought it would be and all at once, for no good reason, I'm engulfed by the reality of the whole afternoon. The body in the water, the sad little shrine under the tree. My voice sounds hoarse and my eyes are suddenly swimming.

Even in the dark I know Finny can tell I'm not faking that I'm bright or shiny anymore, but he doesn't say anything. He puts his arm around me, pulling me against him. His shirt feels soft and worn-out against my cheek, and his arms are warm around my shoulders. I lean into him, breathing against his neck, and he doesn't move or turn away.

"You knew, right?" I whisper. "About how she died, how long it took?"

Finny sighs. Then he presses his mouth to my temple, fast and light like I might not want him to, but he has to do it before he loses the moment. "Yeah, I knew. But I didn't have the whole story or anything. I didn't know. I mean, you never told me."

"I should have. I should have talked to someone who would listen. Someone besides her, I mean."

"Sometimes you can't." He kisses my temple again, only this time he leaves his mouth there. "Hannah," he whispers. Just that. Nothing else.

And suddenly I understand why he keeps touching my cheek.

It's never occurred to me that maybe the raw, stinging place wasn't what he wanted after all. That scrubbing my face in the snow was just about the scrubbing and not about the consequences.

"It didn't leave a mark," I say, remembering how the spot was red and raw for weeks. "The snow. It scraped my face, but I healed just fine."

Finny only holds on tighter. I wonder if it bothers him that even though I'm telling the truth, I'm still lying. It did leave a mark, just not the kind that shows.

"I was so mean to you when we were little," I say, pressing my forehead against his shoulder. "I wish I wasn't, though."

"You weren't the only one."

"It doesn't make a difference. I should have been nice."

"I pushed you down," he says, like he's offering me a trade, some kind of forgiveness.

"I think I might have deserved it."

"You didn't," he says. "I thought you did, but you didn't. No one does."

I nod and know that this is the thing I want so badly to hear, when I'm supposed to want something else. I'm supposed to want a rescuer or a hero, someone who can give me reassurances and answers and charm my parents. I'm supposed to want someone who can fix me. But I don't.

Kissing him is like the wildest, most thrilling thing that

has ever happened to me. It's like diving into the deep end over and over. He touches the curve of my lip with his tongue, just once, so softly, and I think the whole world is ending, the sudden warmth of his mouth jolting through me like a shock. I hold on like I'm falling off the top of a tall cliff or I'm lost at sea, like he's the only solid thing in the whole tilting world.

"Oh my God!"

Ariel's voice is like a fire alarm, and we break apart in a startled lurch that sends the hammock rocking wildly underneath us.

She's leaning over us, looking spooky in the dark. "Oh my God, Hannah, if you don't get up and come inside right now, I'm telling Mom."

Finny pushes himself up out of the hammock and stands over her. "Hey, just settle down."

"Don't tell me to settle down!" Ariel shrieks. "What do you think you're doing with my sister?"

There are a lot of things Finny could tell her, but he says none of them. Instead, he starts to laugh.

Ariel huffs and stamps her foot in the long grass. "Don't laugh at me—this isn't funny!"

Without any warning, Finny reaches for her. He lifts her easily under one arm and carries her, kicking and wriggling, to the back steps, where he sets her down.

"You need to stand there and be quiet," he says. "I'm going to go home now, but first I'm going to kiss your sister, and you're going to not make a scene about it."

Telling Ariel what she's going to do is never a good idea,

but Finny must know some secret trick for dealing with twelve-year-olds, because it works. She stands with her arms dangling limp at her sides, staring at me and looking small and ghostly on the steps.

Finny doesn't hesitate or look back to see if she's listening to him. He just crosses the lawn to me like he never expected anything else from her. He kisses me once, sure and unhurried, then pulls me up out of the hammock and walks me to the back steps, where Ariel is shifting from foot to foot, looking mutinous.

"'Night, Hannah" he says, starting toward the gate. He passes Ariel, who watches him silently from the steps. "'Night, you holy terror."

She doesn't say anything. When he's gone, she darts down the steps toward me and hits me hard on the shoulder with her closed fist.

"Ow," I say.

"Hannah, he's so bad!"

"Ha! So are you."

That makes her laugh like a giddy little loon, knocking into me and banging her forehead against my shoulder.

In the mudroom, she keeps on giggling and pulling at me, only now her voice has dropped to a whisper, which is a whisper in name only. Ariel is capable of whispering the same way a toaster is capable of flight. "He's a big stupid waste of space and you shouldn't be doing things with him."

The way she's scolding me is uncomfortably reminiscent of Lillian. "Why? Because I'm too good?"

Ariel shakes her head, giving me a look that says I have completely missed the point. "Because he's too tall for you!"

That makes me smile. I take her in my arms, one hand resting on her waist, and together we waltz around the little mudroom, twirling in a circle, laughing when I accidentally steer us into the corner of the door.

Then Ariel stops, with her arms still knotted loosely around my back, and says in a low, confidential voice, "Seriously, though. You are in so much trouble."

I stare down at her. "What kind of trouble?"

Ariel lets me go, shaking her head. "I tried to tell her not to worry, but she wouldn't listen. Decker's out looking for you right now."

In the kitchen, my mom is sitting at the table. She's got a can of grape Shasta in front of her, but she's not drinking it. When I come in through the hall, she glances up and at first she looks like she's never seen me before in her life. The way she stares at me across the kitchen is completely disorienting, and it takes me a long, baffled moment to understand that the expression on her face isn't anger or frustration but terror.

She stands up, shoving the chair away from the table with the palm of her hand and then, when the corner catches on the table leg, she kicks it out of the way. "Where have you been?"

"Nowhere," I say. "I mean, just with a friend."

The way she's looking at me is shell-shocked, like she's spent a long time staring into the sun. "Ariel said you'd gone to the movies with Angelie, but when I called Angelie to see when you'd be home, she said she hadn't seen you all day!

Why would you lie to your sister, and why didn't you take your phone with you?"

I give Ariel a quick, searching glance, but her expression is blandly innocent. I've never thought of her as having the ability to look innocent.

The ice maker in the freezer starts to whir and click, filling the kitchen with the sound, and I don't say anything about the phone or tell her I'm fine, that I didn't lie to my sister, that Ariel knew what I was doing and who I was with.

My mom doesn't wait for me to answer, though, and I understand that as far as she's concerned the question was rhetorical.

"You're grounded," she says.

And I stand with my back against the edge of the granite island, trying to work out what just happened. I have never been grounded in my life. Grounded is for girls like Lillian, who have difficult attitudes and smart mouths and who drive their mothers crazy. Grounded is not for girls like me. I've never even had my allowance docked.

I stare across the kitchen at her, trying to work out what this is going to do to my newspaper-collecting and my access to crime-scene photos—and my thing with Finny, whatever it is. "For how long?"

My mom doesn't answer right away, and I realize that she doesn't know how to do this any better than I do. "For—" She stops, shaking her head, then puts her palms flat on the table and draws herself up, looking breathless but unbending. "Until further notice. Until I say that you're not."

15: Grounded

The next week is probably the longest of my life.

I'm allowed to go to work because I'm Kelly's only summer help, and my mom believes that it's important for me to honor my commitments, but I have to come right home afterward, and Decker has to take time off to drive me. Mrs. Ortero or one of Pinky's brothers has to go over to Harris Johnson every day to get Pinky and Ariel.

I focus on collecting papers, magazines, anything I can find that might have something to do with the murders. My ears feel funny. They buzz and crackle, ringing constantly like a faraway alarm, or like the wind is always blowing. I can't tell if it's something I'm imagining or just a natural consequence of the heat, of being shut in. My skin feels too tight for my insides, and I can't help thinking that maybe these past few weeks are just what a nervous breakdown looks like. You throw out all your better judgment and your inhibitions and leap headlong into recklessness with the biggest, roughest boy in school and disappoint your mother. You start spending every stupid minute on your floor, cutting up newspapers and old advertising circulars until none of the pieces even make sense anymore.

Even though it's almost four in the afternoon, I'm in my shorty pajamas with my rag rug rolled back and my papers spread out in front of me, thinking about Finny and how the last time we saw each other was like the best, most perfect thing that had ever happened in my life—and now it's been so long that it's not like anything.

He hasn't called, which is disappointing even though I don't know what I expected. He doesn't seem like the kind of boy who really calls people. I don't even know what this is or what he thinks it is. Maybe it's nothing.

For a little while on Tuesday, I considered calling Angelie to confess to her about my weird, ongoing thing with Finny, or to ask if when boys ignore you, it ever means they really, really like you. But even before I hit speed dial, I knew it would be a bad idea. There's just no way a conversation like that would end with anything good. Anyway, lately she hasn't exactly tried to get ahold of me either. She usually calls in the afternoons, when she knows I'll be home from the photo shop. But ever since our conversation about Hailey Martinsen and about how much it sucks being stuck at home, we haven't really talked.

And Lillian is no help.

On Thursday, when I finally try to tell her how Finny kissed me in the backyard, she just stares down at me from the edge of my desk and says, "Yeah, because that's not the worst idea you've ever had."

If this were some other summer—last year, maybe—we

could at least talk about it. I could whisper to her in the dark, under the sheets with a flashlight between us, or lying side by side in the hammock. I could tell her everything.

Except I couldn't really. Because even before all this, before she got sick, she would never tolerate the idea of me going around with someone like him.

It's weird to realize that I have something Lillian doesn't now, because she was always the confident one. She used to know so much more about boys and dating and sex than I did. She knew so much more about everything. But then Trevor happened, and now the boys who brought her lilac twigs or mix CDs have all moved on, gone before she was even actually dead. Because none of them wanted to date a girl whose bones showed through her skin like it was made out of paper.

Time's kept going, and I've finally done something she hasn't.

Lillian only sighs and shakes her head, flopping down into my desk chair. "I can't believe you actually want to be with him. With *him*. Don't you worry about how you'll look to everyone else? Don't you ever think about what people will say?"

"Like what?"

She shrugs listlessly. "Oh, I don't know—maybe like, 'Look at Hannah, she's totally lowering herself. She's wasting her whole summer hanging around with some loser.'"

I understand that she's finally getting right down to the heart of something real and ugly, and it sort of surprises me that it's taken her this long to say it out loud. "Are you sure you don't really mean that you worried people might be saying, 'Look at Lillian'? That you worried so much about what everyone thought?"

"It was all that mattered," she says softly. "All I really cared about. Isn't that funny?"

I kneel over my stack of newspapers with the scissors clenched in my hand. "I don't want to talk about this."

Lillian sighs and rolls over so she's lying on her back with her head hanging limply over the side of the desk. "It didn't happen all at once," she says.

I look at the bones in her face, remembering how she shrank so slowly that the difference wasn't daily or obvious. It only really showed up in pictures. "No kidding."

"I mean, I didn't think, 'Today I'm going to starve myself until I die.' I just thought, 'Maybe I'll try to lose a couple pounds. Maybe a size smaller. Just one size—that's not so much.'"

"What happens then?"

"What do you mean?"

"If you can go down a size, what happens then? Why is it important?"

"Because if I could just drop a size, then I'd be happy."

"Yeah," I say, and I wish my voice were kinder. "That worked out well for you."

"Hannity, I'm not trying to make excuses. It wasn't rational. I'm just saying what I thought when I was in it."

In it. Like a holiday play or a swimming pool, when what she really means is she dove straight down the rabbit hole after it. I shake my head, staring down at the stack of cut-up newspapers in front of me. "What you thought was that people were paying attention to you."

It just comes out, spilling off my tongue before I can stop it. Too vicious, too mean. I know that but it's too late to take it back, and the voices in my head won't stop. They're shouting it now, chanting along, singing it like a jump-rope rhyme, *pay attention, pay attention*. It's maybe the meanest thing I've ever said to her.

At first I think I might as well have slapped her, but then she tugs her hair and nods. "Yeah, sometimes. Maybe it was for attention sometimes. On days when I felt like I was invisible, or when my mom was on some rampage about how I should join drama or choir and kept telling me if I just got a little smaller, I'd be really pretty. It was like—it was this hobby I had."

But after that it was a monstrous, ugly thing. There must have been a window between well and sick where it became undeniably clear that starving was a black hole and not a toy. "Back then, when it was a . . . hobby, what made you want it, though? Why did you hold on to it?"

Lillian looks down at me over the edge of the desk and her face is so unbearably miserable. "Because it made me special."

I curl over my bare legs, picking at the scrape on my knee. When I peel up the edge of the scab, I see a little pink sliver of new skin, raw and tender. It itches. "Why couldn't you just be special in a normal way?"

She crouches over me, and I hate the way her mouth

always looks so superior when she's annoyed. "Come on, you don't believe that unique-snowflake bullshit, do you? That everyone's special in their own way? That every tiny microscopic flower is precious? It's not. I wanted to be unique or important. To matter."

"You did matter."

"To who? To Jessica and Carmen and that bitch Angelie Baker? To my mother? Please, she spent the last three years drinking a perfectly decent chardonnay on the couch and waiting for me to stop being so *dramatic*." She says the last word like she's swinging a hammer at me.

"You were special to me."

Lillian grins, skull-faced and nasty, which is this new smile she got after she started looking sick. "You think drooling rejects like Finny Boone are special. You think people are important just because they exist, or that everybody matters. But they don't."

The room goes perfectly silent, so still I think it's gathering dust. And then the voices rush back in, thudding in my ears. *Special special special.*

Hands shaking, I flip through a glossy insert full of hardware ads and coupons for laundry detergent. With quick, uneven strokes, I cut out a big cherry-red SPECIAL! It's printed in a bold, chunky font, surrounded by lightning bolts and stars. I swipe the back of it with the glue stick and stick it to my floor. The flood of whispers stops, goes still and slow, and trickles away. The word sits there next to the end of my bed, bright and ragged on the varnished wood.

Lillian laughs a dry little laugh and rolls her eyes. "Nice. Your mom is going to love that, gunking up her hardwood with adhesive."

"It's water soluble," I say automatically, staring at what I've done. All that matters is, for the first time this afternoon, the voices have tapered off, faded out.

The silence lasts for only a few seconds, though. Then the noise is all around me, the chorus of whispers buzzing and hissing, crashing in my ears like waves. And this time, I can almost make out the clearest word, repeated again and again. It sounds like *memorial*.

I hunch forward and sort through the stack of clippings, shuffling around for a photo of the memorial for Cecily Miles on the corner of Muncy and Vine, near the meadow and the culvert. I stick the picture carefully to my floor, just under the bright red SPECIAL, ignoring the way I can feel Lillian's eyes boring into my back.

She hops down from the desk and crouches next to me. "Why did you do that?" she whispers, and her gaze is so intent and so steady that I think she must be looking at someone else. Not at the awkward little girl who followed her everywhere and did everything she ever wanted. Not at me.

I ignore her and paste down another scissored word and then another. The only thing that quiets the storm of whispers is finding the words and cutting them out. I hunch over the stack of clippings and glue them down, plastering my floor in headlines and photos, a big capital *P*, DEAD and LOVE and LOOK.

Lillian watches with her chin in her hands.

"This is getting kind of out there," she says, and I know I must be scaring her now, because her voice is very gentle. It dawns on me how backward that is—that I'm the one scaring her. I can't stop.

She sighs and leans closer, like she's trying to see past the curtain of hair that hides my face. "It's really hot up here. Maybe you should get a drink of water. Or go down and see if Ariel wants to play cards. You could make ice pops or paint your nails." She reaches out, using her fingertips to turn my chin and make me look at her. "You haven't put up your hair or worn makeup in days."

Her fingers are cold when they touch my skin, and I can feel the chilly gust of her breath on my cheek. When she was alive, I could tell if she hadn't eaten by the way her breath smelled. There was always a reek of sickness to it, like something dying. Now that she's dead, it doesn't smell like anything.

✳   ✳   ✳

Later, when the house is dark and everyone's asleep, I lie in bed with my covers thrown back and my window open, restless with the way the room still seethes and clatters around me, the way it pulses with whispers. The heat radiates from everywhere, pressing down. Lillian looms over me, balanced in her familiar place on the footboard.

"I think I'm being haunted," I say, and the words sound small and helpless in the dark.

She shakes her head and laughs. "Did it really take you half a year to figure that one out?"

199

"Not by you," I say, and she goes absolutely still. "There are these . . . voices now, all the time. I hear them whispering, but I can hardly ever tell what they're saying. And other things too. A couple times, I've seen things."

Now Lillian is paying close attention, staring down at me in the dark. "Why didn't you say something before?"

I shake my head, fighting to find the words, struggling to describe the bloody reflection in Finny's kitchen and the day at the river. I try to explain the white, sunken face staring up at me out of the water. I don't tell her the simple truth—that I didn't say anything because I wanted so, so badly for it not to be real.

She listens with her head up and her hands clasped between her knees. "And they're like me? You're sure?"

I fold my hands on my chest and nod, even though I'm not sure if she can see me. "Why is this happening?" I whisper, and I mean all of it—the murders and the crime scenes and Lillian dying and the rotting drifts of birds and the heat and everything.

She makes a low, thoughtful noise, hugging her own shoulders. "Maybe it's something particular about you. Maybe they know something that ties you to them."

If I had to guess, though, I would pick something simpler. I think they might just be looking at me because for the past month, I've been looking at them. "I think they want me to help them," I say. "Not just read the papers and fill the scrapbook like I've been doing, but really help them."

Lillian is quiet for a long time before she speaks again.

"Okay, let me ask you one really important question. You seriously don't think it's weird that both times you saw them, you were with Finny?"

I stare up at the dark ceiling, the gently fading stars. I can feel her watching me, holding very still. I don't want to think about the answer to that.

"Okay," she says finally. Her voice is tiny and dry, a tacit agreement not to force the issue. "But how will we be able to help them if they don't show up for more than a few seconds, and when they talk you can't understand them?"

"The same way you and I did that other time, maybe. Like with Monica."

"Okay, but we don't have a board."

"No," I whisper, feeling cold all over. "We do."

When I turn on the lamp, the light makes a dull yellow circle that splashes over my walls. I slide out of bed onto the floor and pull back the braided rug in front of my bed, uncovering the collage of scissored-out letters. It's an alphabet of mismatched consonants and stray vowels, pictures arranged haphazardly on the floor, pasted in a sloppy arc. It's scary to really look at what it is I've made—not a spirit board, but a brutal gallery of chaos and confusion and sadness.

Lillian just sits on the footboard, hugging her knees and looking at my handiwork like it's the big reveal in one of those movies about psychopaths. "That's pretty intense, Hannah. I'll give you that."

I nod. Then I get up and go down the hall into the bathroom. I take the little jelly glass from next to the toothpaste caddy, then bring it back to my room and tip it upside down on the floor.

Lillian settles herself across from me with her legs folded under her, reaching out to rest her fingers on the glass. When she tries to pull it closer to the center of the collage, though, her hand won't make contact. It keeps slipping right through.

She shakes her head. "I can't. You'll have to do it yourself."

I stare down at the glass, sitting in the middle of the floor. It suddenly looks very small and very stupid. "Will that work? Me by myself?"

I have a sinking fear that without Lillian to help me, the glass will sit motionless on the board and I will sit with it, staring as hard as I can, seeing nothing.

But it's a groundless fear because the whispers are filling up the room, and even though the yard is dark and the moon is down, there are shadows moving on my wall now, stretching and squirming, reaching spidery fingers up toward the ceiling.

When the glass starts to move under my hands, it's slow at first. Barely a jitter. Then it gathers speed, skimming fast and silent over the pasted-down letters. It takes all my concentration just to keep up with it. It keeps lurching like it wants to twitch out from under my hands.

"Who is this?" I whisper, barely breathing, not taking my eyes from the scraps of paper littering the floor. "Who's here?"

The glass moves in a confident swoop, scraping across the floorboards to rest over the grainy newspaper photo of Cecily. Her picture smiles up at me with uncomplicated joy.

There's no suggestion of the bloody girl I saw reflected in Finny's kitchen.

"Cecily," I whisper. "Is there something you need to tell me? Something I'm not hearing? Please, do you know who killed you?"

The glass jerks in my hands, moving to circle NO.

"Can you tell me anything about that day? What happened to you? Tell me about the person who killed you. What were they like?"

"Don't confuse her," whispers Lillian. "Try to keep it simple."

The glass moves over the floor, slow and deliberate, pointing out the word NICE. Then it glides back down to the jumbled alphabet. With slow, deliberate strokes it spells out NOT SO NICE.

"He changed once you were alone?"

The glass swerves hard, signaling NO again and again, spiraling around it like a lost butterfly.

Lillian leans forward, mouth open, eyes fixed on the floor. "You mean, he didn't change? How can he be nice and not nice at the same time?"

All at once, I'm surrounded by whispers so loud that they threaten to fill the whole sleeping house—a high rushing in my ears like static.

At the sound of Lillian's voice, the glass turns ice-cold and I yank my hands away, tucking them under my chin. The pads of my fingers are burning.

The glass is still scraping over the morbid collage, moving on its own now. It sweeps wildly across the floor, and I sit with my back pressed hard against the sideboard of my bed and my knees pulled up, lacing my fingers together so tightly that the joints feel like they might come undone.

YOUR FRIEND, the invisible hand spells with terrible certainty and then starts over again. YOUR FRIEND, YOUR FRIEND. The glass moves in loops and spirals, picking out the letters and the jaggedly cut words. Pointing out the undeniable. YOUR FRIEND IS DEAD.

Then, just as fast as it started, it stops. I'm suddenly aware of a dry, raspy noise and a moment later I realize it's coming from me. My breath sounds like heavy sandpaper, scraping in and out. Lillian is sitting perfectly still, staring down at the board with her hands resting limply in her lap.

The glass sits motionless in the middle of my floor, shining wistfully in the light from the lamp. YOUR FRIEND. YOUR FRIEND IS DEAD.

I clasp my hands tight against my chest, struggling with the realization that whoever was guiding the glass couldn't see Lillian—didn't know she was there until Lillian spoke directly to her—that maybe ghosts don't ever see each other. That even in spirit form, a person can still encounter the horror of brushing up against something dead.

Across from me, Lillian's expression is anguished. She's got her arms wrapped tightly around herself, rocking back and forth in the dim light.

It's there every single day, in every conversation and interaction. I think about it all the time. But even with all the awkward, roundabout ways that we allude to it, we never really acknowledge it. I think she's always been able to just push it away and shut it out. We never talk about the fact that she's dead.

Her rocking intensifies, panicked, frantic. Then all at once she closes her eyes and goes perfectly still, and it's like I'm watching her swallow it, force it down until it disappears again.

She was always so good at knowing how to make things small. It was in the way she would never eat anything with her hands. Even sandwiches and muffins had to be cut apart into tiny pieces and eaten with a fork. Like if a bagel could be broken into small enough pieces, it would get so small that it just stopped existing. She did it with everything. Even me.

16: Ungrounded

On Friday, Pinky comes over with a box of plastic butterfly barrettes and a change of clothes to spend the night. When she shows up, I'm sitting on the couch with a damp dish towel draped over my shoulders like a cape, staring into space while Ariel sprawls on the floor, cutting up magazines to make a paper chain.

Since the night of the séance, the voices have gotten quieter. They haven't disappeared, but at least the noise has settled down to a low hum, buzzing quietly from somewhere in the neighborhood of my jaw.

Pinky crosses the room and flops down next to me. "Can I brush your hair?" she says, reaching up and running her fingers through the end of my ponytail, which is definitely in need of brushing.

"I don't know, maybe later. It's too hot for anything right now."

She shrugs and gives my ponytail one last pat, humming a vaguely bouncy tune under her breath. It sounds like "Camptown Races."

For the next hour, Pinky and Ariel play Slaps and Lillian

sits perched on top of the entertainment center, watching them.

"Another riveting night at the Wagner house," she says, which is pretty hilarious considering it's been months since she felt like doing anything fun, even before she died.

Still, I can't help thinking that she kind of has a point.

"We want to go for ice cream," Pinky says after they go through the cards a few times, slumping against my knees. "Will you take us to Dairy Queen?"

"I can't," I tell her, giving her a mock sad look that is also a real apology. "I'm grounded, remember?"

"Please," Ariel says from the floor, lying prostrate at my feet. "Please just ask? Maybe she'll let you go since it's not really as good as being ungrounded. You'll just be with us."

Her voice isn't shrill or overly dramatic. Not like normal Ariel, but more like she's just asking for a favor, hoping for me to say yes. It's weird, but the way she sounds reminds me of a conversation last winter, when everything seemed like it was never going to melt or thaw out. Like I would never feel warm or okay again.

✳ ✳ ✳

We were all in the kitchen. Decker and my mom were making herbed roast beef with popovers, and Ariel was at the table doing her homework. I was sitting across from her with my notes spread out but not studying. I was flipping through my German book, pretending to memorize the unit vocabulary but at the same time, I wasn't really doing anything. It was six weeks after Lillian died, and I still spent every day feeling like I was floating in midair and this was all just a long, ugly dream.

My mom was mixing the popover batter and talking quickly, in time to the rhythm of the stirring. The wire whisk clinked against the bowl. She was talking about me.

"I just don't know—she keeps saying she's fine, and what kind of things should we even be looking for? Her grades are okay. I mean, what am I supposed to do?"

"Mom," Ariel said from the kitchen table, but my mom didn't answer.

She just kept right on worrying to Decker, talking about me like she was alone in the room. Like I was some other species.

"Mom!"

"And she keeps up with school and chores and never gives anyone any trouble. She's so good at coping with things, at adjusting."

Ariel stood up from the table and slammed her geography book shut. "Mom. If Hannah was on fire, she would still say she's okay."

I think of this and how my mom spent all those months hovering over me, like she was so determined to do whatever she thought I needed, but Ariel was the one who actually just let me be sad, because she was the only one who understood that sometimes that's the only thing you can be. My mom wanted me to go back to the girl I'd been before—the one who was never any trouble. Ariel was the one who wanted me to get better.

And there are so many things about her that drive me crazy sometimes. How she always plays the music too loud and doesn't remember to wash her hands after eating Popsicles, and how she sometimes has a disturbing way of sounding exactly like our mom. But even when I was really sad, she never once tried to fix me, never treated me like a problem that needed to be solved.

❋ ❋ ❋

She's still lying on the floor, looking up at me and waiting for an answer.

Suddenly, I want more than anything for her to understand that I like being with her, and Pinky, too.

"Yeah," I say. "That sounds fun."

When I ask our mom, though, she frowns and shakes her head. "Honey, I don't think that's a good idea."

At first I think that this is still part of the conditions of my grounding. Since the night it happened, my mom and I have been almost unnaturally polite to each other, always smiling, but careful not to get in each other's way.

But then she turns toward the street and looks out the window at the setting sun. Her mouth is thin, worried, and I know she's thinking of other reasons for us not to go walking out in the neighborhood unsupervised.

Ariel has followed me into the kitchen and is standing with her shoulders slumped and her elbows splayed out, leaning on the back of a chair. "We won't stay out late, I promise. We'll go to Dairy Queen and come right back and not stop at the plaza or the park or talk to strangers."

Which is the biggest lie ever, because Ariel is incapable of not talking to every single person she sees.

My mom sighs and clasps her hands, looking more nervous than usual. "I don't want you walking over there alone," she says. "Maybe tomorrow."

"But we wouldn't be alone," says Ariel. "We'd be together."

My mom shakes her head and her mouth goes pinched and small.

Ariel gets a fierce, stubborn look, and Pinky has begun her long process of sulking, which she uses like a superpower. They look cranky and restless, and the night is going to be miserable if we don't get out of the house.

"I could call Finny," I say. "I bet he'd come with us."

Everyone stops and turns to look at me.

My mom is leaning over the kitchen island, chopping a handful of carrots, watching me with her eyebrows raised. "And who, pray tell, is Finny?"

I'm still debating the best way to answer that question when Ariel beats me to it. "He's a boy from school."

I expect her to say more, maybe even tell about the shoplifting or, God forbid, the hammock, but she just shrugs, trying her best to look casual. "I think he wants to be Hannah's boyfriend."

My mom freezes with her hand poised on the handle of the knife and her little pile of chopped carrot. Then she takes a deep breath and puts down the knife. "Oh, really? And how can you tell?"

She's not directing any of her questions at me, and I

can't figure out if it's because she doesn't trust me to tell her the truth, or just because she knows that Ariel has a huge mouth.

The way Ariel stands with her hip cocked to one side and her eyebrows raised is nerve-racking. I'm so sure that we're nearing the story of the hammock and I brace myself for an interrogation or possibly a sex-talk.

But again, Ariel surprises me. "He just likes her, and he talks to us at school sometimes. He's nice," she says, which makes my eyebrows sail up in spite of myself. Ariel is becoming a competent little liar. Either she's not as put off by him as she pretends to be, or she really wants ice cream.

Pinky doesn't say anything. She gives me a worried look, then stares down at her hands and stays out of it.

Ariel is expounding on Finny's various finer qualities now, chattering on and on about my scraped knee, which is a story that's designed to convince my mom that he is exactly the type of person she can trust to take us down to the Dairy Queen alone. "He's really big and strong, almost as big as a senior. No one would hurt us, I promise."

My mom isn't listening to her anymore, though. She's looking at me. "If you're going to be spending a lot of time with this boy," she says, "I want to meet him."

I nod, and take out my phone. It had to happen eventually.

❋   ❋   ❋

It takes Finny less than twenty minutes to show up at our house. When I open the door, he doesn't say anything about my calling him out of the blue, or how long it's been since we've seen each other, or why my hair looks like I styled it with a porcupine.

I invite him in, feeling unbearably awkward. "We can go in a second, but first I'm supposed to bring you in to say hi to my parents. Sorry."

He shakes his head. "No big deal, I don't mind."

The way he looks at me is easy and warm, like everything is just that simple.

Then there's a dry little throat-clearing noise behind me, and when I turn around, my mom is there, looking surprisingly tiny in the doorway.

"Finny," she says in her painfully polite voice. "How nice to finally meet you."

Like there is a level of importance to their meeting. Or a *finally*.

Decker is cooler about the whole thing. At least he's trying to act normal. He watches us with his arms folded over his chest, and I can't tell if he has any particular idea about Finny or if he just hates him.

Finny doesn't seem intimidated, though. He crosses the living room. He offers his hand to Decker, and Decker takes it, giving him a sharp, searching look. I can tell that they're gripping each other more tightly than is really necessary. The look they give each other is thoughtful, though, like maybe they've reached an understanding.

Before we leave, my mom makes us stand in a row in the driveway while she spritzes us all over with mosquito repellant. I close my eyes against the spray. Pinky just stands with her arms out and waits patiently until it's over, but Ariel keeps making theatrical spitting noises, wincing at the taste.

"Ariel," my mom says, lowering the can. "Keep your mouth closed."

Finny raises his eyebrows, then starts to laugh, throwing his head back. My mom gives him a curious look, like she can't quite fathom someone this rough and this big is standing in her driveway, laughing like no one's even going to think it's strange.

He shrugs another one of his big shrugs and I think he'll leave it at that, but then he says, "It's just funny, you telling her to shut her mouth. Because she doesn't."

I wait for my mom to say something about how this is serious and Ariel is being immature or irresponsible, but instead she just looks up at Finny and smiles back in a bemused way.

By the time we leave the house, the streetlights are on, making Sherwood Street look like nothing but a long row of tiny yellow moons stretching out into the distance. The sky is a clear, perfect shade of cobalt blue.

We're only halfway down the block when Finny moves closer and reaches for my hand. The feeling of him next to me is so right, like something I never even knew I wanted. It's funny, I used to hold hands with Lillian, because it was this thing we did. This way of showing that it was her and me. That we'd known each other forever and that she was always going to pick me first for everything. It was a way of being untouchable and also how she let everyone know who was her favorite, even before high school or middle school or boys.

Holding hands with Finny is different, and not just in the obvious ways. It's easy, without all these symbols and meanings, like we are just holding hands because we want to.

Ariel glances at us and I think she's going to make a scene, but then she links arms with Pinky and starts chattering to her about the orchestra assignment for next week.

At the Dairy Queen, we wait for our turn at the little window and I buy them hot-fudge sundaes and get myself a grape slush. Finny just gets a Coke and then we wander through the crowd, looking for a place to sit.

The evening is warm, and everyone in the neighborhood is hanging around the cluster of wooden picnic tables. By now, it's been two weeks since anything's happened, and I guess that a lot of Ludlow parents must be getting sick of constantly having their kids underfoot. Still, there are way more grown-ups around than you'd usually see in the summer.

I weave a path through crowds of laughing kids. The parking lot is full of cars, and the gutters are lined with crumpled napkins and ice-cream wrappers. Under it all, though, I can see scatterings of dark feathers.

Angelie and Carmen are sitting on one of the picnic tables, while a few feet away, Connor and Mike Lolordo wrestle on a little square of dying grass, struggling to see who can make the other one spill their shake. They're clearly all here together, and I can't help feeling a little disappointed

214

that even though I've been grounded, no one called to see if I wanted to come with them.

Jessica is leaning against the side of the little brick building, frantically kissing Austin Dean, but as soon as she sees me, she pries herself away from him.

"Hannah," she says with her lipgloss smeared halfway down the side of her mouth and a big fake Norma Desmond scream. "My God, it's been so long I almost didn't recognize you! Where have you been?"

She and Carmen both come clopping across the sidewalk in their wooden-heeled platforms to gather me up in frantic hugs, exclaiming over how long it's been.

Angelie doesn't stand up to meet me, though. She doesn't even smile. "What did you do to your hair?"

My face feels very warm suddenly, and I can feel Finny and the girls and everyone just looking at me, waiting to see what I'll do. "Nothing. I didn't really think about it before I left the house is all."

Connor laughs, taking his paper shake cup back from Mike and giving me a smile that might even be apologetic, but Angelie rolls her eyes and makes a breathy *well, duh* noise that prickles on my neck. "But seriously. You look like a crazy person."

Then her gaze lands on Finny, who is standing back almost to the edge of the parking lot, with his hands in his pockets, like he's trying not to take up so much space. "Oh my God, what's *he* doing here?"

"He came with me," I say, and even just saying it makes something soar in my chest. The fact that it's true, that Finny is with me, makes my whole inside feel full of sunlight, and I smile without even meaning to.

Angelie turns back to face me, but her expression doesn't change. "Really."

"Hey, come on," says Mike, whose dad owns a Toyota dealership and who once got a three-day suspension for hitting our art teacher with a huge gob of rubber cement in eighth grade. "You know girls are all about the bad boy. Hey, do you think maybe if I bleached my hair and started vandalizing street signs or something, Carmen would let me near those exquisite titties?"

He gives Carmen a suggestive grin and reaches for her, but she steps out of his way like she barely even sees him. Her gaze is worried and fixed on Angelie.

Over on the grass, Connor is messing around with Ariel and Pinky, teasing them that he's going to steal the chocolate off their sundaes with his spoon. I'm suddenly glad they're distracted, too far away to overhear Mike's comments about Carmen or see the way Angelie is looking down at me from the picnic table.

"You're not okay, Hannah." The way Angelie says it is heavy, like she's saying more too, daring me to disagree. "I don't know what's wrong with you, but you're really just not okay."

The way she's watching me is patronizing, and in the six months since Lillian died, nothing about what's left of our little group has really stabilized. Now it seems like everything is falling apart. So much has changed.

216

Since school let out, Angelie has pretty much completely stopped following Lillian's fashion mandate of outrageous sophistication. Tonight she's wearing a plain, cream-colored tank dress I don't recognize. It's a clean, preppy style, and every day she looks more and more like the conventional girls—the ones Lillian was always so disdainful of. The ones who get involved and organize things and look just like everybody else.

I'm wearing an old Warped Tour T-shirt of my mom's and a pair of twill shorts I never wear, no accessories, no makeup. I don't look like anything.

There's a gap between us, maybe only a few feet. We're too different in height to stand nose to nose anyway, but she's up on the picnic table, looking down at me like she's waiting for me to scuttle off somewhere.

"What is your problem?" I say. My grape slush is so cold, the plastic cup feels like it's burning my hand. "Why are you acting like this?"

"Hannah," she says, giving me the most patient, long-suffering look. "There's something going on with you. I mean, come on—lying to your mom that you were at the movies with me, hanging around with boys like that. I haven't seen you in weeks and now you show up here, with him, looking like you just rolled out of bed, and it's like I don't even recognize you."

Once, Angelie and I slept together in the daybed at Jessica's sleepover when Lillian was away on vacation. We talked about our favorite bands, and she let me paste plastic jewels on her fingernails. Now, I kind of want to yank her down off the picnic table by her hair.

Ariel has stopped capering and is standing off to the edge of the picnic area, watching us. I have a strange feeling she might be thinking that this is partly her fault because she was the one who told the lie, but she doesn't say anything.

"Angelie," I say, and it's the weirdest thing, but I'm smiling. "Do you ever just wish that we could be kids again, like back in fifth grade?"

She looks at me like I have lost my mind. "No," she says. "No, because fifth grade was fricking miserable. I was the tallest kid in our class, and I had terrible glasses, and you and Lillian just expected everyone to be as perfect as you were!"

I don't answer right away. Her version of things is twisted and confusing and so, so flawed. "We weren't, though. We—"

Angelie hops down from the picnic table and comes right up to me, sticking her spoon in my face. "I spent the last five years trying to figure out how to be just like you guys, okay? And now she's dead, and you're here looking like a homeless person and prancing around with a giant retard. So don't go telling me how things were."

And just like that, everything inside me seems to go numb, like I've turned to stone.

Jessica is watching us with her eyes wide and her mouth slightly open. Her expression is close to excitement, but Carmen looks worried, like she just wants the evening and the whole summer to go back to normal. I know the feeling, just like I know she won't actually say anything. Of the five of us, Carmen and I have always been the ones who never start arguments or really stick up for ourselves. Carmen, because she's quiet and nice and never wants anyone to think she's being loud or bitchy, me because I never had to.

Because Lillian would always do it for me.

"Excuse me?" I say, sounding cool and sweet, just like Lillian always used to.

And Angelie feels it. Her face goes stark and rigid, because this, right here, this is Lillian.

It's awful to remember how dismissive she could be, how easily she talked to us. She was the one in charge, and it didn't matter if I could only watch slasher movies between my fingers or if Jessica was scared to go off the high-dive. Lillian ran roughshod over all of us.

Angelie stares down at me, hurt and angry, because even from beyond the grave, Lillian has this unshakable hold on her. On all of us.

"Oh, you were done?" I say, and I hate it.

Angelie looks almost shocked, like she might even apologize, take it all back, just the way she always used to. Then, she draws herself up and lifts her hands like she's about to grab me by the shoulders but doesn't quite dare. "Get out of my face, you nasty flat-chested bitch."

I wonder if this is how people get into fights. She's a lot bigger than me and will probably murder me if we actually wind up hitting each other.

I don't care. For the first time in maybe my whole life, I feel dangerous and magical, like a dragon or a mermaid. A

219

fury, standing there with my half-gone grape slush and my jaw clenched, ready for whatever comes next.

When Finny moves beside me, I feel it more than see it. He doesn't say anything, but I can sense him there, looming.

"Oh my God," Angelie says, looking up with narrowed eyes. "Who invited you into this conversation?"

I understand that Angelie is dangerous in a way I've never realized. That she probably even has the power to hurt Finny. He's standing with his hands in his pockets, looking down at her. His expression is unreadable, then he frowns slightly but doesn't say anything. Maybe he was invincible against Connor last year when he yanked him off me in detention, but this is a completely different world. One that can't be solved just by being the biggest. All his easy confidence disappears when he's faced with the pack of little witches who laughed at his shoes.

Without saying a word, I drop the plastic cup, then step up onto the picnic bench and grab him around the neck. It takes everyone by surprise, even him. But it's easy. I stand with my feet planted on the wooden bench and my arms around his neck, and look straight into his sea-green eyes. The way he looks at me makes something go shivery and hot in my chest and in the next second, I'm kissing him in front of everyone.

He doesn't react right away, but then his hands move to my hips. And in the few seconds between Angelie's shocked gasp and Finny's hands, something changes. I understand that I'm not doing this for them anymore. We're beyond that now. We're someplace better, and I smile against his mouth, keeping my eyes closed and my arms around his neck.

When the kiss is over, I stand looking down at everyone, and for a strange moment, I think that this must be how Lillian felt all the time.

But no. Her feeling was bad enough to make her break herself apart from the inside. Mine is wild and powerful and final. Done. The thing is, Lillian never would have proved her point by just doing what made her happy, letting Angelie see how she felt. Lillian's way was always to lash out, at herself or someone else. And maybe I can fake that—I can tilt my head the same way she did or mimic the way she talked—but in the end, maybe the only thing I'm completely sure of is that I am not her.

Angelie stands blinking with her spoon in her hand, looking at me in pure, undisguised horror. "Oh my God, why, Hannah?"

"Because Finny is an excellent kisser," I say, and his face goes red all the way up to the roots of his hair, but he's smiling.

Angelie's mouth has fallen open, glossy and sticky-looking. I jump down from the bench and stand with my arms at my sides, smiling up at her.

"This is so screwed up," she says, shaking her head. "I can't even believe you'd be this dumb. I mean, it's like you have no survival instincts whatsoever."

"What are you even talking about?"

"Oh come on, Hannah! Why do you think the police are

cruising up and down the streets all day, watching boys like him? Why do you think they're stopping us all the time at the mall or the pool to ask if we've seen anything, if they didn't have some kind of evidence it was one of those delinquents? For all you know, he's probably the fucking killer!"

No one moves or says anything, and it's like we've all stopped breathing. If my jaw gets any tighter, I think my teeth will break. We're six inches from each other, so close I can smell her spring-clean bath gel and her flavored lipgloss. I'm staring into her eyes, searching for some way to demolish her, when Finny reaches out and just barely touches my arm.

"Come on," he says, looking out over the neighborhood. "It's late. Let's get you guys home."

"That's right," says Angelie. "Go home with your giant psycho killer. Bye, psycho—bye!"

I don't argue. I just give her a little wave and my brightest, fakest smile. "You're a raging bitch, Angelie. So have fun with that." And I look around at Carmen and Jessica and Connor before I turn to go. "Eventually everyone else is going to figure it out too."

As we start down the little blacktop path toward home, no one says anything. I can tell that Finny's upset, angry or embarrassed over what just happened. I can read the damage in his face, but I don't know what to say.

"You called Angelie a bitch!" Ariel says after a few minutes, prancing around us as we head down the bike path. "That was awesome."

Pinky is quiet, trudging along beside me, scraping the

toes of her sneakers along the asphalt. She looks rumpled and sleepy.

I think about Angelie and how I spent all these times wondering why she could sometimes be so mean, why she wanted to hurt me, but never had the answer. I know why now, and it's got nothing to do with sadness or Finny or my hair. It's just the dark, toxic sludge of residual Lillian.

Residual me.

Finny stays quiet, like if we just pretend the scene with Angelie never happened, then we can act like all these other things never happened either, like I never laughed at his shoes and no one ever called him a retard and a psycho.

"Come on," he says. "If we cut through the park, we can take the path under the train tracks." His voice is flat, like nothing matters.

I bump against his arm and reach for him, trying to take his hand, but he doesn't reach back and after a second, I let my hand fall. "Can't we go back around on Beverly Street? It's just, I promised my mom we wouldn't go through the park."

Finny just keeps walking in the direction of the tracks. "So don't tell her. Beverly takes twice as long."

I don't tell him that maybe I want to take the long way, walk home next to him in the dark, with my head quiet for once and his hand in mine. Even if that's what I want, he doesn't. What he wants is to get as far away as he can from Connor and Angelie and all the rampant ugliness of the last half hour.

"I know you're not any of those things she said," I whisper, just under my breath, just for him.

He glances over with an expression that's unreadable, and because it's unreadable, I know exactly what it means. It's a look of total defeat.

"Well, I do," I say.

"You'd be the first," he mutters, looking away, and in the silence that follows, I've got nothing to do but reach for his hand. This time, he lets me take it.

The air near the river is thick with the smell of honeysuckle and chokecherry bushes, so warm that it's almost like walking through a curtain. It's getting dark now, and the park is rustling softly all around us. Finny's hand is big and comfortable in mine, and I wonder what he did all week while I was stuck at home. If he was lonely or missed me or thought about me at all. It's funny, but even though I've seen his house, I still can't really picture what he does in his everyday life when he's not busy with school or misdemeanors or me.

The path that leads under the railroad tracks to the Sherwood Street side is cracked and weedy. It slopes sharply, bordered by tall, brittle grass. Finny starts down first and helps Ariel and then Pinky along the steepest part. The asphalt path is narrower here, winding down the little hill, and even though the sky is still a deep jewel-blue fading to dusky purple, the shadow under the bridge is dark and cool and private.

Just as I'm stepping under the bridge, I roll my ankle on a

patch of loose gravel, and the sole of my sneaker slips off the edge of the path. I knock my foot against something heavy, and Finny catches me by the back of my T-shirt to keep me from falling facedown into the weeds.

I almost walk on by, but the impact is still throbbing in my foot and there was a certain weight to it, a feeling. Not like the hard, irregular shape of a rock or a branch but a solid softness. I stop and turn back to see what I tripped on.

The darkness under the bridge is almost a living thing, oozing through the hot night air, getting all over my skin. From somewhere around us comes a high-pitched tinkling noise, drifting in from nowhere and everywhere all at once.

I dig in my pocket for my phone, fumbling for the light. In the pale glow of the screen, I can make out a mass of shapes, slopes, and angles.

"What is it?" Ariel says behind me.

I don't move. There are long strands of fishing line hanging from the underside of the bridge, tied to glass beads and safety pins and paper airplanes that sway like wind chimes, knocking against each other a little. I know that you're never supposed to touch things when you're dealing with a body, but there's this soft, hopeful voice in my head that says *maybe it's not. Maybe it's just nothing—some thrown-out trash, a pile of random junk that someone left in the park because they didn't want to deal with it.*

But even as I stand there listing all the things it could be, I know.

The screen times out, goes dark, and I have to hit a button

to make it light up again. I do it without thinking and when the light flares to life again, I'm stunned but not surprised. I'm looking into the face of a girl, and there's blood in her hair and splashed down the side of her neck. There's a smell. It hangs in the still, humid air, and I can taste it in the back of my throat.

She's lying on her back like the others, staring blankly up at the rough underside of the bridge. Her face is pale blue in the light from my phone, but I have this bad idea that it might be blue anyway. The way her eyes are turned up to the underside of the bridge is almost mesmerizing.

"Hannah, Hannah." Ariel says it like the air is being squeezed out of her, her voice breathless and fast. Her fingers are painful, clawing at me, digging into my wrist. "Hannah, that's one of the horns from summer band. That's Abby Brooks."

17: Chimes

"I know her," Ariel says, so frantic and shrill that the words all run together.

The air under the bridge is warm and still, whining with mosquitos, and time feels pointless and far away. The hanging objects are still swaying gently, rustling in the dark around us, tinkling in a way that sounds almost ghostly. A paper plane brushes my bare shoulder, and all I can think of is how weird it is that I don't scream out loud.

The truth is that this whole time, even when I was breaking into Lillian's room or sneaking into the safe to look at the crime-scene photos, I've only been playing detective. It was so easy to just focus on the how and why of it. Easy to sit on my floor with Lillian, searching through printouts and newspaper articles for clues, when all I was really doing was distracting myself from how the horror and the danger are actually real.

There are shadows everywhere, distorting the collection of beads and paper planes, making huge, dark scrawls against the underside of the bridge. Pinky clings to me with her arms around my waist and her face pressed against my shirt.

The girl is lying at our feet just barely to the right of the path, an oblong shape in the dark. Then Finny reaches down. His face is slack as he brushes away a little drift of plastic soldiers and leans over her.

"Don't touch her," Ariel says in a loud, bossy voice, sounding panicked but more like herself.

Pinky takes a sharp, hitching breath, then starts to cry.

"We need to call the police," I say.

The words seem right and obvious, but knowing what we are supposed to do still seems a million miles away from actually doing it. What comes next is simple enough, except that we're standing at the bottom of Muncy Park next to a dead girl, and I don't really remember how to use my phone.

Pinky is still clutching me around the waist, crying into my shirt. She's not sobbing, just making this thin, whimpering noise that goes on and on.

"Should I just dial nine-one-one?" I say to no one in particular. I've known forever—since kindergarten—that it's what you're supposed to do in an emergency. It's the rule, the procedure, but I don't want to call 911 and talk to a stranger. I want my police officers, McGarahan and Boles. I don't want some anonymous first responder coming out to see this small crumpled girl surrounded by random junk like she's part of a trash heap. Like just some piece of meat.

For a few seconds, we just stand there in the dark, looking at each other as I try to remember how to type in the numbers. I have a strange bottomless fear that even if someone picked up, I would never be able to think of what to say.

I'm still frozen in place, staring down at the screen, when a voice speaks out of the dark. "What are you kids doing down here?"

Then comes the light, shining full in our eyes, making us wince and shield our faces with our hands. It's the kind of white blinding light that only cops ever use.

"What do you kids think you're doing?"

The voice is deep and official, and Finny glances at me with his face bare and startled in the harsh light. I can see a wordless panic in his eyes.

"Please, you have to help," I say, shading my eyes with my hand.

The officer approaches, followed by a second, shorter one. They come toward us, crunching down through the long grass. When the one with the flashlight asks my name, I tell him in a calm, patient voice that sounds almost mechanical, like a voicemail system or a talking doll.

The officer comes closer, keeping the flashlight trained full in our eyes. "And do you mind telling me where you live, Miss Hannah Wagner?"

"Over on Sherwood, by the elementary school. Can you get that light out of our faces, please?"

The officer doesn't answer, but after a moment, he lets it fall. The beam plunges toward the ground, shining in the grass at our feet, and I can see the shape of his face for the first time, silhouetted against the sky. I can't make out the details, but he's rounder than Officer McGarahan, with a short-sleeved uniform and a bristly mustache.

When the light drops, it washes across the crumpled body at our feet, but the officer is still focused on us, only watching us.

"Are you okay? Can you tell me what happened?"

"There's a dead girl under the bridge," I say.

For a second, the whole park is very quiet. The officer says nothing, just stands there with the light pointed at the ground by our feet, and I can tell from the way he stays perfectly still that he knows exactly what I mean.

Not a dead girl but a murdered one.

❉ ❉ ❉

It only takes five minutes before we see the lights from the squad cars.

Police officers file down the bank with nightsticks and flashlights. They come wading out to us through the knee-high weeds, and it's like something from a space movie, a parade of alien lights bobbing along in the dark.

They lead us away from Abby and then we are not huddled over her in a nervous cluster anymore. She's still down in the dark suffocating space under the bridge, and we're someplace up on the flat expanse of grass by the playground. It's weird to see Ariel there, standing apart from the crowd with the colored lights from the squad cars hitting her from the side and the teeter-totter right behind her. It looks staged.

I'm standing with Pinky by the tire swing, and the sand is soft and uneven under my feet.

We're only there for what feels like a few minutes before we're approached by two plainclothesmen, who we're informed are detectives Herkabie and Medina.

"Whose idea was it to walk through here?" says the one with the mustache, giving us a stern, searching look.

"Mine," Finny says tonelessly, looking at them with his head up and his shoulders back. His voice is deeper than normal, but also tense. Dry. "I was the one who wanted to cut through the park."

"And did you know what you were going to find down here?"

The question is aggressive, and right away I understand that they were never really asking who wanted to walk through the park. What they want to know is if our being here means something sinister. If Finny brought us here on purpose.

He stares back at the detectives but doesn't answer right away. All I want is for him to just deny it, to tell them flat-out that he has nothing to do with any of this.

His expression is stubborn, almost defiant, and he says, "How would I know there was anything down here?"

Which is not the right answer.

I feel a knot tightening deep in my chest, and I struggle to breathe normally, one inhalation and then another until it adds up to something.

Detective Herkabie nods and makes some kind of note in a little spiral-bound book. "Son, we're going to need you to come down to the station and answer some questions."

231

"What?" Ariel is the one who says it, who almost shrieks it.

I know that I'm the one who should be saying it instead, the one who should rush to defend him, but the words won't come. Suddenly, all I can see is the strange, vacant look on his face, the way he knelt to touch the body. The way the haunting started with him and how all the times the apparitions have been the clearest, the most real, were when I was with him.

One of the detectives has taken him over by the slide. They're talking in low voices—or at least, the detective is talking—and I recognize that they are one second from taking him away, steering him toward the squad cars.

The whole scene is so unreal, high-contrast like a nightmare, and I can almost hear Lillian's voice asking me if it worries me that I saw the ghosts when Finny and I were together, if I think it's weird. Asking if I should be wishing for him or kissing him or be wandering around in the park with strange boys.

Ariel makes a choked, ferocious sound, wrenching free of me and darting across the grass to Finny. "He didn't do anything!"

Her voice breaks and she dives into the crowd of uniforms, shoving her way between them.

Pinky is still holding onto me, but she's stopped crying. Her hands are clutching at my shirt and she's shaking her head back and forth against my shoulder.

Next to Finny, Ariel looks small and willful and wild. She's glaring up at the detective, but it isn't the normal, theatrical Ariel glare. It's fierce and frantic. Near tears.

"He was walking us home," I say, and I sound older and more composed than I did a second ago, but the words feel strangely wooden. "He wanted to make sure we were safe. We took a shortcut. That's all." I can hear my own doubt, though, creeping up into my voice. The things I'm saying are true, accurate things, but I can't ignore the way my heart is hammering in my throat.

And the question that keeps prickling in the back of my mind is, *How much do I really know about Finny?*

It's been a week since the last time I saw him, and no matter what I might speculate or guess, I've really got no idea what he does when we're not together. And when Lillian confronted me about seeing the ghosts when I was with him, she was right. I was the one who pushed away the possibility because I didn't want to think about it.

"And if all that's true, and you're telling me everything, then this should be no big deal," the second detective says. And to his credit, he says it gently. "We're just going to ask him some questions."

I nod numbly. My hands are shaking, and the simple fact is, I'm very glad Pinky's there. That I can hold on to her and look like I'm doing it because she needs it, and not because my grip on her shoulder keeps me from falling apart completely.

The detectives glance across the playground at each other and exchange a meaningful look. Behind them, I can still see the flurry of activity down in the tall grass by the bridge.

233

The coroner is crouched over the crumpled, plastic-wrapped body. I start feeling breathless, like I might cry, so I hold on to Pinky like my life depends on it and focus on the second detective.

"We're just doing our jobs," he says, leaning over me in a way that is supposed to feel warm and reassuring.

But I can hear the other, deeper meaning in what he says. His tone is knowing, like he's on to the boy with the Clorox hair.

I stand with my arms locked around Pinky, sorting through the pieces, trying to work out exactly what's happening. There are so many things that don't quite seem to line up, but the one I keep coming back to is, *Why would Finny want to lead us down under the bridge if he knew there was a body there?* That would be stupid, and maybe Finny is a lot of things, but stupid isn't one of them.

"Can I talk to Officer McGarahan?" I say. "Or Officer Boles," I add, when Finny's head jerks toward me.

One of the cops comes tromping over to us across the sand. "They're not on duty. Why do you want to talk to a couple of beat cops?"

"Because I know them," I say, sounding remarkably like Ariel. "And I don't know you."

He sighs and shakes his head. He's stocky, with a pale, moony face and a little bit of a belly, even though his shoulders and arms are skinny. He doesn't look anything like how a cop should look.

"Now, Miss Hannah, what I need you to understand is,

this is a serious situation." He's not saying it to me, though. He stands with his arms folded, watching Finny.

"Please," I say. "I want to talk to Jason McGarahan. He knows me."

The officer nods heavily. "And we'll see about that. What I need from you right now, though, is for you all to come on up to the car with us, okay? We'll all go down to the station and talk about what we saw here tonight."

Ariel is standing so rigidly that she's shaking all over, and I have this crazy idea that in a minute she might explode. "Why are you looking at him like that? Why are you acting like he's done something wrong?"

But the answer is simple: his hair and his clothes, his disciplinary record, his academic record, and his size. But mostly they're acting that way because he spends hours alone in the park and is strange and quiet and all the things that Lillian said. All the ways he's not just exactly like everyone else.

"I understand you're worried about your friend, but you need to calm down. We just need to ask him some questions."

I try hard not to look at Finny, but I can't help it. He's standing in the light of the squad cars with his hands dangling at his sides. He looks the way he did when we walked home after that day at the river. There's something so broken in his eyes, something so destroyed, and the suspicion and the doubt all fall away in one huge, violent rush. The circumstances are against him, but the truth is very clear. This is not him.

"You have to let him call his aunt," I say. "You have to let him tell her where he is."

"Of course," the officer says. "Once we get to the station, he can call anyone he wants."

He's trying so hard to sound like this happens every single day, like it's nothing, but the way he keeps his stare trained on Finny is not reassuring. His face is stony, turned away from me, and I am so incredibly certain that he's lying.

18: The Station

Finny is at the police station.

Finny's being questioned like he could actually be considered a legitimate suspect. Like he could have done something so appalling and so terrible as killing a little girl from Ariel's band class and leaving her in the low, dead grass under a bridge.

But just for an instant, I thought it too. I stood there while they took him and didn't say anything, even though I should have rushed straight in with Ariel to defend him. The doubt was a tiny prickling thing, a lit match burning brightly for an instant, then gone. It lasted for barely a moment, but that was enough to do the damage. To keep me quiet.

And now I'm here, sitting on a plastic chair and tearing tiny pieces off a paper napkin while my mother hovers over me and says things like "This is completely ridiculous. You can't do anything to help" and "Please be reasonable" and "Hannah, we need to go home."

Ariel's slumped on the hard industrial couch next to Decker, leaning her head against his arm. I keep thinking maybe she'll fall asleep there, but her eyes are open, wide and unfocused. Pinky's mother has already come to take her back to the Orteros'. It's almost midnight.

Over by the coffeemaker, Lillian is leaning against the counter, scowling down at all the little paper packets of artificial sweetener.

"I don't know why you're acting like this," she says. "Just be logical for a minute. Think about the facts. He's a loner, clearly troubled, and he was the one who wanted to walk through the park. The police aren't just making a big deal over nothing. There's a ton of circumstantial evidence that supports questioning him."

I want to scream that I've already thought about those things. I thought about them when I stood in the lights of the squad cars after finding Abby's body. I thought about them when they turned him by the shoulders and put him in the backseat. And that's why right now, I feel like the bottom has dropped out of my stomach.

Instead I stare back at her with my hands clenched into fists, like I can burn right into her with my eyes. She was always so maddeningly good at justifying everything, arguing it and debating it from every vantage point, like just because you could line up all the right words to make a case for something—a case for self-destruction or denial, a case for starving—that was the same as presenting a true, verifiable fact.

But Lillian's facts were never all that solid even though she *acted* so logical, and I know some other ones. Killers don't get people's bracelets back. They don't pick the glass out of your scrape or save you from social indignity when your friend dies. When the police come and escort them into the car and they look back over their shoulders to where their girlfriends are standing on the sandy shore of the playground watching— when that happens, killers never look destroyed.

My mom keeps fluttering her hand above my arm like she's about to touch me, but she's not quite brave enough, just like she's not brave enough to force me out of the chilly, fluorescent waiting room and into the car. So I sit there, drinking cup after cup of hot cocoa made from powder and telling myself that Finny's okay. That this will all be a bad, blurry memory by tomorrow, that he didn't see the look on my face when I watched them take him and thought for one heart-stopping second that maybe they were right to.

Jolene showed up just before they took him into the back offices with the detectives. I'm glad that she's here to go in with him, but her fingers were wound tight around the strap of her purse and she looked so frightened. Now there's nothing to do but sit here and wait for someone to come out and tell us something, wait for a door to open. Something to change.

"Hannah," my mom says in a tiny whisper. The sound of her voice surprises me and I look over. "Please tell me what's going on. Why are they so focused on this boy?"

It's awful how easy it feels to just sit here next to her and keep my mouth shut. But what can I tell her? That they picked him because he's big and quiet and lights off firecrackers and sometimes steals things and that when we were little he used to take Brandon Siberry's lunch money just because he could?

My mom sighs, turning me gently by the sleeve of my T- shirt. "You have to be really careful, Hannah. How much do you actually know about him?"

I look up at her, trying to read her face. She looks so worried, but I have nothing to tell her. The answer isn't the kind of thing she wants to hear. *I know nothing and everything.*

The way she sits with her back straight and her ankles crossed makes me feel nervous, like a bomb is about to go off at any second. My mom adjusts her position, then takes a deep breath, reaching for my hand. I let her take it, even though I want to pull away.

"I shouldn't have let you go," she says. Her voice is thin and she hasn't been crying, but her eyes are wide and scared.

"It wasn't because we went to the Dairy Queen," I say. Since the night of the grounding, I've mostly avoided looking at her when she's looking at me, but now I stare right back, meeting her eyes. "It's because someone out there is a psychopath. They're crazy, but it's got nothing to do with us."

The way she looks at me makes me feel like she's seeing something else, her own reflection, maybe. It's weird to feel yourself disappearing, becoming imaginary, becoming the person someone else wants to see when she looks at you. I stare back, feeling more scared than ever.

My mom just looks away, squeezing my hand too hard. Her mouth is a tiny worried flower, lipstick pink.

"You don't have to believe me," I say. "But don't try to tell me that I don't know what he's like."

Really, though, I'm saying it to Lillian—to Finny, even though he's somewhere behind a whole parade of closed doors—and it might be an empty, useless thing to say, but I don't care, because it still feels true, and sometimes the feeling is the only thing that matters.

Lillian looks away, shaking her head, but my mom just nods. She doesn't ask me if I'm sure. She doesn't argue or try to tell me what I really mean. For maybe the first time in my life, she is listening to the words I'm saying and not telling me the words she thinks I should use.

She slips her arm around behind me and I let her. With my shoulder resting against her, we sit staring out at the empty waiting area.

"You can't do anything to help him," she says with her hand resting on the back of my chair, stroking my hair. "If there's anything to find out about him, they'll find it. You know that, right?"

I nod and lean my head against her shoulder, just quickly, just to feel the reassuring there-ness of her. Then I go back to drinking my cocoa and tearing up my napkin. Lillian is standing with her back against the wall and her arms at her sides, giving me a look that plainly says this is not her idea of a good time. I think this night will last forever.

When Officer Boles walks through the double doors of the lobby, my heart leaps in my chest and I want to fling myself at him. His expression is blank and unsmiling like always, though, so I don't.

"Where's the Boone kid?" he says to the woman behind

the desk, without even giving her any kind of acknowledgement or saying hello.

She looks up him and smiles in a tired, mechanical way. "They're interviewing him in room three. Andy and Chris are talking to him."

Boles nods like that's about what he expected to hear, and starts for a door at the back of the waiting room.

I set down my lukewarm cup of cocoa and hurry across the scuffed linoleum to him, feeling light and small and helpless. "Where's Officer McGarahan?"

When Boles sees me, he stops his charge toward the back offices, and his forehead creases. "Hannah. What are you doing here? Didn't they tell you you could go?"

I stand in front of him, still clutching my tattered napkin. "You have to tell them," I say. "Tell them this is just a big mistake—that it's all wrong."

Boles stares down at me, and I think that if he tells me this is just another avenue of the police investigation, the way it has to be, I will scream.

He doesn't, though. He just shakes his head. Then he steps around me, heads straight for the door to the interview room, and starts banging on it. When Detective Medina comes out to see why someone's pounding on his door, Boles stands over him, eyebrows raised. "Does anyone want to tell me what's going on in my park?"

Medina considers Boles, with his arms folded across his chest. Then he starts to explain the whole messy situation—how we were down in Muncy after dark, which is a violation of the new curfew, and when the patrol unit came through to check for activity, we were standing over a body.

"It doesn't mean anything!" I tell them, and my voice sounds shrill and angry.

"Now, calm down," says Medina. "I'm not trying to be the asshole here, but we just found you and your friends in an area that was supposed to be closed to the public after dark, at the site of a homicide. We just want to get the full story."

Lillian comes creeping up behind me and wraps her arms around my neck. "It doesn't matter what you say," she whispers. The words are icy, but her voice sounds almost sad, like she knows that whatever happens next is going to hurt. "They're not going to believe you. No one ever believes teenage girls about things like whether or not the guy they're running around with is a killer. No one ever treats us like we know what we're talking about."

I square my shoulders and ignore her. "He took us through the park because he wanted to get us home. That's all. The path under the bridge was right there, and it's faster than going around to the road."

Boles nods, but the detective is looking skeptical. He hooks his thumbs in his pockets and sighs. "And even though you knew there was a killer out there, you chose to walk down into an isolated area with a sixteen-year-old boy to what? To protect you?"

Boles is still watching my face, and his gaze is shrewd. "Look, Hannah, is there anything you want to tell us?"

I think about that. The truth is, I could tell them all kinds of things, only then I'd have to explain how I know them. The truth is too crazy to say out loud, and how do I explain to the police that all my information is the product of séances, ghosts, and crime-scene photos I wasn't supposed to see? Still, if I could just give them something useful, point them in the right direction, maybe it could still be enough to help them catch the Valentine Killer.

I stand between them, keeping my gaze fixed on Boles, trying to make him see how important this is. How crucial. His eyes are dark, set deep and close together under heavy brows. "Do you remember a girl named Monica Harris? She was killed last winter behind the bowling alley on the corner of Costello and Vine."

Detective Medina only sighs, but Lillian and Boles are both staring at me.

Then Boles shakes his head. "Are you telling me that an unsolved murder from a year ago has something to do with three homicides this month?"

I shrug, but I can almost feel him measuring me, searching the gesture for a buried nod.

He's staring at me with the strangest expression. "And why exactly would you think something like that?"

"I don't know, I just thought . . . I mean, it was February. There were hearts." My voice sounds small and apologetic. "The Valentine Killer leaves hearts, and I thought—"

Boles doesn't give any indication of what he's thinking. His gaze is steady and sharp, like he's reading something else on me, right there on my face.

Detective Medina is paying attention now too, but he's looking at Boles, not me. "What's she talking about? I thought the Harris murder was straightforward, a mugging that went bad, maybe."

Boles shakes his head. "There were a few cardboard cutouts lying in the parking lot near where the body was found, but everyone just considered it incidental. The holiday decorations around there are always getting pulled down or vandalized."

I've got my arms crossed tight over my chest like I'm holding myself together, but it's not enough to protect me from Boles's revelation, and I take a step back without meaning to. So everything Lillian and I learned from our makeshift spirit board was true—there was a paper heart at the scene of Monica's murder. It just didn't make it into the official police report or the paper, because at the time, no one thought anything of it. At the time, it just seemed completely random.

Medina starts to say something, but Boles holds up a hand. "Now why would you ask about hearts, Hannah? Did someone say something to you? How did you know about the valentine decorations?"

I hesitate, cycling through possible answers. *Lucky guess. Ouija board. The ghost of my dead best friend.* "Kelly told me."

Boles nods, his gaze never leaving my face. He knows it isn't true, not because it's so impossible that Kelly would tell me secure information or even because I look guilty—

although I know I must—but because a few ruined holiday decorations wouldn't have even seemed important enough to remark on, and because Kelly didn't have the crime-scene account that winter. Royal Crest did.

I try to think how I'll answer when he calls me on the lie, of what I can say to explain my uncanny knowledge of the heart, but he doesn't say anything else. He just looks at me in that same shrewd, unsettling way he always does. Perfectly blank.

✳   ✳   ✳

It's after midnight by the time we get home. All the lights are on. The kitchen still smells like Decker's garlic pesto sauce from dinner.

The whole place is way too hot, and Ariel hasn't said anything since the police station.

As soon as I walk into the house, the barrage of ghostly whispers seems to come from everywhere, pressing in, making the middle of my eardrums throb. I can still smell the dark, stinking memory of the air under the bridge and my feet feel heavy. I can't stop thinking about the weight of Abby Brooks shifting under my shoes, her body rocking stiffly. I can't stop remembering that these shoes touched her. That her death touches me.

When I can't stand it anymore, I take off my shoes and put them outside by the back steps. Then I go up to my room, where I find Lillian sprawled across my bed, reclining with her hands clasped behind her head and looking gaunt. "I can't believe you actually told them about Monica!"

"Why not?" I say, and I say it like a challenge, like I'm daring her to give me her best shot. It's weird to realize that she can usually make me doubt myself, but not about this. "Why not point out that she was beaten to death behind the bowling alley and they never caught the guy? It's not exactly a secret, Lillian."

"No, but you know what *is* a secret? That paper heart."

"So? Why would I hold back something that important?"

"Um, I don't know, maybe because it sounds kind of crazy?"

I just look at her. Then I shake my head and glance away. "Well, whatever. It's not like they believed me."

I expect her to gloat, to give me some kind of triumphant smile or at least an "I told you so," but she just sits up and wraps her arms around her knees. "What now?" she says, and it's weird because I can't remember her ever saying that to me before. She was always the one who knew what to do next.

"I have to find out who's doing this," I say, staring up at the string of rainbow Christmas lights. "Otherwise they're going to keep Finny there, maybe charge him with murder, and I should have stopped them."

I was totally stoic the whole way home, but finally saying it out loud makes my voice tremble. I might as well be saying this is all my fault. I did this to him. I wavered for one terrible moment, but it was the moment that counted.

Lillian nods, hugging her arms across her chest, cupping the points of her shoulders. "What are you going to do?" she whispers, and her voice is so frail, like the thinnest, saddest song.

"Someone knows something they haven't told us. Even if it's something small or that doesn't seem like it matters. They have the clue, the thing that will tell us who's out there doing the killing. The girls know, Lillian. They have to. And I'm going to find out what it is."

19: White Rabbit

For a second, we just sit there looking at each other. The room feels so empty and so small. The storm of whispering is roaring in my ears, making it hard to think, hard to concentrate on any one voice.

I yank back the braided rug and set the jelly glass down in the middle of the floor. I'm still wearing my mom's Warped Tour T-shirt and my shorts. My back feels sticky from the heat. It's one o'clock in the morning, and the neighborhood is dark and silent out my window. Even though the moon is still high enough to send long rectangles of light across the carpet, I reach across my nightstand and turn on the lamp. The bulb casts a warm orange glow over everything, the shade draped in an old silk scarf I got from the dollar bin at my mom's consignment store. Warm but not cozy.

On the bed, Lillian is sitting with her knees up, watching as I position my fingertips on the edge of the upturned glass, trying to ignore how cold it feels under my hands.

"Hello," I say, speaking into the stillness of my room, and my voice sounds very loud.

The rushing static grows louder in my head, so thick and

heavy it suddenly seems hard to breathe.

"One of you—any of you—please, can you tell me the thing that will help catch the person who killed you?"

And in that moment, it sounds like all the frantic voices in the world are shouting over one another, clamoring to be heard. Then, as abruptly as it started, the noise stops. The room is suddenly so quiet that I think I might scream.

The glass begins its slow crawl across the floor, coasting gently at first, then picking up speed. I make sure to keep my hands firmly planted, even though I can feel my heart hammering in my chest and I want more than anything to pull away. The glass slides over to the newspaper clipping of the makeshift shrine near where Cecily's body was found. It coasts along the edge of the photo's caption, circling the word *memorials*.

"What about them?" I whisper, but the glass only jerks hard to the side and slides away toward the bed before turning sharply and stopping on a glossy rectangle scissored from a flyer for laser eye surgery.

LOOK.

The room is cold enough to make my ears throb. I keep my hands held out in front of me, though, tucking my arms closer against my sides, waiting for an explanation, or at least a sign.

When it comes, it's not the jumble of noise that's been filling my head for weeks. It's clear and calm, speaking out of the corner by my bed.

"He'll pick you," says the voice, so fierce it seems to ruffle my hair.

I can feel her there, standing just beyond my field of vision, perfectly still in the corner of the room.

"Monica?" I whisper, fighting the urge to close my eyes and tuck my hands under my chin.

"No," says the voice, louder now in the impossible stillness of my room. "Hailey Martinsen."

I nod a stiff, frantic little nod, staring straight ahead at the clippings plastered all over the floor. There's the soft scraping sound of shoes scuffing on my floor, and that's how I know she's there—really there, in the horrible solid way that Lillian has been here for months—and that if I turn my head, I'll see her, with her dark eyes and her bloody hair and her orange nail polish chipping off her fingers. I'll see the unutterable deadness of her, the face that looked up at me out of the river.

"What happened to you?" I whisper, and the words ache in my throat, like I'm begging for whatever she says next to not be true.

Hailey makes a sad, wordless noise, and when I turn my head, she's standing in the corner just like I'd known she would be, but worse. Worse with her slumped shoulders and white lips, her hands hanging limply at her sides. "I was walking home from ballet when he found me. He told me to come down into the meadow and see, that he'd found a nest of baby rabbits."

The trick is so obvious, almost too obvious to work. But maybe that's the genius part of it, that even though any girl should know better, it will always work anyway. Maybe a

251

girl like that, a nice, hopeful girl, will always go down into the long grass to see the rabbits, always follow with a smile, trusting so easily, trusting that whatever he promises her is the truth.

"He'll pick you," says another voice, speaking from the deep, black shadows near the closet, where the lamplight doesn't reach.

I turn my head to see Monica. Monica, who I once made a Salem witch–themed shadowbox with for an English project about *The Crucible*. Monica, who died with blood in her hair and snow in her eyes, in her pink nylon parka. She stands with her coat zipped up to her chin, her hair caked with ice, face purple all down one side. "He'll pick you if you're small. If you're soft. If you look like you'd be fun."

The whole room is suddenly so cold that I think my skin will crack apart. "Fun to what?"

"To break."

And then no one says anything. I am almost too cold to breathe.

"What can I do?" I whisper. "How can I stop it?"

"Find him," says Hailey, and her voice is not the high, soft voice of a little girl anymore, not the voice of someone walking down into the meadow to see rabbits. "Find him and make sure that he's punished."

"Find him," says another voice, from over by the door this time.

There's a pale flutter at the corner of my eye, and I turn to see her standing just behind the open door, just in the shadow, one hand glowing whitely in the lamplight. And then another one in the far corner, beside my desk. All four corners of the room are filled now, occupied by the ghosts of four murdered girls with rage in their eyes and every reason to want retribution. Me and Lillian at the center.

"How?" I ask, and my throat is so painful and dry that it's hard to make the words come out. "I'll do whatever you say, just tell me how."

I expect the voices to speak up in unison, to tell me the secret that will reveal the Valentine Killer. Instead the glass races across the floor beneath my fingertips, swift and insistent, spelling the same word again and again. RABBIT, RABBIT, RABBIT.

"What?" I say, the word catching in my throat.

There's a shudder like an electrical current racing through my hands and up into my wrists, like at any second the glass will spin out of control, go racing crazily around the floor or streak down the hall and out the front door. Suddenly it flies fast and hard across the room and smashes against the wall, showering the floor with a rain of diamond-cut glass. The pieces come spilling toward me in a shining wave, then lie still.

The room is silent. The chill is gone. The corners are all empty.

In my throat there's a feeling like a strummed guitar string, trembling, trembling, but even as I try to keep my hands from shaking, I understand that really, I'm holding very still, frozen in place.

There's a high-pitched ringing in my ears, like if I don't do something quick, maybe the world will end. I jump up and cross to the closet, feeling around in the dark for a pair of shoes and then a hoodie— something to put on, anything to make me feel less exposed.

"No!" Lillian says from the bed. "Are you crazy? You can't just go running outside by yourself in the middle of night!"

I turn and face her, and even before her mouth drops open and her eyes widen, I know I must look wild, unhinged.

I know this script by heart. I've said it a million times, only now the exchange is backward and all wrong. Now she's the one with her hands clasped like she's begging me to go slow, to be careful.

"Is this what you think you have to do? Go running out into the night? This is stupid and reckless. It's not you."

I shake my head. She ought to understand by now that who I am is not the girl I look like every day. And maybe it took staring into the milky eyes of dead girls and kissing Finny in the dark, but at least I finally got a good look at what's under my ribbons and my feathers and appliquéd flowers. Even before all this, though, I think I might have known. I think I suspected. I just never showed it to anyone who might punish or judge me for it, because it's not a contest. Because the fact is, the contest has always been invulnerability, and even when you win, you still lose.

Lillian is watching me with sad, regretful eyes. "You were the brave one, not me. No matter what any of them said or did, you were the one who never had to invent yourself. You always just knew who you were."

"So did you, though."

She stares off into the distance, shaking her head. "If I'd known that, I think maybe I would have been a different person. Maybe I wouldn't have ended up like this. Part of not knowing was pretending so, so hard that I knew everything."

We stand in the middle of my room, looking at each other, and I don't know how to make her see that whatever Hannah she's imagining—that girl never existed.

"I'm not those things you think I am," I say. "Yeah, I looked bright and shiny on the outside, maybe. But inside, I was always just the same as you. Underneath, I wanted all the chaos and the scary, messy stuff. I think I was always just this—this strange, secret girl who always wanted to kiss Finny Boone."

It's weird to say it out loud, like I'm confirming all of Lillian's worst suspicions, admitting to imperfection—weakness and desire. Earnestness, honesty, everything she seemed to be so dead set against before she died.

The whole room is cluttered with stick-on stars and colored lights, but the colors are muted now, like all the bright little pieces of my old life are gathering dust. Like I've been holding my breath for days.

All at once, Lillian shakes her head and looks up, her eyes bloodshot and desolate. "No," she says. She says it quietly, not like she's correcting me or telling me how it is, but just respectfully disagreeing. "No, you can still be both. You have to be,

255

because otherwise we're always just ghosts of ourselves. So the hearts and the flowers are still you. Just like even though I wanted more than anything to be left alone, to ignore everyone and live my life, there was still this huge part of me wanting to be perfect and special, wanting to make my mother happy."

I shake my head, but the words won't come now. They won't take shape. Because she was so much more than her mother's dress-up doll, even when she was volunteering for the part, even when she was desperate to just feel okay and trying so hard to get it right. Even now that she's dead.

"You can't tell me that being sick wasn't who I was," she says. "I mean look at me—it defined everything."

Her cheeks are hollow, and I'm struck by the fact that she never called it "sick" when she was alive. The idea that a person can be defined by anything so superficial is terrible. Like this is the one true heart of her, reduced to a bony apparition in her pajamas. It's like trying to shrink me down to nothing but my shiny thrift-store dresses, or defining Finny by his broad shoulders and his Clorox-blond hair. The simple version isn't even recognizable when you hold it up against a living, breathing human being. Her ghost will always be so much less of her than the girl I used to see every day.

The bed is wildly unmade and the pillows are all over the floor. Lillian turns to stare out the window, sitting in the middle of my bed with her knees drawn up and her head resting on her arms. She looks so unbelievably small, folded in on herself like a jackknife.

"I miss you, Hannah." Her voice is hoarse and shaky.

Her eyes are too red to belong to a ghost. Why does she always look so real? "I miss you so much."

"I'm here," I say, standing over her, reaching for her. "I'm right here."

Lillian nods miserably, looking up at me with wet lashes. Her mouth is crumpled and hopeless. "But I'm not."

❋   ❋   ❋

I leave the house as soon as it's light. My mom and Ariel and Joan are all asleep, but Decker is already gone.

The air over the city is motionless and heavy but not unbearable yet. The sun is still teetering on the horizon. For the last five hours, I've gone over every possible type of rabbit I can think of, trying to understand exactly what the spirit board was telling me. Does it mean the fake, imaginary rabbits that Hailey talked about—the ones the killer used to lure her down into the grass? On the unlikely chance that I could get someone to believe me without demanding that I prove how I know, I could at least tell the police how he's getting the girls alone. They could put the information in the paper and once the public knows, maybe then the trick won't work on anyone else.

I stand on the corner of Sherwood, tugging on my bracelet, running my fingers along the row of charms. A rabbit will help the police catch the killer, but already my list of possibilities is way too long and even if I could check everything, there would still be a whole army of rabbits I was missing. There's the painted bouncy one on the Muncy playground, this wooden cutout with a saddle that rocks back and forth on a big metal spring. There's the fast, sleek outline of a rabbit on the logo for the city bus, the second level of the parking garage at the mall is the Rabbit Level, and there's a bronze statue of Peter Rabbit and Benjamin Bunny in front of the public library. And that's not even counting things like stores or restaurants or anything else that could have the word *rabbit* in the name.

The possibilities are overwhelming, and as I walk, I'm still coming up with more. There are wild rabbits in the park and rabbits at pet stores. There's a whole herd of plush rabbits at Toy Dungeon. There's just no way to pick one specific place or picture or object out of all the rabbits in the world.

After a few blocks, I decide that I can at least check the bouncy-toy on the playground. It's close to the crime scenes, and maybe that makes it important somehow. It's not much, but it's all I've got.

The footbridge near the three-hundred block of Sherwood is the quickest way to get there, but I stay out of the park. Instead I go all the way around on Beverly Street, following the sidewalk, sticking close to the railing where it crosses the river. There's not much traffic on the roads. It's still too early for most people to be going to work.

Beverly is a little ways below the dam, and the water's shallower here. It rushes along, making a chuckling noise where it runs low and fast over the rocks.

From the road near the shuttered Dairy Queen, I have a clear view down into the park, where uniformed officers are still milling around near the opening to the railroad bridge, searching the ground for evidence. The whole area around the bridge is taped off.

It's been less than twelve hours since I stood over the body of Abby Brooks, but already there's a motley collection of objects starting to form against the base of the streetlamp on the corner.

I'm tempted to cross over to the other side of the street so I don't have to walk by the little shrine on my way to the playground. There's something just so tragic and so awful about the way all these sorrowful gifts have sprung up around the streetlamp. The rawness and the grief of it are almost too much to take.

I'm just about to step off the curb and cross the street, when I stop, one foot still slightly raised, remembering the way the glass moved across the floor last night, circling the word *memorials*. The ghosts were trying so hard to show me how to find him, and *rabbit* wasn't the only clue they gave me. They also said *memorials*.

I kneel over flowers and candles and a teddy bear with a satin-covered stomach and a tiny Mylar balloon on a plastic stick sewn into one paw. There are notes written on pink stationery and loose-leaf paper and napkins, mostly saying things like *Friends forever* and *We miss you*. And flowers. So many flowers. Some of the bouquets are from the grocery store, daisies and carnations mostly, still in their plastic wrappers. But some are obviously collected from the big stone planters in the park or from people's yards. The stems are ragged, torn off by the handful.

I'm careful not to touch anything. Not because I really think I might be disturbing evidence, but because it feels inconsiderate to Abby Brooks. It feels disrespectful to be digging around in the pile of gifts meant to honor her.

I'm just about to straighten up and go, when I see it. Sitting under a flower arrangement near the teddy bear is a small pewter charm, flashing silver in the light of the rising sun. The rabbit is silver, but if it were a real living thing, it would be white, dressed in a top hat, racing along with an oversize pocket watch held anxiously in one paw. It's been weeks since I last saw it, but I know it like I know arithmetic or the words to the national anthem. I've spent long, stifling nights running my fingers along the bare stretch of links where it belongs.

For a second, I just kneel over the memorial with my hands clasped stiffly against my chest.

The first idea I have is that I should pick up the charm. Then right after that comes the idea that I should leave it where it is. The charm is mine. The charm is here, lying on the corner, but how?

And my thoughts leap to Finny. The bracelet was a mess when he brought it back to me, scratched and bent. Missing the rabbit. For a terrible moment, all I can think is that this is what the ghosts were trying to help me see—that Angelie was right, and I've been spending the last few weeks with a killer.

But even as I feel the horror rise up to make a choking knot in my throat, I know that Finny didn't leave the rabbit here. He couldn't have, because he's been at the police station all night. In fact, he's probably still there. He might have had the chance to rip the charm off the chain, but he wasn't the one who put it here.

The rabbit was left by someone else—someone who had the bracelet too.

I turn my back on the sad little shrine for Abby and start down the hill, heading for the footpath. For the long slash of shade under the railroad bridge.

When I come up to the police tape, I stop, scanning the crowd for someone I know. The officers are working the scene in their blue uniforms, kneeling on the cracked asphalt, conversing in twos and threes. McGarahan is over by the far end of the bridge, poking through the weeds. I duck under the tape and start across to him, moving carefully, making sure not to step near any of the yellow plastic markers.

McGarahan glances up, and when he sees me coming toward him, his expression is wary. "Hannah," he says, sounding disoriented. "What are you doing down here? You need to get on the other side of that police line right now—before you get in trouble."

"I know who the Valentine Killer is," I say. And even as I say them, the words sound impossible. They don't make sense.

Some of the other officers laugh these dry, incredulous little laughs. They shake their heads, staring in disbelief, but McGarahan just looks expectant.

I soldier on, determined to say the rest before any of

them can interrupt or make me leave. "I don't know where he lives, but he has a police record and he's been in the foster system, so you can get his address."

"Whoa, Hannah, slow down," says McGarahan. "What's his name?"

And now I stop and take a breath. Once the name is out, there'll be no taking this back.

"Nick Andelman," I say.

20: Break

By Wednesday morning, it's all over the news. The police have the Valentine Killer in custody, and his identity has been confirmed. It took less than an hour for Nick to confess to everything.

I don't know how to feel.

There's a part of me that's still just so disoriented, like I thought everything would go back to how it was before the murders, but the only difference is that now the newspaper headlines are triumphant instead of grim and I'm allowed to leave the house again without supervision.

All my mom can talk about is how amazing it is that they caught him, how relieving. How proud she is that her daughter was the one who actually helped the police. She doesn't even lecture me for the way I left the house that morning without telling her.

I want to feel proud of myself, but I don't. I feel anxious and restless, like I'm still missing some important piece of the puzzle. Still waiting for something to happen.

In the living room, I lie on the couch with my head on the cushions and my feet on the armrest, while the local news runs constant coverage of the investigation.

Lillian is on her stomach, draped across the top of the curio cabinet, staring at the TV. "Freaky."

I nod and don't ask what's freaky. The whole week has been like a dream you don't wake up from, because even after you open your eyes, the picture doesn't change. It's still your same everyday life.

I'm just about to turn off the news and go upstairs when I hear a tiny whisper from somewhere behind me, faint, familiar. I sit up, glancing toward the front hall, half expecting the ghostly silhouette of one of the girls, Monica or Cecily, but I don't see anyone.

Onscreen, they're showing a black-and-white school photo of Nick Andelman. He looks worried and sort of intense. Almost haunted. I stare hard into his eyes, trying to find the thing that made him a killer. It seems like you should be able to read the violence or the brutality in someone's face, but even as I try to see it, I know I won't be able to. There are so many things you can't know just from looking at a person.

The story is a profile piece, like the ones they ran about Hailey and Cecily and Abby, only the tone is wildly different. Their portrait of Nick is a familiar one. Troublemaker, poor student, disciplinary nightmare. The grave-faced anchor reminds us that while yes, he's confessed to the brutal murders of four girls, it's still our duty to consider him innocent until proven guilty.

At first the police only wanted to approach him for questioning, acting on the information of concerned citizen

Hannah Wagner, but they quickly changed their objective as soon as they got a warrant and actually searched his room. The photos are grainy and too saturated, blown up to unnatural size when they flash across the TV screen.

"Looks kind of like your floor," whispers Lillian, and I nod because she's sort of right.

In the picture, Nick's desk is just an old end table, stained and gouged, covered in drifts of spilled confetti and tiny scraps of cut paper. Bottles of glue and silver glitter are lined up against the wall at the back of the table. The police confiscated over seventy pieces of cut-up paper and a Nike shoebox filled with crumpled birthday streamers and crappy toys, all lost or discarded or stolen.

This is the part that makes everything else seem so crazy and so horrific. More than anything, I want to know why. Why he killed those girls, and more than that, why he left the broken things. I want to know the point of my rabbit charm. Why he brought this one random little piece of junk and set it carefully among the other offerings.

The whispering is insistent now, growing louder, and I sit up again, trying to block out the noise. The ghosts aren't supposed to be here anymore. Everything was supposed to go back to normal. I don't know what they want.

Lillian flops over onto her back, one arm dangling toward the floor. "It's weird," she says in a low, dreamy voice.

"What's weird?"

"Nothing. Just that none of this seems very organized. I mean, he killed Monica seventeen months ago and then nothing. That's a pretty severe cooling-off period. And then to come back out of the blue? To start killing at such an accelerated rate, almost a frenzy? That doesn't even make sense."

I shake my head, leaning back against the nubbly upholstery of the couch. "You're worried that a total psychopath doesn't make sense?"

"I don't know, I just think maybe we're thinking about this all wrong."

"Why are we thinking about this at all? We already know who did it. He confessed, Lillian. What, do you think he was lying when he described smashing in the back of Monica's skull? You're trying to figure out why a crazy person would act crazy, and that's your answer right there—he's crazy."

Lillian folds her hands over her chest, staring at the ceiling. "But still."

I sit with my head back and my eyes unfocused, thinking about that. She doesn't say but still *what*.

❋　❋　❋

I haven't seen Finny since the night they arrested him, and it's weird to feel nervous about seeing him now. If it were any of my regular friends, I'd text first or maybe even call, but the thing with Finny is that we've never really been like that with each other. We've sort of always just found each other when we needed to.

Lillian watches from the corner of my room while I go through my closet, looking for the perfect thing, the thing that will make me feel beautiful and exactly like myself, a dress that says *I've missed you* and *I'm sorry for ever doubting you*. The one I finally pick isn't any of the bright sundresses I usually wear. It's bird-gray and plain cotton, but it has a short flared skirt lined with pink tulle, and the hem is sewed with tiny silver star-charms.

The day is hot but overcast, and the clouds are sitting low over the trees, so close they seem to almost touch down and scrape the tips of the branches. The metal charms sewn into my skirt keep sticking to the backs of my thighs.

Finny's house is just as cramped and messy as it was the other day, spider plant wilting on the porch, pizza coupons and lawn-care flyers lying everywhere. Jolene answers the door looking scattered, with her ponytail bristling out of its rubber band.

"Hannah," she says, sounding breathless and distracted. "It's nice to see you again. Why don't you come on in? We were just about to have some lemonade."

As she leads me through the front hall into the living room, I pass the same toy animals and spilled blocks as last time I was here, but now there's a pair of big plastic dump trucks added to the mix.

Finny's in the living room, sitting sandwiched on the couch between two younger boys. One of them is practically a baby— this chubby little black kid, maybe two years old, wearing nothing but a diaper, and sucking drowsily on a pacifier.

The other one looks eight or nine, with penny-red hair and freckles all over his face and arms. He's flicking through daytime game shows with the remote, while the diapered one leans against Finny's arm with droopy eyes.

Jolene points to the couch. "That little guy is Levi, and the one in the blue is Everett. They're staying with us for a few days."

I nod to them, but my attention is mostly focused on Finny. He looks just like he always does, wearing his same too-faded jeans, like a juvenile delinquent or a 1970s punk in his white undershirt. I've been waiting for the moment when I'd see him again, waiting to throw myself at him and wrap my arms around his neck, but the look on his face when he glances up stops me in the doorway.

The freckled one stops chasing channels on the TV and points to me. "Who's that?"

"Hannah."

"Is she going to stay here too?"

Finny shakes his head. "Nope, just visiting."

"Is she your girlfriend?"

The question makes me suck in my breath. I wait for his answer, but he just shrugs and doesn't look at me. I feel pointless suddenly, and stupid to have come here. I think I can hear the rhythmic buzzing of the ghosts, but for once I'm not really sure. It might just be the fast, frantic beating of my own heart.

"Can I sit down?" I say. My voice sounds small, like I'm just waiting to be told no.

He shrugs a big, rolling shrug and nods, but he still isn't looking at me. And that's how I know that everything must be wrong, because I feel like I might break into tiny pieces, and because of how strange it is to have to ask if it's okay, when for as long as I've known him, I've never had to ask Finny for anything.

I sit on the edge of a battered easy chair even though my dress isn't really made for sitting. A few of the metal charms jab me, and I adjust my skirt. The tulle feels rough and tickly against my legs.

We watch a game-show host flip numbered tiles without talking.

I want to do the right thing or say something important, but I don't know what it would be. The whispers are louder now, making it hard to hear the game-show contestants when they answer. I wanted this to be the moment when everything strange and wrong and scary went back to normal. I wanted this to be when everything stopped feeling so lost.

It's weird that before Finny, I never really knew how to be quiet. Even right after Lillian died, when I kind of stopped talking for a while, it was mostly because I felt like there was no one I could talk to. With Finny, it was different. It was like we didn't need to talk, because sometimes it was better just being quiet, and because we didn't have to be saying something all the time. There was no gaping chasm, no frightening space that needed to be filled up.

But now the silence is unbearable. I lace my fingers together to make myself stop pulling at the stars on my skirt. Out of the corner of my eye, I see a pale shape in a pink jacket and in that instant, I know that even here, even with Finny home and Nick in jail, nothing is better.

After a few minutes, Jolene calls Levi and Everett to come into the kitchen and get some lemonade. I'm half tempted to follow them, but Finny stays where he is, so I do too. Then it's just the two of us, sitting in his living room less than three feet apart, staring wordlessly at the TV, where nothing about the game show makes a whole lot of sense or seems to matter very much.

"How are you?" I say finally. It sounds weirdly formal, like I'm meeting a stranger.

He shrugs and doesn't look at me. He's staring down at the backs of his hands, which are scabbed over at the knuckles and covered in nasty bruises.

"What happened?" I ask after it gets obvious that he's not going to say anything on his own.

"I punched the hell out of the station wall," he says, staring down at his bruised hands. "Probably not the best way to prove I'm harmless, huh?"

I nod. I want so badly to reach for him, to hold his bruised hand, but I don't even know what good it would do. All I can think is how it felt to look at him there, in the flashing lights of the squad cars, and feel undone, like I didn't know anything about him. I want to say something, but I've got nothing useful, and it seems like everything is getting more messed up by the second.

The voices are very close now, whispering right in my ear. I lean forward, trying to catch a phrase or a word, but the only thing I can make out is Nick's name, repeated again and again.

"Is it weird?" I say, scuffing the soles of my sneakers on the carpet, trying to keep my voice under control. "That Nick did something so awful and screwed-up? I mean, because he used to live with you?"

Finny just stares off in the direction of the TV, like he's tuning out, not really seeing what's there. "I don't know. It's not like I knew him enough to really be surprised. I told you, he wasn't like my friend or anything."

Without thinking or stopping to doubt myself, I reach over the arm of the couch and take his hand, careful of the bruised places.

"Don't," he says, but he lets me do it.

"I want to."

I'm surprised that I've never told him how much I like him. I always just figured he could see it without me having to say it, but the truth is that sometimes it's important to say it anyway. I try to say it, say something, but the words won't come, and he shakes his head.

The weight of his hand in mine is defeated. "It's not going to be okay, Hannah."

"Why? Just because for a few days they thought it might be you? They don't even know you!"

He takes his hand out of mine and leans back, looking away from me.

"Because you're you, and I'm . . ." He trails off, digging his fingers into the tops of his thighs and looking away. "I'm kind of a fuckup, okay?"

He says it like he's so sure, like he's trying to get me to

agree with him, but I already know that I won't do that. I will not tell him he's broken or inferior. I've had enough practice living with Lillian, and I'm not about to sit here in his living room, with picture books and plastic toys lying all around us, and help him tear himself down.

"Stop," I tell him.

He glances over, squinting at me. "What?"

"Stop acting like you need to protect me from yourself." And I sound angrier than I ever usually sound. "I'm not a victim or a fragile little thing. And maybe there's all kinds of dangerous stuff out there, but not you. Okay? I don't need to be kept safe from you."

Finny's looking at me in this sad, pleading way, like he doesn't quite believe me. The truth is, why should he? No matter what, he's stuck being everything people think about him, someone who steals and lies and destroys things, destroys everything. The person he is not.

"Don't listen," I whisper, reaching again for his raw, bruised hands, even though it feels wrong to tell him how he's supposed to live his life when I'm the one who's still surrounded by voices. "Whatever they said, whatever they told you about yourself, it's not true."

He shakes his head and pulls his hands away. The sensation of his fingers sliding out of mine makes me feel lost, like when he kissed me for the first time and then stopped.

"Look," he says—thickly, like something hurts in his chest. "You should probably go."

❊ ❊ ❊

By the time I get home, I'm crying.

My biggest fear is that someone's going to come into the front hall and ask me what's wrong. Ariel should be home from music camp by now, but the house is empty and it's a relief to not have to see anyone. I stand with my back against the front door, wiping my eyes with my fingertips and trying not to smear my makeup.

As soon as I'm inside, though, the storm of voices fills the halls. I want to scream at them to shut up, to just stop talking and let me have some quiet. I did what they asked.

The truth is that I shouldn't even be crying, because I was the one who left him first. I was the one who stood in the middle of the Muncy playground, looking mistrustful and betrayed, not saying anything.

Ariel's sneakers aren't in the front hall, and there's a note on the refrigerator, but I don't go in right away to read it. I want to hold very still until I stop feeling like the world is pitching and tilting all around me. Until the voices go silent and the noise in my head stops and I can just shut myself in my room and not think about anything for a while.

When I open my eyes, Lillian is sitting on the lowest stair with her chin in her hands. I want her to go away and leave me alone, to stop looking at me like that. Like I'm this interesting bug she just found.

When I stare back at her, she doesn't get up from the stairs or ask what's wrong. She frowns a little, tipping her head to one side. "They said he cried."

"What?" I want the question to be flat and dismissive,

but it comes out sounding miserable and stuffy, even to me.

"On the news. They said his confession was tearful. That the interrogation only took like half an hour, because he broke down almost right away."

I shake my head, trying to get my voice under control. "That's not weird, though, Lillian. He killed people. I mean, wouldn't it be worse if he didn't even feel bad about it?"

She gives me a long, shrewd look. "But real psychopaths don't feel remorse. They can fake it maybe, but it wouldn't look convincing."

"So then he's not a psychopath. He's just a really messed-up guy, and now he feels bad."

Lillian snorts. "Well, if he felt so damn bad, then why would he do it in the first place?"

I shake my head and walk away from her into the kitchen. The note on the refrigerator is from Ariel, saying she's going out really quick and that she'll be back in half an hour. Reading it, I feel a familiar jolt of panic, like she shouldn't be wandering around the neighborhood without me, before remembering that with Nick in custody, the danger is over. It's finally safe to be alone.

I go upstairs to change out of the dress I thought looked nice an hour ago, kick off my shoes, and throw myself down on the bed and forget everything, but when I get to my doorway, I stop.

Lillian's scrapbook is lying in the exact middle of the floor. And that's all wrong, because I know, without a doubt, that when I left to go over to Finny's, it was on my desk.

The narrowest sliver of something red is sticking out from between the pages, and I walk across to it like a person in a dream.

I reach for the book, already knowing what will be there waiting for me to shake it from between the pages. The card is a red paper heart pasted to a white doily. The lines and curves and scallops are clumsy-elegant. The paper is rough and cheap. The words *Come and get her* are printed on the front in black ballpoint pen. On the back, it says *Better hurry if you don't want to find another dead girl. You know the place.*

The valentine is crisp and heavy in my hand, lacy under my fingers.

It's for me.

21: Lock and Key

I bolt from the house, tearing down the front steps, out onto the sidewalk and toward Muncy. The soles of my shoes are beating time to my heart, making a frantic *slap-slap* noise on the cement.

When I get to the steep embankment near the playground, I don't stop or slow down, cutting across the street, sliding my way down the weedy hill toward the bike path. The police tape is gone. The bridge sits dark and empty, a gaping mouth.

The space under it is empty now, bare of plastic party favors and bodies. I scramble down the little asphalt path and then stop, turning in a circle, searching for Ariel. I'm staring into the deep shadow under the bridge, still breathing hard, when someone comes crunching through the dry grass above me.

A voice calls, "Hey, Hannah!"

The sound makes me jump, and when I glance up, I have to shade my eyes against the sun. Connor Price is standing at the top of the bridge, leaning his elbows on the railing. Ariel is beside him, grinning down at me. She doesn't look afraid, and for one soaring second, I have the idea that I'm wrong about everything. That this is all just a big misunderstanding and the card was a mistake or some kind of joke. That it was never really there at all.

Above the railroad bridge and the trees, I can see the clouds coming in. They pile up in a dark bank of thunderheads, towering above us, purple and bruised.

"What are you doing?" I say, looking up at the two of them, and my voice sounds all wrong.

Ariel gestures to me. "Come with us. Connor's going to show me a nest of bunnies down by the bridge."

I stare up at her, frozen on the path. The words seem to be drifting down to me from a long way off, chilling my skin like ice water, and I can feel the frantic pounding of my heart thudding in my ears and in my teeth. Until just now, I was so ready to believe that everything would be okay after all, that maybe Connor just happened to run into Ariel here. But he's standing inches away from her, much too close for this to be anything accidental, and then there's the matter of the rabbits. He told her about the rabbits.

He smiles at me—a warm, generous smile. There on the edge of the train tracks, he's like a magazine ad. The perfect fake-worn-out T-shirt. The perfect hair.

"Come on," he says to Ariel, pushing himself away from the railing. "Let's go down and see them. Hannah can come if she wants." The smile he gives me is disgusting.

I want to scream at her to run, run away and find help, but he's right there behind her, blocking her path. There's no way she'll be able to outdistance him.

They're halfway down the embankment when he reaches over and takes her hand. The gesture is a harmless one, like he's just reaching out to help her along the steep part. I've seen Finny do the same thing, but now the whole production seems ugly.

Then all three of us are standing at the bottom of the hill, baking in the sun with grasshoppers buzzing all around us. The neighborhoods to the west look so still, so peaceful. Idyllic, like nothing bad could ever happen. And that's when my skin starts to crawl. I shiver hard, feeling cold all over.

Connor is guiding Ariel along the narrow asphalt path. He moves his hand to take hold of her arm and then pulls her in the direction of the bridge. "Come on, let's get this party started."

Ariel glances at me and her eyes widen, because something isn't right and she knows it. Connor's fingers are digging into her arm. "Hannah, what's happening?"

He tightens his grip and yanks her down into the dark space under the bridge so we're hidden from the sightlines of the playground. Not that anyone is out right now anyway. The little kids are all inside, and the low dark clouds mean thunder.

Once we're all the way under, Connor steps closer, backing me against the stone wall of the bridge, still holding Ariel by the crook of her elbow as she struggles to get free.

"Why are you doing this?" I say, backing away from him, sliding sideways along the wall like I'm about to make a break for it.

"It's not personal, Hannah." But the way he's looking at me suggests that he means the opposite.

"What isn't?" But I'm only pretending now, only doing the happy little Hannah dance, like I can prove to myself that everything's still okay. It occurs to me that murder is probably the most personal thing there is. Bashing someone's head in is personal. Dying is personal. I'm shaking now, shivering so hard that the metal charms on my skirt echo under the bridge, clanking and jingling.

"Hannah, stop being such a baby."

The voice is sharp and scornful. I look up. Lillian is perched on the narrow cement ledge just under the arch of the bridge, with her hands folded carefully in her lap. The shadow there is deep, but a few feet below her the sun slants in at a hard angle, and I can see by the way her outline wavers around the edges how much effort it's taking just to stay here. She's staring down at Connor with a look of absolute hatred.

He must see a change on my face, because he tightens his grip on Ariel and drags her closer. The three of us are standing in a little cluster, almost stepping on each other's feet. Connor and Ariel are right in front of me, and I stand with my back pressed hard against the cement wall.

Connor glances back over his shoulder at the path, and the instant he turns away, I stare hard into Ariel's face and jam my phone into her hand.

Run, I mouth, knowing with hideous certainty that she has to do it. There'll be one chance, and so she has to go, without hesitation, without questions, without looking back or faltering or trying to help me.

As Connor turns to face me, I take a deep breath and press the sole of one shoe against the wall behind me. Then I push off as hard as I can and slam myself into his chest. I might not be big, but I throw all my weight against him like I'm playing Red Rover, trying to break through the chain of hands. Only instead of trying to break through myself, all I'm focused on is wrenching Ariel's arm out of Connor's grasp.

As soon as his hand slips and she wriggles away, I expect him to go after her. I'm ready to fling myself on his back if I have to and do everything in my power to slow him down, but he doesn't chase her. He turns and grabs me by the shoulders, slamming me hard against the wall of the bridge.

His face is close to mine, his breath hot and damp against my cheek. He's laughing. "Hannah, you are just too much. I mean, you're perfect. This is going to be so much fun." He leans closer, and his expression is sympathetic, confiding. "So, I heard you went crying to the police about Nick."

He's watching my face like he's waiting for me to deny it. I don't. I don't say anything.

"You're pale," he tells me gently, reaching out like he might touch my face again.

"You're always pale," says Lillian. She looks deeply unimpressed.

"I'm always pale," I tell Connor. I sound braver than I feel.

Lillian crawls down from the little ledge, digging her fingers into the cracks in the cement, looking like a giant flower-printed spider in her pajamas. She creeps across the asphalt path to stand next to me.

"How can he be doing this?" she whispers, and her voice is stunned. "I mean, I knew he could be impulsive or really insensitive, but Hannah, this is psychopathic."

I nod, just barely, a tiny little agreement.

"I mean, he actually wants you to beg." She leans close, and her eyes are hard and fierce. "Don't do it. Don't cry or try to bargain with him. Don't ask him for anything. Can you do that?"

I look at her, just briefly, glancing away as soon as our eyes meet. And I nod.

"Are you seriously going to hurt me?" I say to Connor, and my voice sounds convincingly incredulous. "We've been friends for years. I've never done anything to hurt you."

His gaze is chilly though, making my skin crawl, and maybe it's true that I've known him since elementary school, but we were never really friends. The little gestures and inside jokes were all there, but that's all they were. They didn't mean anything. Looking back, the only thing our shared history ever really proved was that we knew the same people, went to the same neighborhood barbecues and birth-day parties. That we happened, again and again, to be in the same places at the same time. The way he's watching me now is almost predatory, and there are so many things you can never tell just by looking at a person.

He leans close, staring into my face. "You really think that? You think you've never done anything to fuck things up for me? So, Nick just walked into the police station on his own? He just went right up to the cops with his wrists stuck out for the cuffs and turned himself in?"

"Well, he kind of did," whispers Lillian, creeping around behind me and leaning her chin on my shoulder.

"Oh, come on," I say. "He wanted to get caught. No one goes back and leaves something at a crime scene unless they want someone to come stop them."

Connor shakes his head, squinting at me in the dim light. "Bullshit. Why would he want to get caught?"

"I don't know, maybe because he felt bad for killing those girls." The chilly weight of Lillian's cheek pressed against mine makes everything seem less terrifying but also less real. "Maybe he thought it was just pretty despicable to go around killing middle school kids. But you're off your game now, Connor. I'm not a kid."

Connor laughs with his mouth open, smiling much too wide. "Are you saying you'd rather it were Ariel?" The way the light comes in under the bridge makes his face look kind of like a monster. "It still could be. Maybe I'll catch up with her later. If there's time. And anyway, don't stress too much, Hannah. You're pretty much perfect for this game. You even like all this shiny plastic shit and Nick's stupid craft projects and everything, so what's the difference? I mean, you're practically a little girl, anyway."

The way he's looking at me is hungry, like someone

sizing up a piece of meat, trying to find the best place to stick the knife.

I start talking faster, trying to buy some time for Ariel to get help, backing away from him even as his fingers dig into my wrist. "How did you decide on Monica? What made her special enough to be the first one?" I say "special" in a hard, scornful voice, like it's a dirty word, and part of me doesn't even mean to.

Connor looks at me like he's really thinking about that, trying hard to figure something out. Then he shrugs and shakes his head. "She was there. We wanted to know what it was like, and there she was, just bopping along by herself with her big white mittens on and those fucking ice skates." He shakes his head, smiling at something too beautiful and far for me to see.

"You knew her," I say, and my voice is suddenly ferocious. "You'd been in the same homeroom with her since seventh grade!"

"And she was really surprised when I smashed her head against a Dumpster. Come on, let's go up into the trees. It's freezing down here."

I shake my head and dig my heels into the soft, damp ground and the loose gravel. I'm desperate to stay with Lillian, scared that if we leave the shelter of the bridge, she won't be able to follow us. But Connor just grabs my arm and pulls me hard, making the soles of my shoes slip and skid over the path.

He yanks me out into the sunlight, dragging me up the

283

other side of the bank by my elbow. His grip is painful, and I can feel my pulse banging away in my forearm and my shoulder.

When I try to squirm away, prying at his fingers with my free hand, he gives me a shake that nearly pops my shoulder out of its socket. "If you don't settle down, I will knock you the fuck out."

He pulls me up the hill and into the middle of the clearing, shoving me so that I fall forward into the grass, landing on my hands and knees.

Connor drops down next to me and pulls me close so we're sitting in the grass with his arm around me, holding me against his side so my shoulder presses into his chest. I hate how easy, how familiar the gesture is, like I'm barely even a real person, just a worn-out doll he's dragging around with him.

"I've really been looking forward to this," he says in a voice so conversational that I want to scream and wrench away from him.

His grip is painful, though, so instead I sit perfectly still and imagine Ariel, following her progress in my mind, tracing her path through the trees and across the bridge. *How far is the edge of the park? How far to someone who can help? How much time could I gain if I can make him talk to me?*

"After Monica," I say, sounding breathless and dizzy, "then what?"

"Oh, we were totally freaking out after it happened. I

mean, Nick was pretty messed up about it. Forget making it, like, a recurring thing—I thought he was never going to talk to me again. I was amped, though. I mean, it was insane—like drugs or something!"

He's right. This whole thing is insane.

I stare out over the deserted park, searching for something else to ask, something that will eat up the minutes. "Wait, so you really *were* doing all this with Nick Andelman? I saw you go up to him at the mall a couple weeks ago, but that was one time. You guys never even hung out together."

The look Connor gives me is profoundly patient. "Of course not. The whole point of a secret pact is not to go advertising to everybody that you know each other. He wasn't even supposed to be hanging out at the mall that day because he knew *I* was going to be there. No mistakes, right? Don't get careless. So I had to remind him, make sure he remembered which one of us called the shots."

"If you think you're so much better than him, then how come he was the one you picked to do all this with?"

Connor shrugs and I feel his arm tighten around me. "It's kind of funny, really, how detention is like this great equalizer. We both had to stay after with Mrs. Phipps one day, back in eighth grade. We were the only ones there. Anyway, we started talking about how you could make napalm with, like, Styrofoam and shit, and Nick said he had a whole batch of this really ghetto stuff that was mostly gasoline and random kitchen chemicals, but that it really worked. He said he knew this abandoned building and that he was going to burn it down, so after detention let out, we went over there. Turned out it wasn't really a building, just some dinky little shed out in the field behind that Texaco on Sixteenth, but we took his napalm and torched the place and it was cool. After that, things kind of went from there."

But it's a pretty big jump from burning down an abandoned shed to deciding it sounds like fun to kill a girl you've known since middle school. I stare up at him, trying to work out the chain of events. "And then after setting a couple fires together, he really wanted to go on a murder spree with you?"

Connor laughs, shaking his head like the memory is one of those funny, rueful ones you talk about at parties because it makes such a good story. "Not exactly. I mean, sure, we talked about how cool it would be to off someone, but Nick was pretty much all talk. I had to work on him for a long time. And then after Monica, he was still practically ready to turn himself in and confess everything. But that would have been it for me too, and no way was I going to let that happen. In the end, I got him to see how it was."

"And how was it?" I say, staring straight ahead, watching the dark opening under the bridge.

Connor laughs and shakes his head. "Well, first of all, no one was ever going to believe that it wasn't his idea. I mean, look at him! And as long as we were careful, as long as we took all the right precautions and didn't hang out together where anyone could see us, we could keep doing it—do whatever we wanted. It was going to be epic."

"And that was all he needed to hear? That you were going to kill a whole bunch of girls and it would be epic? That's really what he wanted?"

Connor's expression darkens abruptly, and it's like watching a cloud move across the sun. "We were all set to start doing some real damage. Then he had to go and get picked up for being fucking stupid and lifting utility knives right where the shop guy could see him. He spent four months in Lehigh, and when he came back, he was too scared to do anything anymore. It took pretty much the whole semester to get him to where I was even sure that he wasn't going to go running to the cops any second."

"They're going to catch you," I say, and I say it like it's just that obvious, that unavoidable.

Connor only leans closer and gives me a warm, conspiratorial look. "I know that."

"Why are you here, then? I mean, why bother with me?"

He shakes his head, looking so earnest, so sincere. "Don't you get it, Hannah? Since the second you gave them Nick, it was never going to be any other way. It's just a matter of time before he pussies out and tells them everything. So before it all goes down, I had to make sure I got my chance to deal with you. Because yeah, they'll get me, but until then, I've got you."

In the flatness of his eyes, I can see that he's completely committed to whatever he's got planned, and before now, I've never truly understood what it means when they say that a person has nothing to lose.

Overhead, the clouds are rolling in fast. The temperature has plunged ten degrees in the past fifteen minutes, and I'm starting to shiver even in the heat. The wind is blowing gusty and cool when Lillian comes drifting out from under the bridge. At first she looks just as solid as she does in my room, but as she steps out into the light and starts to climb the hill, her edges go soft. It takes her a while to reach us, struggling up the stony ground, fighting against whatever it is about the outdoors that makes her weak and thin. She sits down beside me with her knees pulled up, watching as Connor slips out of his backpack, keeping one hand around my arm.

He unzips the pack and takes out a pair of disposable latex gloves that he probably got from his dad's dentist office. The whole procedure is so methodical and businesslike. It's so horrifically ordinary.

He glances over at me, and his friendly smile isn't so friendly anymore. His eyes look flat and cold and terribly, terribly alive.

"Please," I say softly. "I'm your friend, Connor. You've known me forever."

Lillian leans closer, clutching at me, but her hand drifts through my arm in a way that makes me think of ghosts in movies. It surprises me because in my room, she is so, so solid. "Don't," she whispers. "Don't say 'please' like that, like you expect him to give you anything."

The light in the clearing is still warm, the afternoon sun pouring through the branches in brilliant arrows of light, but even as I watch, it's fading, growing darker.

"You can't," I say, and this time my voice sounds almost bossy—telling, not asking. "You can't really do this."

Connor laughs, looking around the empty clearing. "Hannah," he says, like he's explaining something so obvious he shouldn't even need to say it out loud. "No one's stopping me."

The three of us are sitting in a little circle in the grass, like we're about to have a tea party. The trees above us sway and creak. Lillian is staring out across the park at the coming storm. The color of her skin is ghostly, clammy gray, like stone. And then she grabs for me, making goose bumps come out on my arms.

"Look," she whispers, trying to catch hold of me even as her hand keeps slipping right through mine. "Look—look!"

Something is moving under the railroad bridge. At first it's just a flutter. Something pale and murky in the dark. Then a cloud rolls across the sun, and Abby Brooks is standing in the arched mouth of the tunnel with grass stains on her knees and blood in her hair. She's still wearing one blue flip-flop.

Connor follows my gaze, not focusing on Abby exactly, but he sees something. His hand goes slack around my arm and I have a fast, crazy idea that I could yank free and run, maybe along the river toward the footbridge or back out toward the road. He's bigger and faster than me, but I'm small enough that maybe I could lose myself in the brush, hunker down, and hide until he goes away.

Without wasting another second, I wrench myself out of his grip and bolt for the river.

I make it about fifteen feet, just to the edge of the clearing, before he catches up to me and grabs me by the back of my dress. He's laughing.

"Hannah, Hannah, get it together! If you make a big thing about this, it's just going to be a whole lot worse."

I twist in his grip so I'm looking up at him, right into his pale, distant eyes. What I see there startles me. There is nothing in them, nothing in his face. His gaze is perfectly empty.

"Worse than what?" I say, even though I'm brutally sure that there are a million ways this could get worse, a million ways he could hurt me or make me scream and cry, or destroy me. But the idea of pain seems far away, and it feels good to stare into the rabbit hole anyway. It feels good to be Lillian.

He shrugs, smiling his dull, brutal smile. I'm absolutely disgusted that I ever could have thought it was charming. It's just a mask he wears, and now I'm seeing him for what he really is—arrogant and cruel. Vacant.

He gazes down at me, shaking his head. "You're a real trip, Hannah—way tougher than any of those junior high girls. You're going to be so much fun to fuck with."

In one hissing electric burst, I have never been so uncontrollably angry in my life, not even when my dad left, or that summer my mom made me quit piano lessons because I had to watch Ariel every day. Not even at Lillian.

I stand with my chin up and my shoulders back, and it's my turn to laugh. "You think you're actually scary, don't you? You think you're smart. But let me tell you something,

Connor. Anyone who'd pick Nick Andelman for a partner is an idiot. No one with any sense at all would ever beg help off a hulking moron with an IQ of seventy-five."

"Shut up," he says, and he throws me down in the grass so hard that my teeth click together and I almost bite my tongue. "He was never my partner. He did whatever I said, whenever I wanted—I was in charge of everything. I came out of this with everything."

The ground under me is still warm from the sun, the long grass prickling against my back, but the sky overhead is nearly black.

"You can't kill a person without losing part of yourself," I whisper. "When you murdered them, you were really doing it to yourself."

Connor crouches over me, shoving his face very close to mine, clamping his hands on my shoulders and holding me down in the grass. "You think they could ever take something from me? As far as those little bitches knew, I was God."

Behind him, Lillian gasps and points. When I turn my head, Cecily Miles is standing at the edge of the trees, like she's just wandered up from the river. Her hair is a wild mousy tangle around her face, and there's mud splashed up her legs. Her eyes are luminous, lit up with a kind of ecstatic fury.

Connor glances in the direction I'm looking but doesn't seem to focus.

"They're coming for you," I tell him, and maybe that sounds insane, but I'm staring him straight in the face when I say it, and he believes me. I can tell by the way his eyes dart rapidly from side to side and from the catch in his throat when he swallows. "The girls. They're coming."

His hands are clenched tight on my shoulders, holding me down in the weeds. I can smell grass and dirt and the sweet, musty pollen of wildflowers. I can smell the tight, electric feeling the air gets before a good lightning storm. We're crossing into the pocket of calm, where the clouds come in and the light goes wrong.

Connor crouches over me, pressing me into the ground. "You sound deranged. Everyone knows there's no such thing as ghosts."

But I can hear in his voice that he's faltering, not trying to ridicule me, but trying to convince himself that his victims are not climbing up the hill to us. That they're not crowding around him. I lie very still, looking up at him. I hate his breath and the dead, unsettling color of his eyes and his white, straight teeth.

"You're such a coward." My voice is smooth and vicious. When Lillian would fly into one of her rages, it was always chaotic, explosive, but mine is tight and poisonous. Hard as a diamond. When I stare up into his face, I feel nearly incandescent. "I'm amazed you had the balls to kill anyone at all. In fact, I bet it wasn't even you. I bet it was Nick, every inch of the way."

That one gets him, cutting right through the cold, smiling mask. That's when he slaps me.

"Don't talk about what I do," he says, and his voice is a snarl. "You don't even see what I am."

"Bullshit," I say. "You think this makes you interesting? You think it's so profound? You're not special, Connor. You're not a mystery. You're just a run-of-the-mill psycho, just like any other sick asshole out there, and you know what? It's pathetic."

And the whole time, I'm thinking that I just have to wait, wait a little longer, wait for Ariel to find someone, bring help.

The girls are right behind him now, standing over us in the grass. Monica is bright and horrible in her pink jacket, with crystals of snow stuck to the side of her face like they're never going to melt. She smiles and puts a finger to her lips. Then she leans down and blows gently in his ear.

Connor shudders, and I can see the doubt in his face now. It flickers in his eyes like a tiny flame, guttering. The light is turning strangely blue as the clouds come in, and there are goose bumps all over his arms.

Lillian is behind him, leaning her chin on his shoulder and looking down at me, and my God, she's scary-looking, but I love her.

"I love you," I whisper, and the way I say it makes it glaringly obvious that I am not talking to him, and he knows it. He knows that we are not the only ones here. The grass is prickly and dry against the backs of my arms, and my heart is hammering in my ears so loudly that I'm amazed I can still hear the rising wind and the river and the sound of his voice.

The other girls are all around us, and Monica slips her ice-blue hands around his throat. Her skin is translucent, almost see-through, but he starts to cough a little anyway, looking panicked.

"What are you doing to me?" he says, barely above a whisper.

"I'm not doing anything."

"Why are you looking at me like that? Stop looking at me."

When Hailey runs her finger along the top of his ear, he jerks like something is buzzing around his head.

"They own you now," I whisper. "You picked them, Connor, and now they own a piece of you."

His hand is over my mouth, covering my smile, and my heart is beating so hard I think I might die, but the wild, savage joy is in me now, and I can't stop. He takes his hand away and I'm still smiling.

"Don't look at me like that," he says. And he shakes me so hard that my head thumps back against the ground. It hurts in the same way falling hurts in a dream, dizzy and far-away. I blink once because I can't help it, and go right back to smiling, staring up into his nervous, skittering eyes.

Lillian is sitting cross-legged beside us, nestled in the grass. Her arms are wrapped around herself, but if she were solid, she'd be holding my hand.

Connor frowns, reaching for his backpack. He takes out something heavy and oddly shaped, like a marble sculpture or a bookend, but my fear is beating time behind my eyes, and it's hard to make out the details. The end is so much closer than I'd hoped.

"Wait!" I say, sounding breathless. "Aren't you going to arrange your crime scene? What about all the candy and toys? What about the valentine?"

He stares down into my face. "Wow, look at you, Hannah! You really are our biggest fan, huh? All that plastic shit is Nick's business. He's the one who gets all broken up about it, but I don't mind if the newspapers get into it. It's actually pretty hilarious how they freak out whenever they see one of Andelman's stupid little presents."

The rain is on its way now. The air has gone damp and cold, and I can smell the frantic ozone smell of an electrical storm.

It doesn't matter that a shambling pack of dead girls is standing over us, making the air go cold. It doesn't matter that Connor is shivering now and that I can see the panic in his eyes, the knowledge that his victims are all around him. None of that matters. He's going to kill me anyway.

His knees are pressing into the points of my shoulders as he takes a deep breath and lifts the marble bookend, which is mottled brown and shaped like a cherub. The sky is nearly black, and the wind comes rustling down through the trees like a secret. He's going to kill me here in the grass, next to the train tracks, before my sister can find help. I buck and twist, trying to squirm out from under him, screaming loud enough to make my throat hurt.

"Scream all you want," he whispers, and now his face is as cold and blank as a statue. "No one is going to get here before I finish this."

"You're not special," I whisper, and don't recognize my own voice. It sounds low and hoarse, ferocious.

The weight of his kneecaps digging into my arms should hurt, but as soon as he swings the bookend down, I can barely feel anything. It ricochets awkwardly off the side of my head, and I gasp and try to call out, but my scream dies in my throat. My vision goes soft and black around the edges.

Lillian is there beside me, kneeling in the grass. She opens her mouth wide, like she's about to scream, but no sound comes out. Her hands are clasped against her chest, and my head is twisted roughly to the side so that I'm staring into her face.

"No," she says in a sad little whisper, shaking her head back and forth over and over, almost moaning it. "No, no, no—Hannah, please no."

Connor crouches over me with his hand against my throat, holding me down in the grass, and when he swings the bookend again, there's the sharp pain of the collision, then nothing.

22: Red Queen

I'm left floating on the cool updraft of Lillian. Drifting away with her, buoyed up, with the impact of Mrs. Price's faux-Victorian bookend still booming through my head and Connor's knees digging into my shoulders.

Then, without warning, there's an explosion of voices and Connor's weight is gone. Shapes are wrestling in the grass around me, gasping and shouting. Someone kicks out, and a shoe catches me in the shoulder and then I know I must be alive, because it really hurts. When I open my eyes, I'm lying flat on the ground, rain spattering on my face.

Then a blurry shape leans over me, hands reach out, and Ariel comes bursting into focus and throws herself at me, hugging me hard around the neck. Her knees press painfully against my side as she leans across me, digging into my ribs, and I don't even care. I lie gasping in the wet grass, keeping my arms around her while she sobs against the front of my dress. I clutch her tighter and struggle to sit up, holding on to her, watching the scene unfold over the top of her head.

Someone is kneeling over Connor, holding him down in the grass. My vision is starting to come back, but there are black starbursts printed over everything. They're struggling, gasping and swearing, crashing around in the dry grass. There's a hoarse yelp, and the struggle gets louder and more frantic. And then it stops.

The noise starts from far away and grows steadily louder. The clearing fills with an earsplitting shriek that rips through the trees, a wail like the torment of all the ghosts of all the horror movies. It goes on and on and I look wildly around the clearing for them, all the ghosts of all the girls. But they're gone. Lillian is the only one left, sitting elbow-deep in the waving grass with her arms crossed over her chest.

And then the light around us gets weirdly red, throbbing like a heartbeat, and I hold Ariel tighter. There's so much noise, wind and thunder and shouting. I crouch lower in the grass and close my eyes, burying my face in her hair, rocking her and rocking myself until the red subsides and things get quiet again.

"Here," says a hoarse, panicked voice very close to my ear. "Ariel, let me see her."

It's Finny. He crouches over me, raking my hair out of my face as he presses his hand against my temple and holds it there. Blood is running down the side of his arm and falling in scattered drops onto my dress. They bloom into dark splotches, and I look away, staring around the clearing for Connor.

"Where is he?" I gasp. My voice sounds furious and bruised, like it belongs to a monster.

Finny's holding me by the shoulders, keeping his hand pressed hard against my temple while Ariel sobs against me

298

with her arms around my waist and her face buried in my dress.

"It's okay," Finny tells us. "It's okay—Boles cuffed him and put him in the car. The paramedics are coming."

His expression is wary and raw, and when I nod and reach for him, he wraps his whole body around me, shielding me from the wind and the rain, and there's so much noise and so much fresh, damp air. I'm coughing so hard that my eyes water and I collapse against him, tears streaming down my cheeks, sobbing for breath. My throat hurts so bad and the tears are so thick that I can't even tell whether or not I'm crying. I mash my face into Finny's shoulder, digging my fingers into the fabric of his shirt as the sky opens up.

A few feet away, Lillian is sitting plunked down in the grass with her hair hanging in her face and her arms folded against her chest, watching us. Rain pours down around her, but none of the drops seem to make contact. Everything in the clearing is wet except her.

I wait for her to say something, but she doesn't. She's looking at me and Finny—the way he's holding on to me and the way I'm holding on to him. The expression on her face is cool and distant, but her eyes are full of longing, and I know what she's thinking. Or maybe the truth is just that I'm thinking it—that she has never had anyone to come crashing into the storm for her.

I reach out, fumbling through the grass with my hand, but I still can't touch her. She reaches back anyway, letting her hand drift above mine, pretending to hold it.

"You did it," she whispers. "You were strong. You were so brave."

There's a flash of lightning, and I flinch against Finny, squeezing my eyes shut.

"It's okay," Finny says against my ear, keeping his hands cupped over my head like he can protect me from the rain. "It's going to be okay. The ambulance will come, and they'll stop the bleeding."

Lillian just sits there watching me, sad and dry and silent.

Her eyes are so huge that it's painful to look at her. "I have to go, Hannah. I have to." This time when she reaches for my wrist, I can almost feel the pressure of her fingers as they brush against my bracelet, jangling through the charms.

I nod even though my head aches whenever I move it. I'm crying for real now, leaning against Finny, sobbing against his shoulder.

❄ ❄ ❄

It's after ten o'clock by the time the hospital lets me go. My throat feels okay, but there's a huge wad of gauze taped to the side of my head, and my voice still sounds like it belongs to a goblin.

My mom and Decker met me at the emergency room, where I got nine stitches and a CT scan and answered questions the detectives already knew the answers to.

The hospital was bright and fluorescent and cold. I waited and waited for Lillian to show up, to make a joke or a smart remark, or roll her eyes at me for flinching from the needle. But she didn't.

300

Now I'm at home in the living room, snuggled on the couch with Ariel wrapped around me like a monkey and Joan lying warm and heavy against my shins. Decker's in the armchair, leaning back like he's having trouble getting his head around everything that's happened, but my mom keeps standing up and pacing.

Finny's sitting on my other side, looking big and rumpled and out of place in our living room. He's restless, touching the scrapes on his elbows over and over, but I know that's just because this is all still new and that the more he comes over, the more he'll start to look in-place. Just like I know that if we were alone, he'd put his arm around me, or at least hold my hand, but he's too nervous to do it in front of my mom and Decker.

I'm pretty sure that after what happened today, though, he gets to. If there's any way to earn a pass for hand-holding in front of my parents, he's earned it.

I reach for him and he reaches back, lacing his fingers through mine. The look he gives me is startled but relieved.

"That was really lucky that you were in the park," Decker says finally, and I know it's his way of telling Finny thank you without actually saying it. He still looks kind of stunned. "Jesus, that was lucky."

Finny just shrugs. "I was on my way over here." His voice is awkward, and he glances sideways at me. "After I'd had a while to, you know, think about what you said, I figured you were right. So I was coming to talk to you."

The way he says it is apologetic, and he stops before he

301

gets to the story of what happened next. I already know the rest, though—the part where Ariel came bursting out of the chokecherry bushes, screaming at Finny to help her, to come stop Connor Price from hurting her sister because he was out of his mind, and she'd called 911, but she was so, so scared that the police weren't going to get there in time.

And I know that I was lucky. That if he'd doubted Ariel for even a minute or tried to make her slow down and explain, it might have been too late. But he wasn't late, and here in the coziness of my living room, with my sister dozing off next to me and my hand clasped in Finny's, the whole afternoon seems far away, like something that happened a lifetime ago.

⁂   ⁂   ⁂

Later, after Ariel's in bed and Jolene has come by to pick up Finny, I climb the stairs to my room and peel out of my dress. The whole back of it is covered in grass stains and red dirt, and the seams are still sort of damp. There's a huge rip in the bottom of the tulle, and some of the charms have been torn off. The ground around the railroad bridge must be littered with them.

It's still raining hard, a black-sky torrent, water coursing down the glass, springing up in tiny droplets from the surface of the backyard. In the dark, the drops catch the glow from the porch light and shine brightly before plunging down again and disappearing back into the grass.

I put on my pajama pants and a thermal shirt, then sit down in front of my mirror. With careful fingers, I scrape my hair into a ponytail, working around the pad of gauze taped over the purpling goose egg near my hairline.

There's a sharp tug at the top of my scalp as my bracelet tangles in the end of the ponytail, and I wince at the pain that radiates through my stitches. I unwind the bracelet and then take it off, setting it on top of the dresser. The light in my room is warm and soft, making a smeary rainbow across the wall. My head aches, but in a vague, sore way that's only really noticeable if I look up too fast.

As I lay out the bracelet, my gaze falls on the enamel surface of the Queen of Hearts. Her dress is painted red and white, but now the paint is ruined. Someone has scratched the red off every single heart.

The job is detailed, neat and thorough, and Lillian has always been able to make the world bend to her will when she really wanted to. I have a wordless memory of her reaching for my wrist in the throbbing light from the ambulance, fingers jangling through the charms, and I sit very still, feeling like a person in a dream.

I understand, with a painful knot tightening in my throat, that this is her gift to me, her good-bye. That maybe getting rid of the hearts is her way of protecting me from the horror and the tragedy of what happened. But I can't help thinking that it might mean something else.

She's ruined my private little reminder of her authority, X-ed out the thing that always seemed like a symbol for her power. And maybe as little as two months ago I wouldn't have gotten that, but in the last few weeks, I've learned too much about her secret self and mine to misunderstand it. This is her letting me go.

Our whole lives, it was like we were always trying so hard to be perfect—for our families and our friends, for each other—when the funny thing was, we didn't have to. In the end, we were better than that.

I sit down in the middle of the braided rug, over the center of the makeshift spirit board. The rug hides the chaotic mess of clippings, but I know it's there like I know the rain will run its course and that soon I'll stop crying. I'll get up and walk out of my room and down the hall. I'll take a shower and be careful not to get my stitches wet. But for now, I sit in the middle of my room, holding the bracelet and thinking of Lillian.

Thinking of this friend I had. This friend I loved and keep loving—dead, but never really gone.

SPECIAL THANKS TO:

Sarah Davies, who champions my books, provides invaluable guidance, and answers every question (even the completely ridiculous ones), all with grace, kindness, and a healthy dose of practicality.

Ben Schrank, who not only gives me permission to write weird books, but actually encourages it.

Jocelyn Davies, who edits like a champ, totally gets what I'm trying to do (even when I'm not quite doing it yet), and if she panics at the sight of my first drafts, she always keeps it to herself. Jocelyn, you rock!

The Razorbill editorial team, for helping me fix the wonky parts, not to mention the erratic comma-use, and for occasionally reminding me that there are very few circumstances under which a character can end a scene wearing different shoes than they started with.

Tess and Maggie, my Merry Sisters. You guys are indispensable!

The Photo Shop. Thank you for the best college job in the history of the world, not to mention imparting all that detailed knowledge of chemicals, machinery, crime scene photos, and customer service. Those parts are all true, I swear—even if they didn't actually happen.

And David, who read this book over and over and over, all the way into infinity, even when it hadn't changed all that much since the last time he read it, and explained to me very patiently that popcorn is not a meal. No, not even when you're revising.

PLAYLIST

Kids by MGMT

Lazy Eye by Silversun Pickups

Anything, Anything by Dramarama

Paper Planes by M.I.A.

(Don't Fear) The Reaper by Blue Öyster Cult

The Missing Frame by AFI

Sweet About Me by Gabriella Cilmi

Sail by AWOLNATION

Burnt by the Sun by David Byrne

Valerie Loves Me by Material Issue

Young Blood by The Naked and Famous

Shadow on the Sun by Audioslave

The Funeral by Band of Horses

WANT MORE MYSTERY?
MORE DARKNESS?
MORE DANGER?

BRENNA YOVANOFF

ABOUT THE AUTHOR

Brenna Yovanoff once thought she wanted to grow up to become
an editor. Although it turns out she was mistaken, she doesn't
regret her days as a slush-pile reader or the fact that she's
memorised large stretches of *The Chicago Manual of Style*.
Her short fiction has appeared in *Chiaroscuro* and *Strange
Horizons*. She has an MFA in creative writing from
Colorado State University and currently lives in Denver.
She is also the author of *The Replacement* and *Smoulder*
published by Simon and Schuster.